STARSTRUCK
L.A. WITT

A BLUEWATER BAY STORY

RIPTIDE
PUBLISHING

Riptide Publishing
PO Box 6652
Hillsborough, NJ 08844
www.riptidepublishing.com

Starstruck
Copyright © 2014 by L.A. Witt

Cover Art by L.C. Chase, lcchase.com/design.htm
Editor: Sarah Frantz, Carole-ann Galloway
Layout: L.C. Chase, lcchase.com/design.htm

ISBN: 978-1-62649-171-7

First edition
November, 2014

Also available in ebook:
ISBN: 978-1-62649-170-0

STARSTRUCK

L.A. WITT

A BLUEWATER BAY STORY

RIPTIDE
PUBLISHING

To Aleks, for inspiring Bluewater Bay.

TABLE OF CONTENTS

A s Levi Pritchard sipped coffee in a window booth at the Sunrise Café, he tried not to notice how many of the cars parked along Main Street had California plates. Or think about the fact that he was here to have breakfast with a producer.

God. A producer. It was bad enough Hollywood had invaded Bluewater Bay after he'd moved here to escape all that shit. Now Hollywood was calling him. *Fuck.*

He put his coffee cup down and kneaded his temples, trying to massage away the headache that was starting to take hold. Why the fuck was he doing this to himself?

Oh. Right. Because he'd never been able to say no to Finn Larson.

Finn was one of those producers who had to be the progeny of a used-car salesman and a litigation attorney. No one could sell bullshit like that man. When he'd called last night, Levi's brain had screamed, "Oh my God, no, I don't want to see you," but his mouth had said, "I'll see you at eleven." He still wasn't sure how that had happened, only that he was here now.

Well, okay, that wasn't entirely true. Levi knew damn well if he'd said no, Finn would've kept after him. Humoring the asshole with lunch was less of a headache than getting a restraining order. Finn probably wanted to resurrect the action hero who'd put Levi on the map. Levi would just politely decline and hope that was enough to get the man to leave him alone, at least until the next two-bit action flick came along.

A couple of women walked by on the sidewalk, raincoat hoods up and heads down, but he still instinctively turned away. Even though not many people recognized him out here, it was a habit to avoid the occasional stare or, worse, a nervous fan.

"Are you really Levi Pritchard?" The same question every time.

"Yeah." It was getting harder by the year to fake that smile. "That's me."

And then came the inevitable:

"I loved your movies! Why aren't you acting anymore?"

"Will there ever be another Chad Eastwick movie?"

"Guess 'actors' like you have a shelf life, eh?"

He'd loved acting. *Loved* it. It was the Hollywood bullshit he'd hated. So he'd walked away from Tinseltown and never looked back.

And now Bluewater Bay was crawling with everything he'd moved a thousand miles to escape.

That was why he didn't come into town much anymore unless he had to. If he'd wanted to be surrounded by directors, producers, key grips, gophers, electricians, set designers, makeup artists, union representatives, cinematographers, and consultants, he'd have stayed in California. His opinionated pair of Maine coon cats were much better company than those fuckers.

The women in raincoats had to be out of sight by now, so he lifted his gaze to the drizzly scenery. A lot of the businesses on Main Street had come and gone, though plenty had been here forever. He was pretty sure the bakery had occupied the building across the street from the café since this part of town was built in the 1920s. Even the Walgreens they'd opened on the corner had tried to retain some of the small-town charm, keeping the building's exterior more or less the same pre-Depression façade it had always had and only adding their distinctive red, cursive lettering. The sign stuck out as badly as the McDonald's a few blocks down, but even they were more welcome additions than the invasion that had begun two years ago.

Hollywood didn't belong here. Bluewater Bay was one of those sleepy logging and fishing towns on the northern tip of Washington's Olympic Peninsula, a long-ass drive and a ferry ride away from anything interesting apart from the rain forest, which was exactly why Levi had moved here.

Oh, if only Hunter Easton had signed that book deal one year earlier . . .

Right then, a sleek black Mercedes pulled up—California plates, of course—and despite the glare on the windshield that obscured the driver's face, he knew. By the time the door opened, his stomach was acidic with self-loathing over letting the bastard talk him into meeting him here. In public. In his town. Hell, meeting him at all.

But it was too late to change his mind or get the hell out of here because Finn Larson had spotted him and was on his way in, briefcase in hand.

Stomach roiling, Levi waited for him. With anyone else from that era of his life, he'd have called upon every iota of theater training he could remember to make his smile as genuine as possible. With Finn? His guard was up, and he wanted him to know it.

As Finn approached the table, he extended his hand. "Levi Pritchard. My God. It's been—"

"Do you mind?" Levi snapped, accepting the offered hand, if grudgingly. "I really don't like announcing my presence in these places."

The producer gestured dismissively. "It's not exactly a big secret that you're here, my friend." He set his briefcase on the bench, shrugged out of his jacket, hung it on the coat rack beside the booth, and slid in across from Levi. "So how have you been?"

"I'm fine. How are things in LA?"

"Great, great. We've got the green light for some amazing films right— Honey, can I get a coffee, please?"

The waitress paused beside their table, threw Levi an "is he for real?" glance, and then gave an obviously forced smile. "Cream?"

"Yes, please. Thank you, sweetheart."

From the way her eyes narrowed, Levi wouldn't have been surprised if the cream she sent with Finn's coffee was comprised of Drano and rat poison. The loggers and truckers called the waitresses "honey" and "sweetheart" too, but from them, it was a more affectionate variation of "ma'am."

From someone like Finn, it was like verbally copping a feel.

"So anyway," Finn went on, oblivious to Levi's inner thoughts, "we've got some fantastic stuff on the table." He flashed him that used-car salesman grin. "Couple of roles that would be perfect for you, by the way."

"No." Levi shook his head. "Not interested. Let's just get that clear right now."

Finn gave his trademark exasperated sigh. "I don't get you, kid. One minute you're riding the Hollywood wave and loving every minute. The next you're, well, here." He looked out the window and wrinkled his nose. "What do you see in this town anyway? It's got no . . . character."

"It's got more than LA."

Finn snorted and plucked a sugar packet from the ceramic box between the salt and pepper shakers beneath the window. Flipping it idly between his fingers, he said, "I don't get you. I don't think I ever will."

"Well, I like it here. And I like my life, thank you." Levi shrugged. "I'm starting to think I was an idiot for passing up that place in Forks, though."

Finn's eyebrows rose. "Forks?"

Levi nodded. "Found a great house down there, but I wasn't moving there right in the middle of the *Twilight* fad."

Finn cocked his head.

Resisting the urge to roll his eyes, Levi said, "*Twilight* was set there. And filmed there. Remember?"

"Oh, right. Right." Finn laughed, glancing out at the two-lane main drag. "Not sure why places like this are so attractive to people who write about vampires and werewolves and whatnot, but"—he shrugged—"as long as I keep getting paid to make the shows, I couldn't give a fuck why."

Levi sipped his coffee, hoping it would wash some of the bitterness from his mouth. He really should've bought the place he'd looked at in Forks. Then again, even though they'd long ago finished filming the movies, that town wasn't much better than this one. He'd been there recently—it was only a short drive down the coast—and the stink of Hollywood still hung over the place like LA smog.

Maybe sleepy little industrial towns were no more immune to Hollywood than any other place. On the other hand, they'd filmed a shitload of movies in Astoria, which was just a few hours from here, and the place still had the small-town charm Bluewater Bay was desperately trying to hold on to.

Levi liked to think this fad wouldn't last forever, but he wasn't holding his breath.

"Well, maybe all the hype will die down eventually," he grumbled.

Finn chuckled. "I doubt it. Have you seen the ratings for the show?"

Levi bit back a curse. "Great. At least Forks only had to put up with *Twilight* for a few years. Sounds like the *Wolf's Landing* plague won't be leaving this town anytime soon."

"Actually, that's what I came here to talk to you about." Finn folded his hands and leaned forward. "I want you on *Wolf's Landing*."

"You *what*?" He'd expected an offer of some sort, but . . . *Wolf's Landing*?

Finn sighed dramatically. "Come on, Levi. It's just a guest spot, and you'd be perfect for it."

"I'm retired. Absolutely not."

"Levi." Finn shook his head. "Levi, Levi, Levi. I know how you acting types are. Once you're bitten by that bug? You're in."

"Yeah?" Levi raised an eyebrow. "That why I haven't been in front of a camera in years?"

Finn smirked. "Well, it might explain why you're spinning your tires and wasting your time at that decrepit community theater."

Levi ground his teeth. *Leave that group out of this.* "Just because I enjoy acting doesn't mean I want to deal with Hollywood anymore."

"This entire production isn't anything like what you've ever worked on."

"How so? Aside from the lack of pyrotechnicians?"

Finn laughed. "Well, there is that. But Anna Maxwell is an executive producer and one of the directors, and I mean, you and she go way back, right?"

"We do."

"So I don't have to tell you that the rest of the cast raves about her, do I? They say she gives them a lot of leeway to interpret their characters."

Levi fought the urge to squirm. He didn't doubt for a second that Anna gave the cast a shitload of freedom, especially on the episodes she directed. And how long had he wanted to work with a director like that, especially her? The last few had had his character development in a choke hold from the get-go—everything from his mannerisms to his voice inflections had been dictated until he'd had absolutely no room to move. Small wonder critics said his acting had "all the range of an emotionally catatonic Keanu Reeves wannabe" and that he "wasn't cut out for a role requiring more creativity than the tree in the background of an elementary school play." He'd been itching for the freedom to show that there was more to him than "at least he does his own stunts, so we know he's a real boy."

Across from him, Finn grinned. "I'm telling you, kid. This would be a good role for you. And Anna agrees. That's why she's specifically asked to direct your episodes." He pulled back his sleeve and glanced at his gold Rolex. "In fact, she should be here any minute."

"She—" Levi blinked. "Anna's coming?"

"Of course." Finn shrugged. "She's been pushing harder than anyone to bring you on board."

Levi gritted his teeth. "Has she now?"

"Absolutely. She— Ah! Speak of the devil."

A figure swept past the window. A second later, the diner's front door opened, and in walked Anna Maxwell.

Levi stood. "Anna. Long time no see."

"Way too long!" She threw her arms around him. "How are you, sweetheart?"

"Doing all right. You?"

She released him and quirked an eyebrow. "I'll be much better when my old buddy explains why he hasn't once tried to meet up with me for coffee or something."

"I . . ." Heat rushed into his cheeks. "Well . . ."

Anna's eyebrow climbed.

"You're right." He put up his hands. "I should have gotten in touch sooner. I've been meaning to, but—"

"Yeah, yeah. Excuses." She playfully smacked his arm. They both laughed, and he let her slide onto the bench before he joined her.

Finn folded his hands on the table. "So, I've already given him the rundown. About joining the cast."

"Good." She faced Levi. "And?"

Levi opened his mouth to speak, but right then, the waitress stopped beside the table. She deposited Finn's coffee in front of him and asked, "What can I get you all to eat?"

"I'll just have the special," Anna said. "And keep the coffee coming."

Levi glanced down at the menu. "The special is fine for me too. With a Coke, please."

The waitress flashed him a brief smile and jotted down his order. The smile vanished as she turned to Finn. "And you?"

Finn pursed his lips as he skimmed over the menu. "The hash browns, are those grown organically?"

Bless her, the waitress managed to maintain a poker face. "No, sweetheart. They're not."

And there was that exasperated, entitled sigh.

Levi kept his head down, not to hide from her—she knew him—but to keep the producer from seeing him roll his eyes again. Thing #4,781 he didn't miss about Hollywood—you couldn't order a meal without someone at the table being an obnoxious activist or adhering to the latest health craze. Or both.

After she'd patiently explained that no, they had no gluten-free toast, and no, there was nothing organic on the menu, and no, the orange juice was not fresh-squeezed, Finn decided to stick with coffee. Probably a wise move on his part. As it was, Levi still wondered what other substances might be lurking in the man's cup.

Finn sneered at the sugar packet he'd been playing with, and put it aside. Probably because it wasn't certified and notarized as pure organic raw cane sugar harvested from sustainable fair trade fields and presented in a thrice-recycled packet after a virgin sacrifice. He stirred the cream into his coffee, took a sip—no immediate bad reactions, so maybe it wasn't poisoned—and set it back on the saucer.

"So," Anna said to Levi. "Are you in?"

Levi sighed. "I'm out of this business."

Finn waved a hand. "Listen, we know you're 'retired' and whatnot, but humor us here." He looked Levi in the eye. "Come down to the set. See how things are run." He tapped his briefcase. "Give the script a read and see what you think."

Levi swallowed, regarding the briefcase like it was a venomous snake. "Why me?"

Anna touched his arm. "Because we—and by that I mean I—think this is the perfect comeback for you."

"I'm retired, Anna. I don't want a comeback. I just want to—"

"Sweetie, think about it. This is the perfect series for you. It's set right in your backyard. You'd have a fairly small role at first. It's—"

"At first?" Levi blinked. "Whoa. I thought you were talking about a guest spot."

"Well, sort of." Finn shrugged. "You'd be credited as 'guest starring' at first, but the character you'd be playing eventually comes back for a recurring role."

Levi quickly ran through the series in his head—much as he hated the presence of Hollywood here, he did enjoy both the books and the show—and tried to narrow down which character they were talking about. Someone who'd surfaced early on, then came back—

The penny dropped. "You want me to play Max Fuhrman?"

A huge grin spread across Anna's lips, and she nodded.

Oh, damn her. Damn her straight to hell. Anna knew one of Levi's biggest frustrations with the studios was that they kept typecasting him. He'd wanted to try his chops at someone with more emotional range—hell, *any* emotional range—instead of spending ninety percent of his screen time jumping off or out of exploding vehicles.

Someone like Max Fuhrman.

Fuhrman went back and forth between an angsty alcoholic with a hefty case of PTSD and—thanks to a shaman's spell—a sociopath. A lazy actor could make him into a generic villain with the occasional moment of humanity, but Levi saw *so* much potential to portray him as a complex, tortured character.

He swallowed. "Why me?"

Anna shrugged. "Well, you're—"

"Because the man who played Chad Eastwick has just the kind of machismo we need for someone like Max."

Anna exhaled so hard it was almost a growl. "Finn, really?"

"What?" He waved a hand. "Look, it's no secret there's been a lot of speculation about the show having a homoerotic vibe."

Levi's heart dropped. He glanced at Anna, eyes wide, and she gave a little "don't worry, I've got this" nod.

"That's not why I picked him for the role." She glared at the other producer. "Levi has the chops and the versatility to play Max. Yeah, we want someone masculine and powerful, but it has nothing to do with the—"

"Your choice doesn't," he said. "But the studio's only considering him because of that. Between a gay lead, the story's homoerotic undertones, and—no offense—a lesbian executive producer and director, there's concern about the show's image."

Anna rolled her eyes. She met Levi's and shook her head slightly, a silent "don't listen to him."

"Anyway. Bottom line, we want you for this role." Finn pulled the script out of his briefcase and set it on the table between them. "Give it a look. Come down to the set and see what you think."

Levi glared at the script, its three brass brads gleaming in the fluorescent light.

Anna chuckled. "This is the role you've been waiting for, sweetie." It was. It so was.

"And you're not the only one waiting for it," Finn said. "The studio's got two other actors in mind, and they are looking for a reason to sign them over you."

Levi resisted the urge to make a grab for the scripts. Damn it. These two really knew how to corner him—offer the role of his dreams, and make sure he knew it was being offered to someone else too.

Fuck. This really was the single role in God's creation that could coax him back in front of a camera. If Hollywood's bullshit hadn't turned him into such a cynical asshole, he'd have signed the contract in a heartbeat. Especially with Anna as one of the people at the show's helm.

A shrill beep startled him out of his thoughts, and Finn pulled his cell from his pocket. "Damn. Would you two excuse me for a moment?"

They both nodded, and he got up and headed for the door. Well, at least he had the common courtesy to take his call outside. Maybe there was hope for the bastard yet.

As soon as Finn was out of earshot, Levi released a breath and rolled his shoulders.

"Ugh, I can't *stand* him," Anna muttered.

"I doubt anyone can."

"You ain't wrong." She smirked. "I don't think anyone likes him as well as he adores himself."

Levi laughed.

Anna managed a soft laugh too, but it didn't last. She held his gaze. "It's good to see you again, Levi. It's been way too long."

"Yeah, it really has." He paused. "So, uh, all shop talk aside, how have you been?"

Anna shrugged. "Up and down."

"Yeah?" Levi cocked his head. "Seems like things are pretty damned good on the professional front."

"Oh, yeah. Absolutely. But you know the kind of toll that takes at home."

He grimaced. "You're probably working insane hours right now, too."

She groaned, letting her calm, professional mask slip for a second. "I am. And Leigh understands, but I'm not gonna lie: it's making things tough."

"Sorry to hear it."

She shrugged again. "It is what it is. So what about you?" She glared playfully at him. "And why *do* I never see you around here when we used to run into each other all the time in LA?"

He laughed dryly. "We ran in the same circles there. Here? Not so much."

"Fair enough." Her expression turned to genuine hurt. "I figured I'd see you eventually, though."

"I know. I'm sorry. I've . . ." He shook his head. "I guess I've taken the recluse thing a little too seriously. And, you know, once the paparazzi started lurking around town . . ."

Anna wrinkled her nose. "Can't blame you for that. But, well, all the bullshit and paparazzi notwithstanding, it'd be good to see you near a film set again."

Levi ground his teeth, biting back a snide "Don't hold your breath." He forced the hostility out of his voice. "Good to see you in the director's chair. And executive producer too. Congrats."

She smiled, and in spite of his mood, he couldn't help returning it.

"So, am I going to get a shot at directing you?"

And so much for his smile. "I don't know. It's temping, but I . . ."

"You don't want to come out of retirement and deal with all the crap again?"

"Basically, yeah." He sighed. "I've kind of gotten used to not getting calls from my friends and family to ask if this or that tabloid story is true."

"But have you ever gotten used to not being in front of a movie camera?"

Levi flinched.

"That's what I thought." Anna leaned closer. "Look, hon. This business chews people up and spits them out all the time. I get that. You know I do."

He dropped his gaze. "Yeah, you do."

"But look at me, hon. I made it. I had to fight my way through all kinds of bullshit because everyone thought the only thing I could possibly direct were man-hating lesbian movies. And now . . ." She gestured at the scripts. "I'm directing more episodes than anyone else."

Levi exhaled, and then he gave another small smile. "You never have been one to take no for an answer."

"You're right." She arched an eyebrow. "Which is why it shouldn't surprise you that I'm not going to let you say no to this role."

"Oh yeah? And why is that?"

She folded her arms across her chest. "Because this is the opportunity you were dying for before you gave up on Hollywood. I know it's not a film, but this is big, sweetheart."

He let himself grin. "Ever the humble one, eh?"

Anna laughed, rolling her eyes. "It's not big because of me. Hunter Easton's a damn genius and his characters are amazing. You deserve a shot at bringing one of them to life."

"And we both deserve better than what people like him"—he gestured at the place Finn had been standing a moment ago—"put us through. I want to act, but I don't want to sell my soul."

"I know you don't." Her eyebrows pulled together. "But it's a damn shame for someone with your talent to give up acting because of that shit. I'm the last person who's going to tell you anything in that town is easy, and I almost walked away from it myself, but . . ." She touched his arm. "I also know it's in your blood just like directing is in mine. Filmmaking gets in there, and . . ."

"Yeah, it does."

Their eyes met, and he knew she had him right where she wanted him.

"Anna, I—"

"Are you really happy, sweetie? Directing little plays in between hiding in the hills?"

"It's better than what I had before."

"I'm sure it is, but can you really look me in the eye and tell me you don't want to do this again?"

"If it was as simple as choosing between acting and not acting . . ."

Anna nodded. "I know, baby." She paused, gnawing her lower lip. "Okay, let me throw this out there. Max Fuhrman's got a small role for the first couple of episodes. Eight minutes of screen time in one, twelve in the other."

"And then he's there for the whole ride starting at the end of the season."

She nodded. "He is. But if it'll convince you to at least give this a shot, we can just film the first episode and see how it goes. We can have the contract written so you have an out."

Levi didn't want to be intrigued by the idea, but . . . "An out? Meaning?"

"Meaning if you decide after filming one or two of the episodes that you want to bail, you can bow out and we can replace you before anyone's committed too much time and energy."

He shifted uncomfortably. "And you think the studio will go for it?"

"They will if they want to keep Hunter Easton happy, and he wants you for this role as much as I do."

He studied her. "You really want me to say yes to this, don't you?"

Anna grinned. "I do. You were a successful actor before, and you can be again, even if I have to drag you into it kicking and screaming."

He laughed. "I wouldn't put that past you."

"Smart man." She squeezed his arm. "Just read the scripts and think about it. You don't have to make a decision right away." The upward flick of her eyebrow suggested he'd damn well better.

"I'll think about it."

"Okay. Will you come down to the set too? I'm headed back there after we're done eating, and I'd be happy to show you around."

He exhaled. "All right. I'll come down and take a look."

"Good. Good."

Levi shifted a little. "By the way, I should've said this a long time ago, but I am so proud of you."

"Thank you, Levi." She put a hand over his. "You know I never would've gotten this far without all your help back then."

He chuckled. "Somehow I doubt that. We all knew from day one you were going to be kicking Spielberg out of a director's chair eventually."

She snorted. "Let's not go that far." She tapped the scripts in the middle of the table. "Now, read those tonight and then just try to tell me you aren't going to join me."

He laughed again. "Challenge accepted."

Her expression turned more serious, and she looked him in the eye. "And even if for some inexplicable reason you don't accept the role, promise me you won't be a stranger. I miss you."

"I won't. Promise."

"Good." Anna started to say something else, but Finn picked that moment to come back into the diner.

"Sorry about that." He smiled thinly as he took his seat again. "Damn thing is always ringing." He glanced at Levi, then Anna. "Did we come to any consensus while I was gone?"

Anna smiled. "He's willing to come down and take a tour of the set."

"Great. And you're going to read the scripts?" Finn nodded toward the bound pages.

Levi hesitated, but finally reached for them. "Fine. After the set tour." He eyed Finn. "But I'm not promising anything."

Judging by the way both Anna and Finn grinned, Levi may as well have just signed his name in blood.

So much for retirement.

CHAPTER TWO

L evi Pritchard walked onto the set, and Carter forgot every single line he'd memorized.

Oh my God.

He'd known before he'd come to Bluewater Bay that Levi lived around here somewhere but was as much of a hermit as Hunter. People saw him around town from time to time, or caught a glimpse of him launching his boat down at the marina, but Carter never had.

And now . . .

Fuck.

Levi was wrapped up in a conversation with Anna and Finn, and didn't seem to notice Carter. Or the fact that Carter was noticing the fuck out of him.

Wow. He'd had a crush on Levi since forever—slight understatement—and seeing him in person wasn't a letdown at all. Quite the contrary.

Levi must have been in his midthirties now. Maybe even pushing forty, and he made the years look *good*. Another five or ten, and his nearly black hair would probably start going gray.

Carter shivered.

"Well, look who's here." A voice startled Carter, and he turned as his stunt double, Ginsberg, sidled up next to him. "I thought he'd tell Finn to go fuck himself, but . . ."

"Apparently not."

Ginsberg lowered his voice. "You hear they're trying to cast him as Max Fuhrman?"

Swallowing hard, Carter nodded. Considering how often his character and Fuhrman would be interacting, he'd been well aware that the man he idolized was the top pick for the role. "Yeah, I heard. I didn't think he'd actually consider it, though."

"Well, he must be." Ginsberg gestured at Levi's back. "Unless he's just humoring them."

"I don't think he'd come all the way down here to humor them." Especially not if it was true what everyone said about Levi: that he'd long ago shunned all things Hollywood. Word on the street was that when he'd been approached for another sequel to the Chad Eastwick films, the action franchise that had made him famous, he'd responded with anatomical instructions for storing the script.

"He would make an awesome Fuhrman," Ginsberg said.

"No kidding."

"Not to mention some eye candy around the set." Ginsberg elbowed him playfully. "Too bad he's straight, eh?"

"Yeah. Too bad."

Though it was debatable. There'd been rumors since the dawn of time that Levi was gay, or bi, or curious, or *something* other than perfectly straight. Another actor maintained that he and Levi had dated on the down-low for a while, but Levi had always vehemently denied it. Some people said it was revenge after a bad breakup. Some said it was the alleged ex's attempt to date his way from B-list to A-list.

But Carter had always wondered.

Maybe it was wishful thinking. Not that he had a shot in hell, but the odds might tip slightly in his favor if dudes were on Levi's radar.

Right then, Levi glanced in his direction, and for a split second, they locked eyes. The script in Carter's hand almost fell to the floor, but he managed to hold on to it, using his momentary fumble as a reason to break eye contact. And he didn't dare look again. Great. First time Levi had ever seen him, and he was being a clumsy idiot. Fabulous.

When Carter finally worked up the nerve and turned around again, Levi was gone. So were Anna and Finn. Damn it. "That didn't take long."

Ginsberg scanned the set. "Wow. Yeah. Fastest set tour I've ever seen." He glanced at Carter. "You think he's gonna sign?"

Carter shrugged. *I hope. Please, please, let it mean something.* "Well, everyone says he wants nothing to do with film, TV, or anything." *Which is a damned shame.*

Ginsberg nodded. "Yeah, I thought he'd given up acting completely."

From a few feet away, a grip named Kevin snorted. "You mean he gave up on *trying* to act. Have you ever seen his work?"

Carter glared at him. "Actually, I have. Some of his old, pre-Eastwick stuff."

"Yeah?" Kevin rolled his eyes and yawned. "And?"

"And it's good. Really good." Carter turned toward the empty space Levi had been occupying a few minutes ago. "It's a crime they kept casting him in those stupid action movies."

"Maybe if he'd been a little better at—"

"I don't think he's given up completely on acting," Ginsberg broke in. "I mean, even if he doesn't get cast on the show, I heard he's been working with that community theater in town for the last couple of years."

Carter blinked. "You don't . . . you don't mean the Bluewater Bay Theater Company, do you?"

Ginsberg nodded. "That's what I've heard."

"No way. Wouldn't his name be on the marquee?" Carter shrugged. "I drive past it all the time, and I've never seen it." *And I would have noticed.*

"Don't know."

"And seriously, what the hell is a guy like him doing at a shitty place like that?" Carter glared at Kevin, daring him to pitch in his two cents. The guy wisely kept his trap shut.

"Well, around here, it's really his only option aside from . . ." The stuntman gestured at the set.

"Hmm. Good point. Maybe that's why he showed up."

"One can hope, right?"

Oh, I'm hoping . . .

Carter pulled his phone out of his pocket and thumbed a quick text to Hunter: *Anna + Finn got Pritchard to come to the set.*

Almost immediately, Hunter started typing a response, so he must've been at his desk. Working on the eighth *Wolf's Landing* book, no doubt.

You're kidding. They must've threatened him or something.

Carter chuckled. *LOL Don't know. But he was here. Def. him.*

Good. Did he seem interested?

Before Carter could respond, the outside door opened, letting in the blinding daylight. When it banged shut and Carter's eyes refocused, Finn had reappeared and was speaking into his cell phone. The producer was a pro at keeping a poker face, and he gave them nothing—no signs of frustration, relief, concern, or optimism.

Well. Carter would know soon enough if Levi was joining the cast or not. For now, he sent a message to Hunter saying he couldn't tell if Levi was interested, and then he picked up the script again. Half an hour ago, he'd known this scene by heart. Now, it was like he'd never even looked at the damned thing.

As he reread it, refreshing his memory, he pushed all thoughts of Levi out of his head. He'd let the man take over his mind again later.

But first, he had a scene to shoot.

CHAPTER THREE

A s soon as Finn had gone back into the abandoned warehouse-turned-soundstage, Levi muttered a few curses at the closed door.

Anna shook her head. "He drives me crazy. Sorry he had to come along, but he and the showrunner make the final decision, so I couldn't really avoid it."

"It's all right. Honestly, watching you try to blow up his skull with your mind was entertaining as hell."

She laughed. "Was I that obvious?"

"I know you, dear. And you've done the same to me before, so . . ."

"Only when you deserved it." She held out her arms. "Now give me a hug so I can get back to work."

"Yes, ma'am." He gathered her into a hug for the first time in way, way too long. Damn, she was right—they really should have met up when she'd moved here. Still embracing her, he said, "I promise I'll keep in touch this time. Even if I don't take the role."

Anna grinned as she released him. "Damn right you will."

"I will!" He showed his palms. "Just don't blow up my skull."

She threw him a menacing look, and then giggled.

He shifted his weight, gravel crunching beneath his sneakers. "I do have one question."

"Sure. Shoot."

He studied her. "Out of curiosity, does the current cast have anything to do with why you wanted me to come tour the set before I made my decision?"

Her eyes widened, and he'd have recognized that "who, me?" look from a mile away. "I don't know what you're talking about."

"Uh-huh." He raised an eyebrow. "So it had nothing to do with using a little bit of man candy to weaken my defenses?"

Anna casually inspected her nails. "No idea what you mean."

"Sure you don't."

Their eyes met, and the devilish sparkle in hers made him laugh.

Batting her eyelashes, she asked, "Well, did it work?"

"No. I'm not making career decisions based on . . ." He gestured at the soundstage.

"I know you're not." She smiled. "But I can't imagine you'll turn down a role where you get to engage in some sweaty man-grappling with Carter Samuels."

Levi's throat tightened. "What? He doesn't have a stunt double?"

"Of course he does. But whenever possible, he does his own stunts." She grinned, and he was sure she *almost* winked as she added, "Just like you."

Fuck. He was so fucked.

She knew it too. Brat.

Anna watched him for a moment. "Truth be told, I don't know how you've lasted this long in 'retirement.'"

Me neither.

He rubbed a stiff muscle in the side of his neck. "I've considered it a few times, but all it takes to remind me why I quit is a solid night's sleep without agonizing over some reporter getting a little too close to the truth about my personal life."

Anna pursed her lips. "I suppose I can't judge you for that."

"You know it even got to the point my own ringtone almost made me break out in hives?" He blew out a breath and kept kneading the muscle. Then he lowered his hand. "I want to act again. I *don't* want to deal with people speculating about who I'm fucking."

"I don't blame you."

"Speaking of . . ." He cleared his throat. "And, uh, is what Finn said true? About the studio being concerned about gay—"

"Oh, fuck them." She groaned. "Yes, they've been making noise about it, but I couldn't give two shits what they think. Everyone knows Carter's gay, but his character is . . . well, so far, he's straight."

Levi raised his eyebrows. "So far?"

"Honey, have you read the books?" She smirked. "Let's just say that if Gabriel ultimately turns out to be completely straight, I will renounce my lesbianism and take up cocksucking."

A laugh burst out of Levi. "Really? Maybe I need to catch up on my reading . . ."

"You should." She turned more serious. "And the thing is, the fans have caught on to that, so the studio is worried. With Carter and me both being openly gay, the studio is convinced the show is going to become hyperfocused on sexuality instead of, you know, shape-shifters and stopping the bad guys."

"Naturally." Levi paused. "So, uh, that means they have no clue about me, right?"

"Absolutely not." She stepped a little closer and lowered her voice. "I'd never out you. You know that."

"I know. But the rumors . . ."

"Trust me, nobody buys them." She glanced back at the soundstage, as if to make sure they were really alone. "The studio, Finn, everybody—they're all convinced you're the heaping dose of heterosexuality this show is missing."

Levi snorted. "Wow. I'm . . . flattered?"

"It's studio politics, sweetie. I feel squicky jumping on the whole 'Levi's the straight man we desperately need' bandwagon, but—"

"No, it's okay. Honestly, as long as *they* don't know."

"They don't, and they *can't* right now."

"They won't hear it from me." He scowled. "If the most recent session with my family was any indication, I won't be coming out anytime soon anyway."

She grimaced. "My God, are you *still* trying to iron things out with them?"

Levi nodded. "It's better than it was a few years ago. Just, you know, a slow process."

"Familial amputation is a lot faster, you know."

"Yeah, well . . ." He shrugged. "Things are improving. I mean, I only really see them during our family counseling sessions."

"How do you manage that?"

"Skype."

"Well, I guess that prevents you from throwing anything at them."

"More often than they probably realize," he muttered. "Anyway, it's getting better. Though, ask me again after they come visit."

She cringed. "Is that happening anytime soon?"

"Allegedly, they're coming to see the play I'm directing in town. So, next month."

"Good luck with that."

"Thanks." He hooked his thumbs in his pockets. "Anyway, if the studio's that hung up on me being straight, it's no big deal. As far as anyone else is concerned, I am."

Anna pressed her lips together, and he wondered if she was going to launch into one of her lengthy dissertations about hiding who he was, but she just sighed. "Okay, well. I should get back to work before my crew decides to take a long lunch." She gestured at his Jeep. "You go read those scripts and let me know, okay?"

"Will do. The theater's got rehearsal tonight, but I'll read them afterward."

"You'd better."

They embraced one last time, and then she headed back into the soundstage.

When she was gone, Levi closed his eyes and ran a hand through his hair. She had always been the persuasive type. So was Finn, but Anna wasn't conniving and slimy about it. She simply stated her case, pushed all his buttons, and didn't let up until she won.

But Levi wasn't ready to give in yet.

Sliding his hands into his pockets, he strolled back toward his Jeep. As his boots crunched on the gravel, he replayed their conversation, the discussion with Finn, and the tour of the set. Finn's sheer presence had been enough to keep Levi's guard up. He was a walking, talking reminder of all the reasons Levi hadn't read a single script that had been sent his way in the last few years.

Anna, though . . .

Damn her, she knew why, for all Levi said he'd left Hollywood and never looked back, he did look back once in a while. Every time Finn tried to twist Levi's arm like he was trying to sell him a used Honda, Anna would quietly clear away the slime and sleaze with a matter-of-fact comment about giving him the freedom to really dig deep and make Max Fuhrman into something even more complex than he was on the page. And suddenly Levi's hackles would go down, and he'd stop just short of swooning over this opportunity.

And then of course, though Anna would never confess to deliberately making it happen, Levi had caught a glimpse of Carter

Samuels. Whatever Finn had been saying at that moment had faded into the background with the usual film set noise.

Good lord. The kid was cute on camera, but he was gorgeous in person. The blond-blue look had never been Levi's thing, but Carter made his pulse jump. Remembering that fleeting eye contact made him stumble over nothing, and he glanced around to make sure no one had seen him. Thank God, there was no one else in sight. Face burning, he continued to his Jeep.

If working with Carter was part of the deal, Levi could almost convince himself to sign on the dotted line right then and there.

Almost.

He unlocked his Jeep and got into the driver's seat. He started the ignition, but didn't leave immediately. While the engine idled, his gaze drifted to the old warehouse. What scene were they shooting right now? Something in a dank, atmospheric place, judging by the lighting and set dressing. If he told Anna he was considering the part, would she let him hover in the background and watch them film?

Laughing to himself, he shook his head, and then put the Jeep in gear. Just what he needed. Fuel Anna's persuasion by confirming he had a wicked crush on one of her cast members.

He pulled out of the parking lot and headed for the highway that would take him into town. And of course, his mind went right back to the warehouse and that stunning blond lead.

It wasn't just that Carter was smoking hot. The man was as talented as he was gorgeous. He'd been drastically underutilized for the first couple of years of his career, relegated to pretty boy sidekicks and wisecracking cannon fodder, but then he'd been cast on *Wolf's Landing*, and now he was the star he deserved to be. He'd accumulated a whole pile of awards for his role on the show, and even though Levi wasn't sure he could untie his tongue when they were face-to-face, Carter was one actor he dreamed about working with.

And fantasized about—

You're old enough to be his father, idiot.

Still. Fantasies aside, they'd work together. Their characters interacted fairly regularly—first as adversaries, later as tense allies—and that meant he'd finally be able to act opposite someone with some serious chops.

If he took the role, that was.

Of course, Anna wouldn't let him pass it up without a fight. When she wanted something, she got it. End of story. Small wonder she had successfully clawed her way out of obscurity and scored a job as an executive producer on this show. He wouldn't have been surprised at all if she'd parked her ass in a higher-up's office and refused to back down until the guy had thrown up his hands and said, "All right! All right! Produce the goddamned thing."

The thought made him laugh, but at the same time, he kept his guard up. Just because Anna could persuade him didn't mean it was the right thing for him to do. And hadn't he promised himself hundreds of times that he wouldn't do this?

If it had been any other role . . .

If it had been any other producer . . .

If it had been any other costar . . .

He glared at the scripts sitting on the passenger seat, but no matter how much he tried to tamp it down, excitement started swelling in his chest.

Excitement, and some nerves he hadn't felt in a long time.

The cast of *Wolf's Landing* were in a huge fishbowl. Their fandom was, as some of them had joked in interviews, "gently obsessive." While the fans weren't terribly discreet about their fantasies—which manifested in everything from fan fiction to graphic art—about the actors and characters alike, the legitimately scary stalker types appeared to be few and far between. But the collective fandom still watched the cast's every move, flocking to public appearances and blogging endlessly about the briefest mention of an actor in a magazine.

For a lot of the cast members, this was their first major role. He couldn't blame them for basking in the adoration. In fact, he envied their ability to appear at conventions, chat up fans, and genuinely enjoy being on Q&A panels. By the time Chad Eastwick had become a fixture at things like Comic-Con, Levi had already turned bitter and jaded, desperate to separate himself from that role as much as possible.

He'd never let it show, but it had been agonizing to have fan after wide-eyed fan approaching him and *raving* about the one character he regretted playing. In fact, he was pretty sure some of them were *still* furious about the piece of Eastwick fanfic he'd anonymously penned a while back. It was still floating around out there somewhere, along with all the angry—and some alarmingly supportive—comments from the readers who couldn't believe its author had gleefully killed the guy in such grisly fashion.

What he wouldn't have given for the opportunity to visit with fans when he was as enthusiastic about a character as they were.

He glanced at the scripts again.

Maybe this was that opportunity.

CHAPTER FOUR

What the hell am I doing?

Carter's stomach clenched at the sight of the marquee above the Bluewater Bay Theater Company. Did this qualify as stalking? Oh God. Probably.

He very nearly accelerated past the theater, but slowed down instead. Go in? Go away? Go find something better to do than try to talk to Levi Pritchard?

A car honked, startling him, and he realized he'd slowed to a crawl in front of the theater. He waved an apology at the other driver, and turned into the tiny, mostly empty lot between the theater and the bank next door. He pulled into a space at the end of a row where he hoped no one else would park and issue his Porsche a door ding.

You're really going to do this?

Oh hell. Why not? What's the worst that could happen?

He didn't let himself entertain that thought as he got out of the car and walked over to the theater. He'd driven by this place a million times, but had never really given it a second look until now. It was a cool building, reminding him of some of the movie theaters in LA that were designed to look old and run-down, except here it wasn't done ironically.

Time had darkened the edges of the marquee, and a relatively recent paint job couldn't quite cover up the slight warping of the wood. Like most of downtown, the theater was probably Depression era, maybe even a little older, and no one had made much effort to update it. The weathered look gave it some charm, though. Some character that those new-but-old-looking playhouses in Los Angeles lacked.

The door creaked on its hinges. Inside, the dimly lit lobby was deserted apart from a couple of teenagers playing on their phones. They glanced at Carter and recognition flickered in their eyes, but they didn't say anything.

A lot of the ironically aged theaters in LA had lined their lobby walls with fresh versions of classic movie posters—*Gone With the Wind, Casablanca, The Wizard of Oz.* Carter suspected this place had had those faded, yellowed posters since the films were first run, showing in this very theater back before it had been converted into a playhouse.

The auditorium door was propped open with a half-rusted metal folding chair, and voices and activity came from the other side. Stomach fluttering, he wondered again and again if this was a good idea.

Before he could talk himself out of it, though, he stepped through the doorway and into the auditorium.

Onstage, three actresses—two middle-aged, one who might've been in her twenties—in street clothes stood with dog-eared scripts in their hands amidst an obstacle course of sawhorses and half-constructed sets. A half dozen theater techs worked in the background, painting the set pieces and talking amongst themselves, but didn't make much noise. Must've been nice—nothing was more fun than rehearsing over the whine of a power saw.

There were people everywhere. Actors studying the script and quietly rehearsing their scenes. Techs. Someone standing in the corner and frowning with her cell phone pressed to her ear. Probably a producer.

But where was Levi?

Carter scanned the room. A few people noticed him—they did double takes and subtly murmured behind their hands to get others to turn and look at him. Well, shit. There was no pretending he hadn't been here. Might as well not chicken out at this point, assuming he could find—

There.

Carter couldn't see much of Levi, but the man's voice was unmistakable. He sat low in a third-row seat, invisible except for when he gestured at the actors onstage. His presence, though. God. Carter could feel him. The second he heard Levi's voice, the hairs on his neck stood up just like when the man had appeared on the set this afternoon.

Like Carter, the actresses onstage were focused on Levi, watching him intently as he gave instructions.

"Marti, you're getting there, but I still don't *quite* believe you. I need the people in the back row"—he gestured over his head, making Carter's heart skip—"to feel how hard this news is hitting Sadie."

The middle-aged woman nodded. "Okay."

"All right," Levi said. "Start at the top of page four."

The actors all flipped back a couple of pages, and began going through the lines again. Carter took a seat in the back row. It wasn't a play he had ever heard of. Might've been written by one of the locals, or maybe it was an obscure show the company had found God knew where.

After a few more attempts and more guidance from Levi, the woman finally breathed some life into her lines.

"Good, good!" Levi rose, unaware he was taking Carter's heart rate with him. "That's perfect, Marti. Carry that through the whole scene and you're golden."

The woman smiled, her cheeks coloring under the overhead spotlights.

Levi took his seat again. "Let's run through the entire scene one last time, and then we'll call it a night."

Carter's heart went into his throat. This was it. While the actresses did their final run-through for the evening, he tried to find the nerve that had brought him this far in the first place. He'd known when he moved here that Levi lived in the area, and he'd desperately wanted to connect with him ever since, but he'd never known how to cross paths with him until now. Did that make it right? Did that make this *not* creepy?

But then, if the guys on the set knew Levi was working here, it was probably no big secret. The theater was public, so it wasn't like Carter was chasing him down at his house, which was likely secluded and tucked far away from town for a reason. As long as Carter took "no" for an answer and didn't push, then he wasn't being a stalker.

Whatever helps you sleep at night, man.

The actresses wrapped up their scene, and Levi dismissed the entire crew after a brief pep talk. Carter rose, ready to pull him aside as he came up the aisle, but a paint-and-plaster-splattered tech beat him to the punch, cornering Levi with some paperwork. They slowly made their way toward the door, faces buried in a stack of file folders.

"The lifts haven't been used in years." The tech gestured at something on a form in front of Levi as they passed Carter. "If we want to raise and drop the sets the way you're asking, we'll have to completely refit it, and it's going to blow our budget."

"Fuck," Levi muttered. "All right, get some estimates and get it done." He handed the papers back to the tech. "Let's keep it reasonable, but I'll pay it out of my pocket if it goes over budget. The theater needs an upgrade anyway."

Carter didn't hear the response because they disappeared through the lobby door. He started to follow them, but a pretty brunette suddenly materialized beside him.

"Excuse me, are you . . ." She blushed. "Are you Carter Samuels?"

He smiled. "Yeah, I am."

"Really? Would you mind—" She gestured with her phone.

"Sure."

He'd gotten pretty damned good at taking selfies with fans, so he took her phone, and they posed for a quick picture. Though he was eager to catch up with Levi—what if he left?—he gave her a chance to make sure the shot turned out, and waited until she'd hurried off to show the other cast members before he slipped out to the lobby.

Fortunately, Levi hadn't left yet. The tech he'd been talking to earlier was gone, but a small group of actors were listening intently as he spoke, though Carter couldn't hear what was being said.

While Levi talked with his cast members, Carter hung back and tried not to notice that they'd noticed him. Two other women—one of the actresses he'd watched earlier and another who he guessed was a tech because of the dust on her jeans and T-shirt—asked for a photo and an autograph, and he was as gracious as possible. He even appeared, he hoped, calm and cool—thank God for a few trips down the red carpet and four appearances on Comic-Con panels. Those had taught him well how to hide his nerves.

While he posed and chatted with them, his heart pounded and his tongue threatened to stick to the roof of his mouth. He wasn't sure if waiting made it better or worse. It gave him time to get used to being in the same room with Levi before he had to actually speak to him, but it also gave him more time to get worked up and nervous.

The women left, and suddenly Carter was alone with his thoughts and those ever-present nerves.

How do you talk to someone who doesn't know he shaped who you are?

Carter took a few deep breaths. This was definitely a bad idea. He should've waited to see if Levi accepted the role on the show. At least then it wouldn't seem creepy or weird for them to be in the same place at the same time. In the same room. Breathing the same air.

Fuck. What the hell is wrong with me?

Movement caught his eye; in Carter's moment of distraction, Levi had left his conversation and was disappearing into the night.

Carter hurried after him, catching the door just before it closed. "Hey, Mr. Pritchard."

Levi stopped dead in his tracks, looked around, and then faced Carter. His eyebrows jumped. "Uh, yes?"

Calling on every bit of confidence he had to banish the fresh onslaught of stage fright, Carter stepped closer and extended his hand. "Carter Samuels. I work on—"

"Yeah, I know who you are." Levi hesitated, but then shook Carter's hand. "I watch the show."

"Oh. You . . ." Carter suddenly couldn't remember how to shake hands. "You do?"

Levi nodded. He gently freed his hand. "And I also, uh, saw you on the set today."

You saw me? You noticed *me?*

"Right. Yeah." Carter shifted his weight. "Look, I'm not gonna go all fanboy on you, but I've, uh, kind of been wanting to meet you since I moved here."

Levi held Carter's gaze, but drew back a little, and Carter couldn't decide if the guy was uncomfortable, embarrassed, amused, creeped out . . .

Carter cleared his throat. "I wanted to pick your brain. One professional to another." Now that he'd said it, he suddenly felt like a school bus driver asking Mario Andretti for driving tips. One professional to another? Yeah. Right.

"Pick my brain?" Levi's eyebrows rose. "About?"

"Your technique." Carter swallowed. "I've always admired you. The things you do with a character are just—" So much for not going all fanboy on him. Lowering his gaze, Carter added, "If you'll let me buy you a drink, I'd love to just ask about how you do it."

Levi laughed bitterly. "You'd be better off talking to a stuntman. I just do what they do, except with lines." He started to walk away.

"I don't mean your action roles."

Levi stopped midstep. "What?"

Carter chewed his lip. "I mean films like *Broken Day* and *Stir.*"

"You've . . ." Levi turned around. "You've heard of those two?"

"Heard of them?" Carter laughed nervously. "I have them on DVD. My copy of *Tin Horse* was stolen, but I—"

"*Tin Horse?*" Levi stared at him, eyes wide. Moving slowly, almost cautiously, he came back toward Carter. "You had a copy of *Tin Horse?*"

Carter nodded. "I've been looking for another one for three years. It's . . . it's my favorite of all your films." *It's one of my favorite films* ever.

"Mine too. I haven't heard someone else mention it in ages." Levi paused and cleared his throat. "All right, let's go get a drink. This one's on me."

"Really? I can pay, it's—"

"No, no." He smiled sheepishly. "I'm the one who was about to storm off like a dick. Consider it an apology in a glass."

Carter laughed. "Okay. Second round's on me, though."

"Deal."

Holy shit, he's really taking me up on it? I'm having a drink with—

Right. Not going all fanboy.

"So if you've heard of those titles, you must be into indie films."

"My mom calls it a mild obsession."

Levi chuckled. "Is 'mild' an attempt to be gentle?"

"Maybe . . ."

They glanced at each other and laughed. Something electric shot down Carter's spine. He'd worked around enough actors—even a couple of Oscar winners—that he'd long since gotten over any inclination to get starstruck.

But . . . Levi Pritchard.

Levi Pritchard was walking with him. Talking with him. Sharing a laugh with him. They were going to sit down and have a drink and talk shop and— Okay, so apparently he was still capable of getting starstruck.

There was a tavern three doors down from the theater, and only a few heads turned when Levi and Carter walked in. Most of the locals knew each other, but largely ignored the "foreigners" as he'd heard a few of them refer to the cast and crew.

A hostess showed them to a booth in the corner, and they ordered drinks—a light beer for Carter and a Coke for Levi. Carter wasn't particularly hungry since his stomach was full of butterflies, but he perused the menu anyway. Or tried to. His gaze kept drifting from the words and pictures to the man on the other side of the table. Jesus fuck. Was he really sitting across from Levi Pritchard? The man who'd inspired him to be an actor in the first place?

He gave up on the menu, and let himself look at Levi. The overhead light picked out details and imposed heavy shadows on his face, including a faint, silvery line spiking upward from his cheek to his temple. Where the scar met his hairline, a few stark white hairs crisscrossed with the darker ones. Carter didn't remember ever seeing that scar before, and God knew he'd looked closely at a few of Levi's pictures.

Levi's eyes flicked up, and Carter quickly shifted his to the menu in front of him. The skin on the back of his neck prickled. He wondered if Levi was scrutinizing him the way he'd been doing, but he was afraid to look.

Their server appeared. "What can I get you gentlemen?"

"Um, let's see . . ." Carter scanned the menu and realized he hadn't read a single word of it. "You go ahead. I'm still deciding."

Levi ordered a plate of nachos, and Carter quickly decided on steak fries. When the waitress left, their eyes met briefly, and they both cleared their throats and looked away.

From the corner of his eye, Carter watched Levi poking at ice cubes in his soda with his straw, and he struggled to kick-start a conversation.

Levi beat him to the punch, though. "By the way, I'm sorry again for almost storming off like that. Isn't very often I run into people who know me as anything other than Chad Eastwick."

"Don't worry about it." Carter waved a hand. "I can, uh, relate a bit."

Levi laughed. "Yeah, I suppose you can, can't you?"

Groaning, Carter rolled his eyes. "I will be Gabriel Hanford until the end of fucking time."

"Just be glad he has some depth."

"I am, believe me."

Levi was quiet for a moment. Then he met Carter's eyes through his lashes. "So I'm curious. How did you stumble across my old stuff?"

"Buddy of mine saw *Broken Day* at Sundance. We found a—" His cheeks burned. "Okay, it was a bootlegged copy. But I did buy a legal copy as soon as I found one!"

Levi chuckled. "It's all right. To be honest, I can't begrudge a bootleg on one of those films. At least that means someone put in the effort to get their hands on it."

"It was worth the effort. Great movie."

"Thanks."

Silence threatened to settle in, so Carter asked, "How did you even go from roles like that to the action movies?"

Levi sniffed. "Because someone in a suit thought I looked good with a gun and a few smears of fake blood."

Oh, he wasn't wrong there . . .

Carter cocked his head.

Levi rubbed the back of his neck and sighed. "My agent talked me into taking the role in the Eastwick films because he said it would get me on the radars of people who counted." Rolling his eyes, he added, "Do a few Die Hard roles, and sooner or later, you'll get cast in *The Sixth Sense*."

"So they say," Carter muttered.

"Right?" Levi watched him. "You have plans for after *Wolf's Landing*? I mean, other kinds of roles you want to play?"

"I want to try everything, but I'm worried it's going to be tortured detectives from here on out. At least for a while."

"You never know. Your character's got some depth and versatility." Levi snorted. "I have yet to see a critic say you're a stuntman with lines."

You've noticed what critics say about me?

Mouth suddenly dry, Carter reached for his beer. Which was also dry. Fuck. He cleared his throat. "I guess I'm just afraid I'll be typecast as Gabriel forever."

"Could be worse." Levi smirked. "You could be Chad fucking Eastwick for the rest of your life."

Carter laughed. "That role put you on the map, though, didn't it?"

"Yeah. And as far as most people are concerned, it's *all* I've ever done."

"Hooray for being typecast." Carter lifted his beer bottle.

Levi raised his glass slightly, then took a drink.

The waitress arrived with their plates. After she'd gone, and they'd both nibbled at their appetizers, Carter quietly asked, "So, is it true you're considering the role in *Wolf's Landing*?"

Levi bristled. Carter almost retracted the question, but Levi sighed and shrugged. "I don't know. Maybe. I know Finn's bent on convincing me—"

"Oh, fuck, I hate that guy!"

Levi laughed. Like, really laughed. "Do you?"

Carter groaned. "Fucking slimeball."

"Ah, so you've had the pleasure."

"Mm-hmm. And he's trying to talk you into signing on for the show?"

Levi nodded.

"But you're on the fence?"

"Yep." Levi tugged a chip free from his nachos. "People like Finn are the biggest reason I left Hollywood. Roles like Max Fuhrman are the biggest reason I'd consider going back."

"Wow. Tough position to be in."

"Yeah, you could say that." Levi laughed, bitterly this time, and then crunched on the chip.

For a long moment, they were both quiet, munching on their food and sipping their drinks. Carter wasn't sure how to keep himself from blurting out, "I really hope you take the role because I'm dying to work with you," so he just focused on his steak fries.

"Listen, um . . ." Levi muffled a cough. "I still have a few copies of *Tin Horse*. If you want to grab coffee or something, I could bring a copy."

"Really?"

Levi lifted his head, and his smile made Carter's pulse soar. "For someone who actually appreciates that film? You bet."

"Awesome." Carter grinned. "Thank you."

"Thank *you*." Levi held Carter's gaze for a second, but then broke eye contact again. "Just, you know, let me know when and where. Your schedule is probably crazier than mine."

Carter took out his phone. "Fortunately, there's an app for that."

"Must be nice."

"It's a lifesaver." Carter pulled up the shooting schedule. "Actually, I'm pretty free tomorrow. We're doing a few reshoots in the morning, but..." He scrolled through the entire day's schedule. "Yeah, I'm free."

Levi smiled, which buzzed Carter more than the beer had. "Why don't we meet up for coffee, then? There's a place over on Sandy Bluff Road." He pointed over his shoulder. "Annette's."

"Sounds great. What time?"

He shrugged. "Whenever. I don't have a schedule."

Carter glanced at the app again. "Two thirty?"

"Two thirty. I'll be there." Levi's smile broadened a little. "And I'll bring *Tin Horse*."

"Great. See you then."

CHAPTER FIVE

L evi didn't want to be sold on the role of Max Fuhrman. He didn't want Anna to be right. He didn't want to be the studio-prescribed helping of heterosexuality on an otherwise queer show. And he *really* didn't want to give in to Finn's arm-twisting.

Being out so late with Carter had given him an excuse not to read the scripts until today. All morning, though, he'd given them a wide berth, eyeing them warily every time he passed the kitchen island where he'd put them before last night's rehearsal. He circled like a reluctant shark, knowing he'd eventually do it, but talking himself out of it time and again.

Finally, he snatched them off the counter, settled on the couch between the cats, and opened the first episode.

And damn it, three pages into the script, he couldn't have turned it down if he tried. For the first time in years, the thought of signing a contract actually gave him that rush it had when he'd started out.

This was the role he'd been begging for before he'd left LA. The kind of role that reminded him how much he loved—and missed— acting. Even when it had been two-bit action hero roles where the dialogue was a bunch of corny one-liners that must've been dreamed up by failed comic book writers, he'd enjoyed it.

And this role? He loved Max Fuhrman in the books. The man was fucked in the head, and had been since before he was traumatized by some time in combat, as well as his run-ins with the vicious paranormal critters that frequently cropped up in the series. At first, he'd seemed plain old crazy and quite possibly evil, but then he'd started showing a more human side. Morally ambiguous at times, borderline sociopathic at others, but also . . . human. The scene where he'd found out his daughter was dead was *heartbreaking*, and the thought of bringing that moment to life on camera gave Levi goose bumps.

Some screenwriters were spectacular at destroying characters when they transferred them from a novel to a script. Levi should've known that wouldn't be the case here, and it wasn't—the screenwriter had transferred every possible scrap of Max onto the page. This was perfect. It was Levi's chance to get back in front of the cameras, to play a real and complex character, and to be taken seriously as an actor.

For that matter, it would help with his expenses. His plan a few years ago had consisted of "get the fuck out of Hollywood." He'd had plenty of money to pay cash for his house and live for quite a while, and he'd made some investments to keep the coffers from running low, but those investments weren't doing so hot these days. Though he wasn't exactly in danger of being out on the streets anytime soon, a little positive cash flow wouldn't hurt, especially when he was writing checks to support the theater.

Accepting the role didn't mean he was going back to Hollywood. Hell, he didn't even have to leave Bluewater Bay. After a day of shooting, he could retreat to his own home and his cats, and escape. This was *perfect*.

Anna and Finn had included copies of the scripts for later in the season too, when Fuhrman, no longer just a peripheral character, really started to make himself a part of *Wolf's Landing*. After reading the first two episodes, Levi was itching to dive into the rest.

And he would have, except he needed to get into town to see Carter.

Goose bumps prickled his skin.

Carter Samuels wanted to meet up with him. And he wanted a copy of *Tin Horse*. And they'd be working together if Levi agreed to play Max Fuhrman.

There had to be a "but . . ." waiting around the bend. There always was.

Might as well enjoy this ride until it runs out of tracks.

He left the scripts beside his chair in the living room and went into the garage. It didn't take long to find the box he was looking for. All the boxes had been painstakingly labeled with their contents, though the one marked *DVDs–Crew Copies* was pushed back behind *Xmas Decor* and *Textbooks*.

After shuffling a few around, he pulled down the box and set it on his workbench. As he dug out a copy of *Tin Horse*, the image on the DVD case gave him pause. How long had it been since he'd even thought about that film, let alone watched it? He brushed off some of the dust and stared at the cover for a moment, scrutinizing the picture as if he'd never seen it before.

He'd always loved that cover—the wilting rose on a rain-soaked headstone with a few brass shell casings scattered around it. Sighing, he ran his fingers over the image. Damn, they'd all been so sure the film would take off. After it had racked up awards at Sundance, Cannes, Toronto, and half a dozen other major festivals, it had been pretty much guaranteed to break out of obscurity. Cult classic status at the very least.

And . . . nothing.

Negotiations with potential distributors had been promising, but then a controversial film about modern whale hunting had exploded onto the scene. Suddenly it had become The Film Everyone Wanted, and it ultimately went on to become a blockbuster with three members of the cast being offered major roles—one of them had an Oscar now—while *Tin Horse* had faded back into the woodwork. Within two years, it was "Tin what?"

But still, somehow, it had made it onto Carter's radar.

And Carter had certainly made it onto *his* radar. There was no mystery there. From the first time Levi had tuned into *Wolf's Landing*, he'd been struck by the wild-eyed kid. He usually snorted derisively when an actor was declared a heartthrob or whatever, but he got it with this one. If Levi were still a teenager, he had no doubt Carter would be in many, many of the magazines he had tucked between his mattress and box spring.

Except Levi wasn't a teenager anymore. He was pretty sure he had at least fifteen years on Carter, and younger men had never really been his cup of tea. Particularly younger men who were out and proud to the whole damned world when Levi still couldn't tell his volatile, conservative family or their therapist that his ex's name, Kim, hadn't been short for Kimberly.

Though Carter's character, Gabriel Hanford, was steadily making his way through the women of Wolf's Landing, Carter himself was openly gay and had been out since day one. He was out, he was hot, and he'd hunted Levi down at the community theater to talk about a film Levi couldn't believe he'd even heard of. Was that all he'd come to talk—

Yes, of course it was.

Levi scowled as he put the box back up on its shelf. He would've loved to delude himself into believing Carter might be interested in more than just picking his brain, but a young, hot A-lister with his choice of any gay man on the planet? Levi had a shot at him like he had a shot at a singing career, and there was a reason he'd never done musical theater.

But if they could at least work together . . .

What the fuck is the matter with me?

He wasn't starstruck. Levi Pritchard didn't *get* starstruck. Half the women—and, discreetly, men—he'd dated in LA had been A-listers. The notches on his bedpost read like a list of Academy Award nominees. Hell, he'd slept in the shadow of two Oscar statuettes for that year and a half he and Kim had been "roommates."

But something about Carter screwed with his equilibrium.

Might as well get used to it if we're going to be working together.

And the next step toward that seemingly impossible task was sitting down to a late lunch with him and talking about films. One on one with the too-young, too-out guy he'd secretly had a crush on since *Wolf's Landing*'s pilot episode, talking about the thing he was most passionate about. He might as well swing into Ink Bay and get "It's Not a Fucking Date" tattooed across his arm so he wouldn't forget.

Shaking his head, he grabbed his keys and the DVD, and headed into town.

"Another refill?"

Levi glanced up at the waiter, then at his Coke glass, which contained nothing but melting ice cubes faintly tinted by the remaining soda. "Sure, thanks."

The waiter took his glass and Levi glanced at his phone. Five minutes till three. He set the phone down and gazed out the window as he drummed his fingers on the table. At what point did "late" become "he's standing you up"? Especially when it was two guys meeting for a bite to eat and a DVD, not a date?

A minute later, the waiter reappeared with a topped-off Coke glass. "You ready to order, or still waiting?"

"Still waiting." Levi forced a smile. "Shouldn't be too long."

"Sure, no problem." The waiter returned the smile, and Levi couldn't help thinking he saw a flash of pity in the kid's eyes.

He shifted his gaze back to the street outside. Did he really expect someone like Carter to take time out of his life just to get a copy of an obscure DVD? A DVD of one of *his* films? Then again, he had heard of the film, and his enthusiasm had seemed genuine. It was possible he—

Holy fuck. There he was.

Carter practically ran past the window and when he came in the café's front door, his cheeks were flushed like he'd sprinted halfway across town. "Sorry I'm late. My phone was dead, and then we—"

"It's all right." Levi chuckled and pretended he wasn't so fucking relieved. "Relax. Sit."

Carter exhaled and took a seat on the other bench. "Anna was directing today, and I fucking adore the woman, but goddamn, she cannot stick to a shooting schedule to save her life."

"Can't she?"

Carter whistled. "No, she cannot. As soon as she says, 'Let's do one more take, just to be sure,' we all know we're going to be there for another two hours."

Levi laughed. "I've worked with directors like that."

"Have you? Do tell."

"Well, did you ever see the second Chad Eastwick?"

"Of course."

"You remember that scene where my character's brawling with Clint Jasper's character and we end up fighting waist-deep in the water?"

"Oh, yeah. That was a kick-ass scene."

"Says the man who didn't have to film it." Levi clicked his tongue and shook his head. "It was in October, and that water was *maybe* forty degrees. Clint and I were fucking numb. I mean, it made the scene look good, because we both looked exhausted, but it was hell to film."

Carter grimaced. "Ouch."

"Yeah. The best part? My stunt double was supposed to do like half the shots, but he got stung *bad* by a goddamned jellyfish—"

A laugh burst out of Carter. "Oh shit. You're kidding."

"Hand to God." Levi chuckled. "I don't know if he was allergic or if it was a particularly nasty jellyfish or what, but he was done for the day. So the director said we'd have to finish the scene another day after he'd recovered, and I was like, 'Nope. Let's do this.' Because there was no way in hell any of us were getting back in the water after that."

"Good thing the rest of you didn't get stung."

"Oh, we did. Both of us. *And* we got cut up on the rocks too. Not all the blood you saw was fake, I'll tell you that."

Carter's jaw dropped. "Jesus Christ. Were they trying to kill you?"

"Sometimes I wonder. But the most priceless moment was when Clint was standing there, covered in fake and real blood, shivering like hell and pouring vinegar on a jellyfish sting. I don't know if he was trying to be in character, or if he was just royally pissed, but he had that perfect villain snarl right then, and said, 'If he asks for one more take, I'm going to find a jellyfish and shove it up his ass.'"

"Now *that* I can relate to!"

"Oh yeah?" Levi lifted his eyebrows. "Similar experiences?"

"Ugh. Yes. When we were shooting *Butcher Shop 2* in— Did you see that one?"

"Yeah, I saw it." *Three times on the big screen.*

"Oh. Wow. Really?"

"Hell yeah. It was a great film."

Carter's jaw dropped. "I . . ."

"I don't live under a rock," Levi said playfully. "I do go to the movies sometimes."

"Yeah, I guess . . . I guess you would, wouldn't you?" Carter swallowed and shook himself. "Um, right. Anyway. You remember in the climax scene, when Sam Blaine flings blood in my face?"

"Yep, I do."

"So the director kept making us reshoot it and reshoot it because I kept anticipating the 'blood' and I kept flinching."

"Understandable."

"Right? So we did take after take until he was finally happy. You know—throw it in my face, then go to makeup and clean it all off, which is a huge pain in the ass since red dye and blond hair go so well together, redo my makeup, and do it all over again. And again. And again." He groaned. "*Finally* we get it right."

Levi cringed. "Don't tell me there was another problem."

Carter nodded. "A neurotic cinematographer."

"Oh God . . ."

"Yeah."

"I'm surprised there wasn't a mutiny among the entire crew."

"There almost was. And there was almost an even worse one the next night after we filmed the tanker explosion. I think the lead pyrotechnician actually had to be physically restrained from beating the shit out of the cinematographer."

Levi laughed. "I can't say I'm all that surprised. Let me guess— perfectly timed and coordinated 'one chance to get it right' explosions, and the lighting was wrong?"

"Bingo. You run into the same problem?"

"Not exactly the same. Usually the director just decided the explosions weren't big enough or something. That's why the Eastwick films always went so far over budget."

Carter snorted. "I wonder how much of that was bonus pay for the pyrotechnician to not blow up the director's trailer for spite."

"No kidding." Levi chuckled. "Oh! I almost forgot." He reached for the DVD on the bench beside him. "One copy of *Tin Horse*."

Carter's eyes lit up. "Sweet!" He took the DVD from Levi and held it to his chest like some fans clutched their autographed photos. "I've been looking everywhere for a copy. I cannot *wait* to watch it again."

Levi smiled. "It's nice to see some enthusiasm about that one, believe me."

"I still don't get why it's not bigger than it is." Carter set the DVD on the table with his phone on top of it. "I mean, okay, I know how distribution works and all that, but it's still bullshit."

"Trust me, you're preaching to the choir."

"Annoying as fuck, isn't it?"

"*Oh*, yeah."

"Ah, well." He tapped the DVD case. "Thanks again."

"You're welcome." Levi glanced at the DVD. It was surreal, seeing someone else in possession of that film. "I was in love with it from the first page of the script."

"It's an awesome story. How different was it, making an indie film instead of a studio-backed one?"

"Huge difference. *Huge*."

"Really?"

Levi nodded. "It's all about making the story, not making money." He smirked. "You just kind of assume you're not going to make a dime off the damned thing. No one's expecting a blockbuster when they're shooting an indie film."

"No, I guess they wouldn't be. Must take some pressure off."

"Big-time. Of course, you also don't have a lot of money to start with, but even that's a plus in a way."

Carter tilted his head. "It is?"

"Yeah. You have to get really, really creative when you're shooting on a budget, and that can be a lot of fun. Sure, you don't get to play with the pyrotechnics and CGI, but there's something really cool about watching a scene you've just filmed and realizing a studio would've spent millions to build scale models and create background CGI, but you pulled it off with fifty bucks worth of fireworks and some Legos."

Carter laughed. "Fireworks and Legos?" He sat up, folding his arms on the place mat. "Which scene was that?"

"The one in *Stir*, where the mobster's mansion gets blown up."

Carter's eyes lost focus for a second. "The one . . . oh, right, when it was on the hill and you and the other character were watching from a distance?"

Levi nodded. "That hill was just a little berm in the director's backyard, and the mansion was made out of Legos and filled with M-80s."

"Whoa. Well, it sure looked convincing."

"I hope so. We spent two days building that thing."

"Two entire days building a mansion out of Legos just so you could blow it up?" Carter put a hand to his chest. "My heart *bleeds*."

"Hey, we all have to suffer for our art."

"Uh-huh." Carter rolled his eyes. "So why didn't you ever make any more indie films? After you left LA, I mean?"

Levi absently stabbed at the ice cubes in his soda. "I think I was just so cynical and jaded over everything, I stayed away from the entire industry. Even the stuff I knew was worlds apart from Hollywood."

"You miss it?"

Levi watched the ice cubes dip beneath the surface of his drink before popping back up again. Finally, he confessed what he hadn't been able to say out loud for years: "I miss it every single day."

He braced himself for the inevitable pressure to sign on to *Wolf's Landing*, but Carter just murmured, "I can only imagine."

A weird silence set in, and Levi realized it was the first awkward moment they'd had since Carter had approached him last night. After their nervous introduction, they had fallen easily into conversation, and they'd slipped right back into it again the second Carter had walked in today.

He cleared his throat. "Say, uh, do you remember the bridge scene in *Tin Horse*?"

Grinning, Carter sat a little straighter. "When you and Victor were getting high and playing Russian roulette under the bridge?"

Levi couldn't help returning the grin—it was a fucking rush to hear someone else talking about that film. "Yeah, that one. You remember the revolver we were using?"

Carter nodded. "Yeah."

"You want to see it? The real thing?"

Carter's mouth fell open. "You have it?"

"I have a *ton* of props from that film. Hell, I have props from pretty much all my films."

"No shit? They let you take them?"

"Well, they let me take some of them. Others, well . . ."

"They just sort of 'disappeared' from the set?"

"Pretty much. After we finish up here, I can take you over to my place to check out the collection." Levi paused. "I mean, if you're okay with that."

"Okay with it?" Carter smiled. "If it means I get to see the revolver from *Tin Horse*? I'm there."

Holy shit.

He said yes.

CHAPTER SIX

Levi followed Carter to his rental house just outside of town. Carter left his Porsche in the garage, and then climbed into the passenger seat of Levi's Jeep. They drove back the other direction, taking the highway across town to the expanse of thick forest and not much else between this town and the next one. Then Levi turned off one of the barely visible side roads, and they continued deeper into the hills.

All along the road, huge old-growth cedars shot up from a carpet of ferns, their broad trunks covered on one side with thick moss. Carter wasn't sure if this was the northern edge of the rain forest, or if it was separate, but it certainly reminded him of the trails he'd hiked out in Olympic National Park.

The pavement ended, and Carter gripped the edge of his seat as Levi expertly navigated the deep potholes—well, the ones he could avoid. They were almost thirty minutes from town now, an exit and three or four turns from the main highway, and there was less and less civilization out here.

As the dusty old Jeep bounced and bumped down the dirt road, Carter wasn't sure what to expect. Where Levi lived, what kind of house it was. There'd been rumors flying around for the last year or two that Levi had bankrupted himself and was just getting by out here in Bluewater Bay. Some people said he'd sold off two of his three Corvettes to make ends meet—his movie wealth wouldn't last forever. Others said he and a bottle of tequila had wrapped the third Vette around a tree. Everyone had seen pictures of the wreck, but the booze part had never been confirmed. All Carter knew for sure was this wasn't the passenger seat of *any* Corvette. The Jeep was in good repair, but definitely an older model.

Levi might've lived in one of the mobile homes they kept passing, the ones clustered between run-down gas stations and cheap motels, or in a mossy trailer tucked behind the trees, next to cars on blocks.

It was just as possible he had a sprawling farm, or a luxury house overlooking the Strait of Juan de Fuca.

Carter had no idea. Every time they passed another home, farm, trailer park, or gated driveway out here in the sticks, Levi intrigued him a little more.

The trailer parks and gated driveways faded behind them, and for a good five miles, there was nothing but trees and the odd service road for the Department of Forestry. At a lone mailbox beneath a pair of towering cedars, Levi turned down a gravel driveway, which wound through the woods for almost a mile before the house came into view.

And . . . wow.

The rumors of Levi hiding in a trailer were obviously unfounded. The house was large, though modest by Hollywood standards, and built from reddish-amber cedar with a dark-green trim. Gleaming solar panels made up most of the roof, and Carter guessed those huge south-facing windows on the top two floors must have a spectacular view of Mount Olympus.

Levi pressed a button on the visor, and the left bay door of a three-car garage slowly opened. As the Jeep rolled into the garage, Carter glanced to the side, and a gorgeous black Corvette Stingray caught his eye.

"Wow, nice. I wondered if you still had your Vettes." He gulped. "I mean, since you were driving the Jeep, I . . ." Fuck. Way to make things awkward.

Levi glanced at him, then past him at his car. "Well, I have that one."

Carter wanted to ask what happened to the other two, but he bit his lip, not sure if he should press. Especially considering some of the relentless rumors.

Gaze fixed on the Vette, Levi killed the Jeep's engine. "I sold the silver one. The red one . . ." His eyes lost focus for a moment. "I wrecked it." He took the keys out of the ignition and finally looked at Carter again. "And *no*, I was not drunk."

"I—"

"C'mon. Props are inside." Levi got out of the Jeep. Carter glanced back at the car, and then followed Levi into the house.

The interior was gorgeous. Bright and open, with enough lighting to compensate for the Northwest's notorious gray days.

Levi dropped his keys on the granite countertop in the kitchen. "Can I get you anything? Beer? Coke?" His expression was taut, his voice flat as if he was keeping something close to his vest.

"No, I'm good. Thanks." Carter smiled, hoping Levi would do the same. He did, but halfheartedly. Guilt gnawed at Carter. He just had to mention the cars, didn't he?

Levi cleared his throat. "This way."

Carter followed him down a hallway lined with nature prints and a framed poster of a sleek Vette. There was also a photo of maybe a dozen guys—he recognized several as cast members from *Tin Horse* and *Broken Day*—smiling and posing, and there were signatures all over the mat around the photo.

He didn't stop to look closer, though, and followed Levi to a set of French doors. As they stopped in front of the room, the dark clouds over Levi's mood seemed to evaporate. With a grin, he put his hands on the brass handles. "I still have to find a place to put some things, but the good stuff is in here."

He pushed the doors open and flipped a switch. The room lit up like a museum gallery, dim except for strategically positioned spotlights. The hardwood floor was unoccupied except for a few standing cases, and similar cases were built into the walls all the way around. The spotlights illuminated the various contents, as well as the odd freestanding display—a mannequin wearing battered gladiator regalia, a blood-stained pinstripe suit, and what Carter was pretty sure was the camouflage from the third Eastwick movie.

"Wow." Carter stepped inside, the hardwood creaking under his sneakers. "I never thought of putting something like this in a house."

"Neither did I, but the guy who sold me the place did a ton of traveling." Levi scanned the room like he was seeing it for the first time. "He collected cool stuff from all over the world, and had it on display. I couldn't think of anything else to put in here, so . . ." He waved a hand at the cases. "Movie props."

"That . . ." Carter struggled to take in the awesomeness laid out around them. "This is fucking amazing."

Levi grinned. "Thanks. Oh, and the gun from *Tin Horse* is right over here." He led Carter across the room, floorboards squeaking under their feet, and stopped in front of a case against the far wall.

And front and center was the .38 special revolver.

"So that's the gun, huh?" He leaned down and inspected it as best he could through the glass. "Damn, it looks real."

"That's because it *is* real."

His head snapped up. "You're kidding."

"Nope." Levi's gaze was fixed on the gun, his expression full of nostalgia. "Our budget didn't allow for a convincing prop, so the director let us use his. We had it modified so it was impossible to shoot, but the cylinder would still turn and the hammer would drop."

"Damn . . ."

"Yeah. That was probably one of the smarter things we ever did. Unlike, say, having me and Steve jumping out of moving cars in *Broken Day*."

"No stunt doubles?"

"Not on that budget."

Carter chuckled. "Guess you couldn't pull that off with Legos and fireworks, could you?"

"If we could've, we would've."

"I have no doubt." He turned his attention back to the case. "Are those the shell casings from the DVD cover?"

"Yep. Nobody else wanted them, so . . ."

"Nice. And that's the switchblade from *Broken Day*, isn't it?"

"It— How many times have you seen that film?"

Carter's cheeks burned and he glanced sheepishly at Levi. "Enough times to recognize a few key items."

"Apparently so." But he didn't seem creeped out or anything. Genuinely surprised, but not in a bad way.

Carter turned back to the case. He was about to ask about the pair of leather gloves beside the gun when something bumped his calf. He looked down to see an enormous black-and-brown tabby cat staring up at him with huge green eyes. "Oh, hello."

The cat made a soft half-purr, half-chirp sound and nudged his leg again. Carter knelt and held out his hand, letting it sniff his fingers. The cat must've decided he was okay because it bumped its head against his fingers.

As Carter petted the cat, he marveled at its size. Long hair notwithstanding, the cat was immense—easily twenty pounds or so. "Jesus, what do you feed this thing?"

Levi laughed. "He's a Maine coon. They tend to get, uh . . ."

"Big?"

"Yeah." He gestured at the cat. "Anyway, that's Link."

"Link?" Carter raised an eyebrow. "Seriously?"

"You'd understand if you'd seen him as a kitten. You see those tufts on his ears?"

Sure enough, Link had long black tufts sticking up from the ends of his ears.

"When he was a kitten, his ears were huge, and those tufts made them seem even bigger. My sister thought he looked like Yoda, but he reminded me more of Link from the Zelda games."

"Gotcha." He glanced past Levi at a second cat who was sitting in the doorway, peering at all of them as though their sheer existence bored it. Same color as Link, but slightly smaller. Slightly. "That must be Zelda, then."

Levi turned around. "Yep, that's her." He squatted and snapped his fingers. "Come here and be social."

Instantly, the aloof cat came to life and trotted across the floor, paws thumping heavily on the hardwood. She wedged herself between Carter and Link, and eyed Carter with a mix of curiosity and suspicion.

"You would push him out of the way," Levi muttered. He scooped up Link as if the monstrous cat didn't weigh a thing. "I guess I should've asked if you were allergic to cats before I invited you over. I don't have a lot of visitors, and I forget sometimes—"

"Don't worry about it." Carter looked up from scratching Zelda's chin. "I love cats."

"So I see."

Carter laughed as Zelda purred so loudly she almost rattled the artifacts from Levi's past life in the case above them. Link wasn't much quieter in Levi's arms. "They're a friendly pair, aren't they?"

"When they want to be." Levi leaned down and let Link jump to the floor with a heavy thud. "Just watch. Next time they see you, they'll just sit across the room and glare at you."

Next time?

Carter tried not to read too much—anything—into that. He scratched behind Zelda's ears, and then stood. As the cat wove figure eights around his legs, he scanned the rest of the cases in the room. "This really is an impressive collection."

"Thanks."

"Thanks for showing it to me."

Their eyes met, and goddamn, he thought Zelda's gentle head bumps were going to knock him off his feet. Maybe it was the perfect, art gallery lighting, or maybe it was because he was alone in a room a million miles from nowhere with *this man* of all people, but the intensity in Levi's eyes took his breath away. The fact that Levi wasn't breaking eye contact didn't help in the slightest.

And just like that, they both turned their heads.

"Anyhow." Levi gestured at the rest of the cases. "This is the collection. All the crap I've stolen from various movie sets."

Carter laughed. "I can't blame you for taking a few things."

"And I didn't really 'steal' most of it. Especially on the indie stuff, I mean, what else were we going to do with it?" He sighed. "I'm glad I kept what I did. Sometimes I think it's the only evidence left that some of these films were ever made."

"Which is a fucking travesty." Carter let his gaze drift to the revolver, the shell casings, the switchblade with the mother-of-pearl handle. "Honestly, even though the movies never did much commercially, I envy you. I would love to be in an indie film. But . . ." He scowled. "Those doors kind of close when you start getting bigger roles. Not that I'm complaining about the bigger roles, or about getting into *Wolf's Landing*, but it'd be cool to do something really out there and different, you know?" *Why are you rambling?*

Levi nodded. "I know exactly what you mean. The minute you do a low-budget indie thing, everyone starts wondering if you're washed up."

"Or if they just cast you for name recognition."

"Exactly."

"Ah, well." Carter shrugged. "Even if I can't be in them, at least I can watch them."

"True." Levi met his eyes. "You, uh, want to watch one? Like, now?"

"Hell yeah."

Levi grinned. "Awesome. Theater's downstairs."

"Theater?" Carter raised his eyebrows as he followed Levi out of the room. "You have an actual . . ."

"I like movies." Levi flicked off the light and waited for the cats to trot out of the room before he pulled the door closed behind them. "Might as well enjoy them as they were meant to be enjoyed, right?"

He wasn't kidding. The room he'd converted into a theater wasn't huge, but the screen that took up one wall must've been at least eighty inches. The carpet was black, as were the walls, ceiling, and the twin rows of leather couches that were basically three attached La-Z-Boy recliners.

Carter chuckled. "Apparently sitting on the living room sofa and watching a movie just isn't good enough for you, is it?"

Levi wrinkled his nose. "Not when I can have this, no."

"I don't blame you. I'd love to have something like this myself. Maybe someday when I buy a place."

"You looking at buying soon?"

Carter shook his head. "Nah. I mean, they're paying me well enough, but part of me keeps thinking the show's going to get canceled at any moment, and the cash flow will stop."

Levi grinned. "It's *Wolf's Landing*. I don't think you have too much to worry about."

"Which is probably what someone said to the cast of *Firefly*."

"Good point."

"So, I'll buy something eventually, but for the moment, my rental's nice enough."

"Yeah, it looked like a nice place." Levi pulled open a drawer and withdrew a thick binder of DVDs. "Take your pick. I have a little of everything in here."

Carter thumbed through the DVDs. Some he'd heard of, some he hadn't, but he was having a hard time even reading the titles with Levi standing right next to him. He managed to concentrate enough, though, to see the disc for *Metallo*, an obscure Italian film from the 1960s.

"Holy shit." He tapped the DVD. "I've been dying to see this one."

"Let's watch it, then." Levi's expression turned deadly serious. "You are okay with subtitles, right?"

"Am I—" Carter arched an eyebrow. "Okay with subtitles? Really?" He huffed and rolled his eyes. "As if any self-respecting film snob would settle for a dubbed version."

Levi grinned. "You're a film snob after my own heart."

Oh, if you only knew . . .

CHAPTER SEVEN

After two and a half hours of subtitles, Levi's eyes were getting a little tired. That didn't usually happen to him. It wasn't even that late—though this room had no windows, it was still far too early in the day for the all-black walls to fool him into thinking it was nighttime.

Must've been lack of sleep last night. And it didn't help that he'd had to struggle *hard* to even concentrate since he had Carter here in his home theater.

Beside him, Carter rubbed his eyes. "Man, that movie was better than I thought it would be."

"It's better than I remember it." Levi stretched, then stood to turn up the lights and retrieve the DVD. "I don't think I've watched it in five or six years."

"I can see why." Carter stretched too, groaning as his back cracked and popped. "That film's intense."

"The best ones are."

"Amen. And the best ones always seem to be in other languages too. Present company's films excluded."

Levi clicked his tongue. "Kiss ass."

"Hey, I just don't want to lose my source of impossible-to-find films."

"Fair enough, fair enough." He rubbed his eyes again. "I'd say let's watch another one, but I don't think I can handle another set of subtitles today."

Carter yawned. "You and me both. Don't know why I'm so tired, but maybe a short one?"

Levi let himself wonder for a moment if Carter was tired for the same reasons he was, but he quickly banished the thought. "Well, if you're game for something short, and don't mind something in English, I've got a whole other binder full of nothing but film noir."

"Film—" Carter's eyes widened. "You're a noir junkie too?"

"Fuck yes."

"I'm definitely game to watch one. What do you have?"

"Everything." Levi reached into the drawer to get his noir binder. "First, though, I'm going to grab a Coke to wake myself up a bit. You want something?"

Carter shrugged. "Sure. A little caffeine would probably do me some good."

"We can look at these upstairs, then." Levi handed him the binder, and they headed out of the theater, both blinking and wincing as they adjusted to normal lighting. Levi had carefully designed the hallway so that it was dim at the theater end and brighter when it reached the stairs, giving his eyes time to adjust, but he still had to squint a bit.

By the time they were upstairs, though, his eyes had adapted, and the afternoon light pouring in through the windows in front of the kitchen and living room didn't bother him in the slightest.

Carter didn't seem to mind either. "That's one hell of a view."

Levi gazed out at the blanket of trees and the snow-capped peaks of the Olympics and Mount Olympus. "It was one of the selling points of this place."

"I believe that. I'd pay for a damned trailer if it had a view like that."

"Me too." Levi smirked. "And five minutes later, I'd knock it the fuck down and build something nicer."

Carter laughed. "Obviously."

"With a view like— What the hell?" He pulled out his buzzing phone. "Sorry. Got a text."

The message was from Anna. *We still on for tomorrow night?*

He swallowed.

"Everything okay?" Carter asked.

"Yeah." Levi exhaled. "Anna wants to meet up tomorrow. To, uh, discuss the contracts. She said Finn usually handles it, but since we'd probably kill each other . . ."

Carter's eyebrows jumped. "Are you signing?"

"I don't know yet." He quickly sent back *I'll be there, no promises re: contracts.* Then he set the phone down and faced Carter again. "Anyway. DVDs."

"Right." Carter didn't push the issue about signing, and while Levi took out some glasses and a two liter of Coke, he spread the DVD binder open on the kitchen island. "Man, you really have everything in here."

Levi shrugged. "I'm an avid collector. What can I say?"

"So I see." Carter slowly turned the pages, inspecting each title before moving on to the next. "At least you're not one of those jackasses who turns up their noses at anything in English."

"Ugh. You've hung out with those types too?"

"Yep. You know you're friends with a bunch of film snobs when everyone tries to be the one who's seen films in the most languages."

Levi laughed. "Oh, yeah, sounds like we've definitely run with the same crowd."

"Oh yeah?"

He nodded. "Buddy of mine has been on a mission since college to find a movie in a language no one else has seen. Smug bastard was insufferable the week he found one in Tibetan."

"Let me guess: *Windhorse*?"

Levi's mouth fell open. "You've heard of *Windhorse*?"

"Heard of it?" Carter sniffed indignantly. "I have it on DVD."

"Nice. I love that film. And next to nobody has seen it."

"Which is a crying shame."

"Amen to that." Levi finished pouring their drinks and nodded toward the binder. "Anything look interesting?"

"Dude, it's noir. It's all inter— *Oh*, this is one of my favorites."

Levi craned his neck, and grinned when he saw the title: *Double Indemnity*. "I fucking *love* that film."

"Me too. It's not exactly short, but . . ."

"But it's *Double Indemnity*."

"Exactly. Guess we know what we're doing for the next ninety minutes, then." Their eyes met, and Levi's pulse soared. One innocent comment, perhaps not worded as well as it should've been, and suddenly Carter's cheeks were a little pink. Levi's probably were too. And he damn sure knew what he *wanted* to do for the next ninety minutes, but he cleared his throat and busied himself capping the Coke bottle.

"Let me just put this away, and we can go back downstairs."

Just before he turned to put the bottle in the fridge, he caught Carter's eye again, and they both froze for a second. The kid's expression was unreadable, but definitely different than it had been a minute ago.

Was he thinking the same thing?

Levi cleared his throat and picked up one of the Coke glasses. "So. *Double Indemnity*?"

"Yeah." Carter looked down at the binder as if he'd forgotten it was there at all. "Definitely."

As they headed back to the theater, Levi was sure of two things:

One, his drink needed to be a lot colder than it was.

Two, this was probably going to be the first time in history he couldn't pay attention to *Double Indemnity*.

Levi could definitely get used to this. When it came to films, he and Carter never stopped talking unless they were actually watching one. Whether it was comparing directors, bringing up obscure films no one else had ever heard of—but they'd both seen or even had on DVD—or snarking about modern Hollywood's attempts to stack up to the artistry of indie films, they could've gone on all night.

But several hours and three DVDs after they'd met in the café, Levi drove Carter home, and the second they pulled into the driveway, the conversation died. As the engine idled, they exchanged a glance, but quickly broke eye contact.

A full minute passed, and it was Carter who finally spoke.

"Today was a lot of fun. And thanks again for the *Tin Horse* DVD. I'm looking forward to rewatching it."

"You're welcome." Levi paused. "If, uh, you want to see it on the big screen, we can always watch it at my place."

"Oh, hell yeah. That'd be awesome." Carter's smile made the world spin faster. "When?"

The sooner the better.

Levi swallowed. "You're on a schedule, not me."

"Well, you have your rehearsals and stuff."

"Just a few nights a week." He tapped his thumbs on the wheel. Then, conscious of how obvious it made his nerves, he withdrew his hands. "I do have rehearsal tomorrow night, but we're usually done around nine if that's not too late for you."

"No, not at all. I could meet you there, or at your place."

"My place is fine if you can remember how to get there." He raised his eyebrows.

"Text me the directions just in case."

"Will do. See you tomorrow night, then?"

Carter's smile broadened. "I'll see you then."

They locked eyes for a moment, just like when Carter made that unintentionally loaded comment, and Levi was sure one of them was going to say something. Or worse—better?—do something.

Then Carter dropped his gaze. "Anyway. Thanks for the lift."

"Anytime."

They exchanged one last look that went on a second longer than it should have, and then Carter was gone, the Jeep door shut behind him as he strode up the walk.

Levi didn't move quite yet. He told himself he was merely waiting until Carter opened his front door, but . . . yeah, right.

The door opened.

Carter looked back.

Levi's heart skipped.

He waved, and so did Carter, and then the door was shut and suddenly Levi could breathe again. Sort of.

On the way down the road, Levi kept glancing at the seat next to him. It was rare for anyone to sit there—the cat carriers occupied it more often than people did—but now that Carter wasn't in it, Levi was hyperaware of the empty space between the console and the door.

He shook his head and tried to focus on the road as he headed out of Carter's neighborhood.

As he drove away from town on autopilot, he kept replaying the day in his mind. Tried to make sense of it. He hadn't felt like this in he didn't know how long. This fluttery feeling? Borderline queasy but in a good way, if such a thing was possible. It had been so long, it was almost alien.

He didn't want to overanalyze anything. It made perfect sense that spending half a day in the company of Carter Samuels would leave him reeling and dizzy and off-balance, and it didn't matter if it was because he was starstruck for the first time in years or . . . or if it was something else.

It didn't matter.

So he didn't think about it.

He just sat back and enjoyed the high.

Levi was toweling his hair dry the next morning when he heard the muffled chirp of his cell phone. At nine in the morning? What the hell?

He went to pick it up, but it wasn't on his nightstand. Shit. He looked around, waiting for another beep. When the sound came, it was still muffled. He ran his hands over the rumpled bedspread, checking every crevice for his phone while trying not to disturb either cat.

The phone chirped again, and it was definitely on the bed somewhere. When it went off yet again, he turned toward the sound. Zelda peered back at him, smug as always. He gently pushed her onto her side, and sure enough, there was his cell. She swatted at his hand as he drew the phone away.

"Hey! It's your own fault for laying on top of my stuff."

She glared at him, then rolled all the way onto her back, stretching her paws out. Absently scratching her exposed belly with one hand, Levi checked his phone with the other. Two missed calls. One from his mom, one from his dad. About ten minutes apart. That was odd. He gulped. They didn't call often, and it always stressed him the hell out when they did.

He debated calling them right away and getting it over with, but it could wait until later. There was no voice mail, so it wasn't an emergency. They could wait.

Besides, he also had a text from Finn that made his stomach lurch even harder than seeing their names:

We need to talk.

Oh. Fuck.

Okay.

While he dressed, he kept eyeing the phone, waiting for a response. He was just buckling his belt when the phone chirped again, and he damn near knocked Link out of the way as he lunged for it.

Meet me at the same café as last time. 1 hr.

Levi wrote back that he'd be there, and refrained from a sarcastic *Can't wait.*

Exactly an hour after they'd exchanged texts, he walked through the door of the café. He hadn't seen Finn's flashy Mercedes outside, and didn't immediately smell sleaze and expensive hair products, so he assumed the man wasn't here yet.

The same waitress who'd waited on them before met him at the front. "Just you today, darlin'?" Her forehead creased, and her eyes were nothing if not hopeful.

He offered an apologetic smile. "No. Two."

"All right. This way." She led him to a table, and he had no doubt she did a little "please God, grant me the serenity . . ." while her back was to him. He couldn't blame her.

Once he was seated, he ordered a cup of coffee, and then played on his phone while he waited for Finn to show up. They'd agreed to meet at ten, and it was five minutes till ten, so he'd be there any minute. In theory, anyway.

Ten minutes went by.

Fifteen.

Twenty.

After a full thirty minutes, Levi wondered if he could say he'd made a good faith effort but left because he thought he was being stood up. Naturally, just as he'd come to the conclusion that, hell yes, he could bail, Finn strolled through the front door.

Halfway to the table, he waved at the waitress. "Hey darlin', could I get a coffee?" He gestured at the table where Levi was sitting.

She responded with a tight-lipped smile. "Of course, sir. I'll be right there." Then she went back to taking an order from another customer, and Levi tried not to crawl under his own table and die of embarrassment.

"We gotta talk." Finn dropped into the booth across from him.

"So you said." Levi folded his hands and tried not to look or sound impatient. Or annoyed. "What's this about?"

Finn pulled out his cell, and Levi gritted his teeth as the man started searching for something. If it was on his phone, couldn't he have just sent it? Did they really have to—

Finn turned his phone around, and Levi's stomach dropped.

He and Carter were walking together down the sidewalk in front of the antique store on Sandy Bluff Road, Carter laughing at something Levi was saying. The photographer had frozen them in a moment of direct eye contact. Though they'd probably turned to one another for a split second, the static image turned the glance into a lingering gaze. The photo wasn't exactly incriminating, but he was all too familiar with how the media could spin, spin, spin an image like that. He didn't recall what they'd been talking about right then, only that they'd been heading from the coffee shop to where they'd parked their cars. A chill ran through him. What if they'd been followed? If Levi had been seen pulling into Carter's driveway, and then the two of them stealing off to his place? No one had followed him past the highway turnoff, he'd been absolutely certain of that, but how far *had* they been followed?

He scrolled past the picture to the headline.

Does 'Chad Eastwick' Have Wolf's Landing *Star in His Sights?*

Below that, *Rumors have circulated about 'retired' action hero's sexuality—is he about to go public with Samuels?*

Well. That explained the missed calls from his parents.

He scrolled farther, and fortunately, the only other images were similar to the first. Just the two of them walking down the sidewalk, though his heart went into his throat when he realized the copy of *Tin Horse* was visible in Carter's hand. Maybe it was a good thing that film wasn't well-known—he could only imagine the conclusions the reporters would draw. And thank God it wasn't *Broken Day*. Of all of Levi's films, that one easily had the most on-screen sex and nudity.

Face on fire, he handed the phone back to Finn, who set it facedown on the table.

The producer shifted uncomfortably. This must've been the one topic on God's green earth that could make him squirm like that. "So, um." He cleared his throat. "You want to tell me what's going on between the two of you?"

"Pictures say a thousand words. Is it so hard to believe two actors might be seen walking and talking around—"

"Cut the crap." Finn's eyes narrowed. "Is there or is there not something going on between the two of you?"

He bit back a response of "What does it matter?" After all, Finn had made it abundantly clear that the studio wanted him in part for his heterosexuality, and he doubted they were playing games. So he went with a flat, "There isn't."

An eyebrow rose.

Levi put up his hands. "It was—"

"It wasn't what it looked like, you were just talking, yadda, yadda, yadda." Finn inclined his head. "Yes or no, Levi. You guys have a thing or not?"

"We don't. We really were just talking." The producer eyed him, and Levi added a growled, "You want a play-by-play of everything we were talking about?"

Finn scowled. "I just want to make sure you're not pissing away your—"

"What is this all about?" Levi growled. "My personal life is none of your business or anyone else's."

"It is when the possibility of your acting comeback is hanging in the balance."

Levi clenched his jaw. Two days ago, he hadn't even wanted a comeback, but now the thought of having it pulled out from under him was enough to twist his gut into knots.

"Now that I have your attention . . ." The producer folded his hands. "Your career's in a very precarious spot right now. You're looking to get back on the scene—"

"I beg your pardon?" Levi growled. "You came to me. I didn't ask for this role."

"No, but you didn't turn it down either." Finn's expression hardened. "And don't think for a second that just because we came to you means you're calling the shots here. Especially since you're not the only one in the running for this role. And for that matter, this is an opportunity for you to get back on the scene in an entirely different capacity than before. I don't think I need to explain to you that breaking out of being typecast is harder than breaking out to begin with."

Levi ground his teeth.

"So if you want this role," Finn said, raising his eyebrows, "then I would suggest you play the game."

"Okay, first of all, no matter what's in the tabloids, just because Carter's gay doesn't mean that if we're seen together, we're sleeping together."

"No, it doesn't. But if there is something going on, the studio wants it nipped in the bud."

"What? Jesus Christ, Finn. It's the twenty-first goddamned century. People are gay. And actors come out all the time!" He shrugged. "Hell, Carter's out."

"Yeah, he's out, which is part of the problem."

"Can't handle the show being any gayer?" Levi didn't even try to rein in his sarcasm.

Finn huffed. "Look, people know Carter's gay, so after all the rumors that have gone around about you, when people see you with him . . ." He waved a hand. "And also, Carter's not you."

"What difference does that make?"

"Carter's young, new talent who's been playing a variety of roles, and he's been out from day one. You, however, are an action hero."

"And as you mentioned," Levi said through his teeth, "I'd like to break out of that, thank you."

"I know you would." Finn locked eyes with him. "But for the time being, everything about you is 'action hero,' and America is just not ready for someone in that role to be gay." He paused, but before Levi could interject, he continued. "Listen, here's the bottom line: This role on *Wolf's Landing*? It's your ticket to more serious ones."

"I know."

"But as far as the powers that be are concerned, you're still Chad Eastwick, and until you've proven and re-proven your chops at something else, that's all you'll ever be. Which means you have to appeal to Eastwick's fans, or the powers that be aren't going to risk their time and money casting you."

Levi's stomach knotted. He knew where this was going.

"You're the Sly Stallone, Arnold Schwarzenegger, Vin Diesel—"

"Yeah, I get it."

"And people might think it's cute when a romcom star comes out of the closet, but the people who come to see Diesel, Stallone, and you?" Finn shook his head. "They don't, buddy. They want macho, manly men."

Levi barely kept himself from rolling his eyes.

"It would be a different story if you were doing musicals and shit, but—"

"I got it. But you saw the article. The rumors have been going around for years. It's not like it would be a surprise to anyone if I *was* gay." Levi's heart jumped. Just saying the words was as close as he'd ever come to admitting it, and he nearly choked. "I'm not, but if I—"

"Doesn't matter. The thing is, people get ideas in their head about their heroes, and they don't like it when those ideas change. Especially when the hero confirms it. I mean, people have been trying to out Steve Bancroft for years, and no one bats an eye because it's just rumors. The minute someone actually comes out, then it's . . ." He shook his head. "Bottom line, Levi? If you want a shot at that serious acting career—and I assure you, this is your *last* shot at *any* kind of acting career—you'd better be what those who sign the checks want you to be. And gay?" He shook his head again. "That ain't what they want."

"Not that it's any of their business."

"It is what it is. And I wanted to make sure this is absolutely clear before you sign on the dotted line." Finn waved a hand dismissively. "I really couldn't care less what you do in your personal life, but the reality is that it can hurt your career. Conveniently coming out *right* when you're trying to get back into the spotlight? It might get you some attention in the media, but it won't get folks to take you seriously." He paused. "Think about Carter too."

Levi bristled. "What about him?"

"The consequences this could have for *his* career."

"He's already out."

"Yes, but his popularity hinges on sex appeal to a female audience. That audience can deal with him being gay when they're not seeing him out and about with another man. When they can fantasize about him without being constantly reminded that he's not interested in them."

Levi folded his arms on the edge of the table. "So it's okay for him to be gay as long as he doesn't throw it in everyone's faces by being, you know, gay?"

Finn shrugged again.

Rolling his eyes, Levi reached for his cooling coffee.

"I'm not kidding about any of this," Finn said. "Neither is the studio. And you might want to bear in mind, your role on *Wolf's Landing* isn't written in blood until your episodes have actually aired. And even then . . ." He locked eyes with Levi. "Let's just say that 'out' Anna had written into your contract works both ways."

"Are you threatening me?"

"No. I'm merely reminding you of the reality of your situation." He flattened his palms on the table and leaned closer. "The reality, Levi, is that Anna and the author have fought tooth and nail to cast you, but the studio has their heart set on another actor. And he'd like the role, believe me."

Levi's chest tightened, but he didn't speak because anything he might've said began with "fuck" and ended with "you."

Finn steepled his fingers. "They're letting you have the role to appease Hunter Easton, and they're looking for a reason—any reason at all—to replace you before you start shooting. If you are gay, and I don't care one way or the other if you are, but you need to understand that opening the closet door right now will close a lot of other doors." Yet another shrug, this one even more blasé than the last few. "Sorry, Levi."

Yeah. I'll bet you are.

Neither of them bothered ordering more than coffee. Levi tipped the waitress the cost of the bill plus an extra twenty, hoping that was enough to atone for subjecting her to Finn a second time.

Then he got the hell out of there and hurried down the road to where he'd parked. He started the Jeep, but didn't move yet. Instead, while the engine idled, he pulled out his phone and speed-dialed Anna.

She picked up right away, which meant she wasn't busy. Considering her shooting schedule—any executive producer or director, never mind both, of a show like *Wolf's Landing* was lucky to have much downtime—that was unusual. "Hey, Levi."

"Hey. I'm surprised you answered."

"Yeah, well." She sighed. "I kind of figured you'd be calling."

His hackles went up. "So you knew he was meeting with me."

"I didn't know until he'd already gone to meet you, or I'd have said something." She exhaled hard. "I'm so sorry, sweetheart. I fought this whole thing like crazy, but the studio is just . . . *ugh*."

"What is their damage, anyway?"

"Besides the fact that they're idiots?"

"Besides that, yeah."

"It just keeps coming back to the same old shit: they're worried about *Wolf's Landing* becoming some sort of queer statement." She clicked her tongue. "But listen, between you, me, and the fencepost, *are* you seeing Carter?"

I wish. "No."

She was quiet for a moment. "That's a shame, to be honest. You two would make a great pair."

Levi bit back a groan. "Thanks. That helps a lot."

He could almost feel her wincing as she said, "Sorry. I guess that probably doesn't help."

No, not really. "It's okay. Listen, I gotta run."

"Okay. Tonight's still on, right?"

He chewed his lip for a moment. He did want this role, damn it. "I'm . . . still not a hundred percent sure."

"Okay. I actually have to go myself. Why don't you think on it for a bit longer, and then text me later if we're on for tonight. Or rather if I should bring the paperwork. I want to see you either way."

"Sounds good."

After they'd hung up, he didn't put the Jeep in drive. His mind was going a million miles per hour, but the vehicle wasn't moving.

There was nothing going on between him and Carter, but he couldn't say that nothing *would* happen. And what if it did? Going public with any man, especially that one, could never be anything but a decisive move. A statement to the world about a part of his life he'd always tried to keep private.

But it didn't just mean broadcasting a piece of his personal life to the population at large. It didn't just mean revealing who he was to those with clout and checkbooks.

It meant coming out, at thirty-eight goddamned years old, to his parents.

His ultraconservative, disapproving, hypocritical parents who'd never quite left the 1950s, who expected their kids to forgive decades of alcohol-fueled misery, and had all but disowned his sister after her long-overdue divorce. They were better than they used to be, enough that Levi and his siblings weren't estranged from them anymore—not completely, anyway—but the Pritchard family was still a long way from functional.

Groaning, Levi scrubbed his hand over his face. If he'd just come out when he was a teenager and gotten it over with, at least this would all be behind him. They'd have disowned him, he'd have moved on with his life, and he could've been out for the last twenty fucking years. He wouldn't be jeopardizing the results—tenuous as they were—of a decade of slow, steady work rebuilding his relationship with them.

He wouldn't be telling his mother he'd looked her in the eye and lied to her at every single family gathering and joint counseling session when she'd asked when he was going to get married, when he was going to settle down, and if he was absolutely sure he wasn't—hushed voice—*gay*.

Levi closed his eyes and leaned his head against the headrest. He should've known this whole thing was too good to be true. Playing Max Fuhrman? Having a shot at the career he'd given up on a long time ago? Making friends with Carter Samuels? Something had to fall apart.

Which opportunity was he supposed to take? His one and only shot at being the actor he'd always dreamed of being? Or the first chance—however slim—he'd had in ages to really connect with someone?

His gaze drifted to his cell phone. The fact was, he and Carter had just met. They barely knew each other, and Levi couldn't justify gambling a career opportunity like this for the minuscule chance that Carter was even attracted to him, never mind interested in dating. While Levi wasn't thrilled about playing games with studio execs, and he was admittedly tempted to pursue Carter as a "fuck you" to the powers that be, he couldn't. This was the one and only time he'd been offered a serious, complex role outside of an indie film, and he was kidding himself if he thought another would come along this side of the Apocalypse. Giving it up for a one-in-a-million shot with a guy who was fifteen years younger than him with the choice of Hollywood's available gay men?

He picked up his phone and wrote a text.

I'll see you tonight. Bring the contracts.

CHAPTER EIGHT

L evi was on edge.

Carter could feel it the minute the front door opened. The man could act circles around anyone in Hollywood given half a chance, but when it came to keeping nerves beneath the surface when he wasn't on set, not so much. Sometimes it was easier to fake a character's emotions than it was to keep your own off your sleeve, after all.

"Something wrong?" He stepped past Levi into the foyer. "You look kind of rattled."

Levi closed the door and turned to Carter, holding his gaze for a moment. Then he gestured toward the kitchen. "Come on in."

Carter tried not to get frustrated. They barely knew each other. Levi hardly owed him an answer. Without a word, Carter followed him.

Levi opened the cabinet, but paused. "Something to drink?"

"I'm okay, thanks."

Levi nodded and pulled one glass down instead of two. Carter grabbed a barstool on the opposite side of the kitchen island, watching Levi put ice in the glass before filling it with Coke. The fizzing of the settling bubbles amplified the silence between them.

Carter tried not to stare at him, hoping he wasn't too obvious in trying to figure out what was behind the tension plainly visible in Levi's neck and shoulders. It wasn't stiffness like he'd injured himself or something. Maybe he'd overdone it at the gym—the man kept himself in spectacular shape, so he must've had a strict workout regimen.

But, no, the way he moved didn't strike Carter as nursing exhausted muscles or anything like that. Levi seemed wound tight, ready to . . . what? Snap?

Levi winced as he rolled his shoulders.

Dude, you know there's a massage therapist in town, right? I've got her number . . .

Levi took a sip and set the glass down with a *clink*. "So, uh, I don't know if you follow the tabloids..."

Carter's chest tightened, and he shook his head. "I avoid them like the fucking plague."

"Smart man." Levi absently ran his finger around the rim of his glass, watching that instead of Carter. "So, I had lunch with Finn today. He, uh, showed me an interesting article."

Something twisted beneath Carter's ribs. "Interesting, how?"

Levi pulled his phone out of his pocket, and Carter cringed. Whatever this was, he was pretty sure he didn't want to see it.

Levi slid the phone across the island. "Apparently someone saw us in town."

"Of course they did." Carter eyed the picture. He remembered walking with Levi yesterday, lost in conversation between the café and the cars, but he hadn't seen a single reporter. Though he'd never admit it out loud, that only added credence to the tabloid's claim that there was something brewing between them. He'd long ago developed a sixth sense for cameras and eavesdroppers, but in that moment, he'd been aware of nothing except Levi walking beside him. Judging by the angle, and knowing the width of that particular street, the image had probably been taken from across the road, likely from the window of a car—sneaky bastards. If he'd been paying attention to anything besides Levi, he'd have noticed. Maybe subtly put a little more space between them. Kept the eye contact to a minimum. Not done such a piss-poor job of hiding the DVD.

But nothing else had existed. It could've been a two-foot-long lens right in his face, and he wouldn't have noticed.

Because... Levi.

Pretending to be unfazed, he shrugged as he handed back the phone. "Eh, let 'em talk. The way these idiots act, I might as well have a gay Midas touch. They'd have you believe every man spotted within a ten-foot radius of me is automatically in my bed." *I wish...*

"Right." Levi laughed, but it sounded forced. He gave the phone another glance, and then pocketed it. "I think I'd just forgotten what it was like to live under a microscope."

"Lucky you," Carter grumbled. "So, what? Did Finn drag you in for lunch just to tell you the tabloids were spreading rumors?"

Levi's fingers drummed rapidly on the granite countertop. "Kind of."

"Kind of?" Carter tilted his head. "What did he want?"

Levi took a deep breath. "He wanted to let me know the reality of my career's future."

"Which is?"

"That until I've established myself as something other than a macho action-hero type, I'd better keep myself on the straight and narrow." Into his Coke glass, he added a muttered, "Emphasis on 'straight.'"

Carter blinked. Well, that explained a lot. "So, he was threatening you with your career if . . . *seriously?*"

Levi swallowed a mouthful of soda and set the glass down again. "Basically, yeah. Apparently they're concerned about *Wolf's Landing* becoming the LGBT show."

Carter's spine straightened. "You're shitting me."

"Nope. With a lesbian producer and—" His eyes flicked up and met Carter's. "Well . . ."

"With me being out."

"Yeah. He's concerned that if I were gay and they added me to the cast, it would just look like they'd gone overboard with the diversity. Especially with all the speculation about 'homoerotic undertones' on the show."

Carter gritted his teeth. "I'm not surprised. The studio that's producing it doesn't want to be known for being the most gay-friendly studio in town." He rolled his eyes. "They fought Anna hard when she suggested me for the role. They pretty much told her to kick rocks until Hunter Easton stepped in and said I was perfect for the role." He laughed bitterly. "Guess we can all be glad he demanded a certain amount of creative control on the show, right?"

"Yeah, guess so."

The silence settled in again, Levi's soda bubbling softly in the background. As Carter searched for a way to steer them back into a more comfortable topic, he realized Levi wasn't actually annoyed about the accusation that he was gay, only the studio's insistence he *not* be gay. Even the most accepting straight men Carter had ever known, the ones who didn't have a homophobic bone in their bodies, would've thrown out an emphatic "I am *not* gay" before the conversation had gone on very long.

His mouth went dry, and he suddenly wished he'd taken Levi up on the offer of a drink. He cleared his throat. "All the studio's bullshit aside, you're, uh, okay with what the tabloids are saying, right? I mean, you're not freaking out that they think you're with me?" He swallowed. "You're still comfortable being around me? When they're—"

"Are you kidding? It isn't like you wrote the article."

"Yeah, but I *am* gay."

"So?"

"So, some straight guys are, you know, weird about that."

Levi shrugged and went for his drink again. "It isn't like it's some big secret that you're gay. If it bothered me, they never would've gotten that picture of us in the first place."

A dozen more questions hovered at the tip of Carter's tongue, but he was afraid to hear the answers. At least Levi was still cool with hanging out with him and watching movies. Bringing his sexuality into the conversation as something more than a rumor had the potential to make things awkward, and he'd already bungled things yesterday with the Corvette conversation.

Levi absently swirled his Coke like it was wine. "Anyway, Finn just wanted to put it out there before I signed the contract. And to let me know my role wasn't written in blood until my episodes actually aired."

Carter snorted. "It's not even written in blood then. They recast Alicia halfway through the first season." He paused. "Except you're a bit higher profile. They probably wouldn't let you go once it came out that you were on the show."

"You would think."

Carter watched him for a moment. "Do you know yet if you're going to sign? I'm guessing this didn't help with the decision."

Levi nodded. "Yeah." A hesitant smile formed on his lips. "I signed the contracts earlier this evening."

"Oh. Awesome!" Carter grinned. "Welcome to *Wolf's Landing*."

The smile finally came to life. "Thanks. I'm looking forward to it."

So am I. Believe me, so am I.

"When do you start shooting?"

"Not for a couple of weeks yet. Might not be until the middle of next month."

"That soon? Wow." He hoped he was doing a good job of hiding the fluttery feeling that he'd had since he'd walked in the door. It was intensifying now thanks to Levi's confirmation that they would—*holy shit, oh my God,* seriously?—be working together.

"Anna said she'd call me." Levi turned around to put the Coke bottle back in the fridge. "But she wants to start filming my episodes sooner than later."

Carter furrowed his brow. "Why's that? Fuhrman doesn't even show up until halfway through next season."

Levi faced him again. "Yeah, but the sooner the episodes are in the can, the sooner they can be 'leaked' and, as you said, my role will be official enough that the studio can't replace me." He chuckled. "Anna can be devious when she wants to be."

Carter cocked his head. "Do you guys know each other or something?"

"Oh yeah. We go way back. I had a small part in a short she directed in film school." He picked up his glass and gestured down the hall. "To the theater?"

There must've been a nerve there—Carter was quickly learning that an abrupt subject change was Levi-speak for "I don't want to go into it."

So he stood and nodded. "To the theater."

Downstairs, they agreed on a French film from the 1980s. While Levi put it in the DVD player, Carter took the same seat he'd occupied last time, and his ass had barely landed on the leather chair before Link jumped up and parked himself in his lap.

"Um, hello."

Levi glanced over his shoulder, and grinned. "Looks like you've made a friend."

"Guess I have." Carter petted the cat, who was purring loudly now. "Heavy as he is, do I have to worry about losing circulation in my legs?"

Laughing, Levi came back to his own seat with the remote in hand. "Nah. If you start getting uncomfortable, just fidget a little. He'll get annoyed and leave."

"Good to know."

Levi settled beside him, and though they'd sat like this last night, the armrest between them suddenly seemed too narrow. And at the same time, too wide. It kept them unnaturally far apart, preventing them from letting things progress however they were destined to progress. At the same time, it felt like a reassuring barrier, a physical presence to maintain their comfort zones and keep things from getting awkward.

Am I losing my mind? I'm losing my mind.

Levi turned on the film, and Carter focused on watching the screen and petting the cat.

The subtitles didn't make any sense. For all his ability to comprehend them, they may as well have been written in Swahili.

He and Levi were going to be working together? Sooner than later? And right on the heels of the producers warning Levi to stay closeted and away from Carter?

In spite of the rapid-fire dialogue he'd never understand without reading that block of text at the bottom of the screen, he let his gaze slide toward Levi.

Was there more to the studio's concerns than just the photo on the tabloid site? Was there something to the rumors that had been flying around since the dawn of Levi's career?

Swallowing hard, he focused on the screen again. Focused his eyes, anyway. His mind was having no part of it.

Of course he'd had thoughts about Levi since the first time he'd seen him as Chad Eastwick on the big screen. And of course he'd fantasized about him after they'd met. But now that the article was out there, now that they'd had a conversation that skirted the laughably hypothetical possibility of them hooking up and all the reasons that would be a disaster, he couldn't get it out of his head. As if the conversation had been some sort of incantation that made a fantasy into something nearly tangible that just needed a little nudge to become real. It was like his mom telling him to stay out of the package of cookies she'd put in the top shelf of the pantry when he was a kid. It hadn't seriously occurred to him, but now that someone had mentioned it . . .

Levi hadn't come out and admitted to being gay. For all Carter knew, Levi's silence on his history with Anna meant there was a *history* there. And even if he was gay, there was no guarantee he found Carter the least bit attractive.

But that sure didn't stop Carter from wishing.

CHAPTER NINE

I f there was one thing Levi had learned after directing half a dozen shows at the playhouse, it was that rehearsal times were more of a suggestion than anything. The people involved had jobs and families, not to mention inevitable snafus like malfunctioning cars and late ferries.

So it didn't really surprise him when Wednesday's rehearsal, originally scheduled for six thirty, started at quarter past eight. Between Marti's late babysitter, Jennifer getting stuck in traffic on the way back from Port Angeles, and Shannon's shift running two hours over, just getting everyone into the theater had become a comedy of errors.

Normally, he didn't bat an eye. He was probably the only member of the company who wasn't on a schedule, so he was usually patient with those who were.

Lately, though? Not so much.

For the past week and a half, he and Carter had been burning the midnight oil watching the kinds of films no one else ever wanted to watch. Old, obscure, weird—anything. Tonight, they were supposed to meet up again, but that didn't look promising. As the actors for the next scene gathered onstage, Levi glanced at his watch. Shit. Well after nine, and they still hadn't run through the last two scenes of act three. And considering how shaky that scene had been the last few rehearsals, they couldn't afford to skip it tonight.

Which meant they were going to run well past their usual time. Which meant there was no way he and Carter would make it back to his place before it was too late to watch even a short film.

Heart sinking, he texted Carter:

Doesn't look like I'm getting out of here on time.

Damn. He hadn't even realized how much he'd been looking forward to their movie nights. It had been ages since he'd known someone who appreciated film the way he did. Someone who loved nothing more than chilling with the cats and a Coke in front of a black and white with subtitles.

Another night, though.

He was just about to put his phone in his pocket when it buzzed. *No problem.* A moment later, *Prob. no time for a movie, but I can meet you there.*

He eyed the message. Then, *Your call. We should be done by 10ish.*

Almost immediately, Carter wrote back, *See you soon.*

Levi smiled as he pocketed his phone. Maybe they wouldn't have time for a movie tonight, but at least he'd get to see Carter.

And why the hell did that make him feel like he was in high school again? He could barely keep himself from grinning. Of course he knew damn well where the feelings came from, just like he knew damn well why he hadn't been able to sleep after Carter had left last night. Or the night before. Or the night before that. He couldn't act on it, though, so no one else—least of all Carter—needed to know.

If there was anything that could take his mind off Carter and this giddy feeling, it was a stage full of actors who still couldn't quite grasp their scene. He was as patient as possible—they were in this for fun, and it wasn't Broadway, for God's sake—but there were moments where he could empathize with a few directors he'd worked with in the past. He'd always thought Leo Tate was batshit crazy and had a hair-trigger temper, but tonight, he was beginning to understand why the man had thrown his notes in the air and stormed out of the auditorium once or twice a week. The mental image made him laugh, which relieved enough of the frustration to keep him calm and collected.

And he had to give them credit. They really were busting their asses to get it right, and though opening night was creeping up fast, he had complete faith they could get this thing together in time. If they were able to work out all the bugs of that insane adaptation of *Guys and Dolls* last winter, this would be cake.

At a little past ten, he was satisfied enough with the scenes from the third act and called it a night. As the cast gathered their things to leave, he went backstage to check in with the crew, who were still struggling with the sets in between trying to either upgrade or completely avoid the playhouse's aging pulley system.

As Levi flipped through some bids for an upgrade, Jack said, "The only companies we can get in here to do the work before opening night are Seattle based."

Levi shrugged. "If we have to pay more, then—"

"It's not budget that's an issue. The Seattle companies are all three-plus hours from here. If the system fails right before a show, we'll never get it fixed in time."

"Damn." Levi scowled. "Well, we'll get it done before the next play, but for this one, we might have to do without."

Jack grimaced. "With that many set changes?"

"I'm afraid so." Levi glanced over the bids again, then handed them back. "I know it's short notice, but I'm thinking we might want to rethink the entire set. Go for something minimalist." He pointed at the rigging and catwalks high above their heads. "The new lighting equipment is functional and versatile, so maybe we can use that to our advantage."

Jack looked up, pursing his lips. "I can talk to the lighting tech." Meeting Levi's gaze again, he added, "You're the director, though. You tell me what you want on the stage, and we'll make it happen."

"I will. I'll have notes for you tomorrow night."

"Sounds good."

Levi picked up a clipboard with the notes for the current set design. "Opening night is in three weeks. Ideally, I'd like the stage completely ready to go within ten days. That gives us time to make any changes in case we have problems." Levi tucked the clipboard under his arm. "Any reason we won't be able to pull this off?"

"Not if we keep it as basic as the last few shows," Jack said. "Get us the details soon so there's time to get what we need, and we've got this."

"Perfect. You and your guys can go ahead and call it a night. I'll get started making notes for the new design."

"All right. G'night, boss."

"G'night."

The backstage area quickly cleared out. Levi wanted to follow them, especially since every minute he spent here was one less he could spend with Carter. But with the prospect of overhauling the set in too little time, he couldn't justify bailing quite yet. Maybe just a few notes to get Jack started, and then he could leave.

He was about to text Carter and beg for another twenty minutes as he stepped onto the stage. As he thumbed the message, he glanced at the rows of plush red seats. They were all empty except one, and when his gaze landed on it, his heart jumped.

"Carter." He slid his phone back into his pocket. "Sorry about that. We ran even further over than I thought we would."

"It's fine." Carter stood and came down the aisle toward the stage. "We were shooting late anyway. I just got here myself."

"Shooting late again?"

"Shooting late *always*."

Levi grimaced sympathetically. "Well, give me another ten or fifteen minutes tops to make some notes about the set, and I'm all yours."

Something flickered across Carter's expression, but then it was gone, and he coughed quietly. "Don't worry about it."

"There's probably not much point in going back to my place this evening." He sighed. "By the time we get there, it'll be pushing midnight."

"Damn." Carter gestured over his shoulder toward the lobby. "Well, there's a couple of places in town that are open late. If you want to grab a drink or some coffee . . ."

Levi tried his damnedest not to look surprised at the invite. No sense pointing out to Carter that a late-night cup of coffee was dangerously close to an excuse to spend time together, which was dangerously close to—

He cleared his throat. "Sure. Yeah. I, uh . . ." He waved a hand at the sets behind him. "Like I said, I need to wrap up a few things here. Won't take long."

Carter smiled. "I can wait."

"Great, thanks."

Before Levi could turn around to inspect the sets that needed to be finished in the next several days, Carter said, "Like being up onstage, eh?"

Levi chuckled. "Can't say I mind it. You ever do live theater?"

"Of course. It's just been a while." He sighed. "Only time I get near a stage anymore is at Comic-Con and award shows."

Levi hesitated, then leaned down and extended his hand. "Come on up."

"Really?"

"Sure." He beckoned. "Tell me there isn't something addictive about being onstage even when there's no one around."

Carter regarded the offered hand for a moment, then clasped his around Levi's forearm. Levi pulled him up onto the stage, and suddenly . . . Jesus.

They were face-to-face. Bright, hot lights illuminated every gorgeous detail of Carter's features. He still had a few traces of makeup on, including the faintest smudges of what must've been one hell of a black eye and maybe a battered cheekbone. The color didn't look quite so menacing now, less like an injury and more like subtle shadowing that brought out the blue in his eyes like *whoa*.

And neither of them had released the other's arm.

Carter seemed to realize that in the same instant Levi did, and they both jerked back as if that lingering point of contact might suddenly turn into a live wire. The boards creaked under their feet, echoing through the empty theater, as they put a few extra inches of space between them.

"So, you're—" Carter looked around the auditorium, as if searching for a topic of conversation, his cheeks probably hot as hell if the color was any indication. "Do you ever act here? Or just direct?"

"Mostly just direct. I've been in a few, but . . ."

Carter turned to him. "I thought you missed it."

"I do. And I've wanted to act more, but—" Levi glanced down at his clipboard just for a reason to break eye contact. "There's, uh, there's no way to say it without sounding like an egotistical asshole, but I don't want the productions here to be about me. It's not a big secret that I direct and sometimes produce, but I don't let them put my name on the marquee. The cast and crew work their asses off, and I want people coming here because of them." He cringed. "That does sound conceited, doesn't it?"

Carter waved a hand. "Nah, I know what you mean."

"And it's hard to find directors. We had a really sharp one for a while, but he moved to Seattle, and no one else wants to do it." He paused. "Well, no one who has the first clue about theater, anyway."

"Seems like they're in good hands now."

Levi laughed softly. "You haven't seen me direct."

Carter smiled and nodded toward the seats. "Actually, I have."

"Oh." Levi felt himself blush, and he didn't even know why. "I didn't realize you were back there."

"That was kind of the idea. I didn't want to interrupt your rehearsal."

"Oh. Uh, thanks."

Their eyes locked for a second, and this time it was Levi who broke away with a cough and a desperate attempt at conversation. "Anyhow. We have to gut the set and redo it before opening night, so I just need to make some notes for the crew."

"Gut it?" Carter turned, gaze sweeping over the partially built sets. "This looks pretty good as is."

"It looks great." Levi sighed, shaking his head. "But the equipment under and over the stage is old. It's screwing up the set changes between scenes."

"Oh yeah?"

"Yep. Comes with the territory when you're using an old-ass theater."

"I guess it does."

Levi rested his clipboard on his arm and faced the sets. "They almost tore this place down a few years ago because it had fallen into disrepair, but we've been trying to update it. Only problem is, the pulley system and the hydraulics for moving larger equipment are fucked up. They could theoretically work for one or two more seasons, but it's not safe, so we're either replacing it or not using it."

"Good idea."

Gazing at the half-painted kitchen interior, Levi sighed. "So now we're trying to think of a minimalist idea that conveys the setting without having to rebuild the whole fucking theater."

Carter's eyes flicked up, then scanned the stage. "What kind of setting is it?"

"Mostly house interiors and a couple of exterior scenes on a city street." Levi glared at the half-built set. "Incredibly simple, really, but with the equipment malfunctioning..."

"Why not just use silhouettes?" Carter pointed at the overhead lights. "Wouldn't take much to imply the shape of a building on the back wall."

"That..." Levi blinked. "Goddamn. That might actually work."

Carter smiled. "I've worked on a production that used that method. If you need a hand with it, let me know."

The thought of having Carter here, even as a stagehand, made Levi's heart thump. He could barely stomach the idea of his parents coming to watch the play. With Carter in the same building, he'd be lucky if he knew which way was up.

"I, uh. Thanks. My guys can probably handle it, but if it's..." Words. Say words. He cleared his throat. "I'll keep it in mind. Thanks. Again."

Carter nodded, seemingly unfazed by Levi stumbling over the English language. "Don't mention it. My schedule's a little crazy with shooting, but I'm happy to help if I can."

"Great. Good to know." Levi tried to go through the various sets in his mind, mentally cutting out the silhouettes they'd need, but who was he kidding? His concentration was shot. Had been since the second he'd realized Carter was here.

He had all day tomorrow to figure this crap out, so he jotted a quick note on his clipboard. "Okay. I think I'm just about ready to get out of here. Let me leave these where the crew will find them." He headed toward the front and center of the stage, where he and Jack often left each other notes and information.

Behind him, Carter said, "So, uh, there's another article making the rounds on the set."

"Another—" Levi froze. He swallowed as he laid the clipboard on the lip of the stage. "What are they saying?"

Carter rolled his eyes. "Someone saw me having lunch with Hunter Easton the other day, and they spent half the article speculating about what you thought of me hanging around with him."

"Seriously? They spot us walking together once, and suddenly I'm Mr. Territorial Boyfriend?"

"You know how it is." Carter shrugged. "If you're snapped in the same frame, you might as well be engaged."

"Yeah, that sounds about right. So what is everyone on the set saying about it?"

"Eh, just gossip." Carter waved a hand and laughed, though it sounded forced. "I mean, people can talk all they want. Two guys can be friends, right? Even if one's gay?"

"Of course. Why not?"

Carter studied him for a moment. "Only one of us *is* gay, right?"

Levi froze. Standing there, center stage and under the hot lamps, where only one person in the universe could see him, he had never felt so out in the open. It wasn't just the overhead glare heating his skin right then. The whole world had sometimes stared into the fishbowl Hollywood had dropped him in, but he'd been able to shut them out. Carter's gentle scrutiny was inescapable.

"Uh . . ."

"You don't have to answer." Carter offered a reassuring smile. "I mean, I'm curious, but . . ."

Out of habit, Levi normally would've looked around, making absolutely sure there was no one else here except for them, but he couldn't pull his gaze away from Carter. He didn't want to, no matter how damning this relentless eye contact might be.

A board creaked under Carter's foot. The space between them narrowed. Levi needed to move closer as much as he needed to retreat, and both canceled each other out, freezing him in place.

"I'm sorry," Carter said softly. "I didn't mean to put you on the spot. I'm just . . ."

"Curious."

Carter nodded.

"Well, I guess with the rumors circulating"—Levi finally broke eye contact—"it wouldn't be right for me to let you get blindsided."

"Blindsided?"

Levi took a breath. "If it ever comes out . . . so to speak . . ." His throat constricted. He'd avoided the words for so damned long, his stomach threatened to revolt at the prospect of finally saying them.

Carter came closer. Levi didn't look at him, but he could feel him there, entirely too close to him on the lip of the stage, under the same hot lights that were bringing sweat to Levi's hairline. "Your secret's safe with me."

Levi lifted his gaze. He wanted to say "I haven't said a thing" or play stupid with "what secret?" but Carter's eyes stopped him in his tracks, and he didn't know a single straight man who would've stared back at Carter like this for five . . . six . . . seven seconds.

Carter swept his tongue across his lips, startling the fuck out of Levi. Before he could berate himself for being so jumpy, Carter blurted out, "Would it be weird if I admitted I've had a crush on you since I first saw *Tin Horse?*"

The hairs stood up on the back of Levi's spotlight-warmed neck. He didn't know quite what to say, quite how to react, only that Carter's expression was gradually shifting to a grimace, as if he regretted asking.

So Levi finally responded in the only way he could: "Would it be weird if I said you're one of the reasons I watch *Wolf's Landing?*"

Carter blinked. Then his shy smile turned Levi's knees to water. "Would it be even weirder if I said you're the reason I'm on *Wolf's Landing* in the first place?"

"How do you figure?"

"Watching your old stuff was what made me want to act." Carter took another step, and his gaze flicked back and forth from Levi's eyes to his lips. Somehow he was close enough to touch now. The door was all but open, the invitation extended, but Levi was paralyzed by nerves.

Carter locked eyes with him. "How often do you get to meet the person who made you realize who you are?"

Levi's throat tightened again. "What?"

Carter swallowed. "Your early films made me realize I wanted to act." He came closer. "And seeing you in *Tin Horse* made me finally admit I was gay."

The universe seemed to condense into what little space remained between them, and took all the oxygen with it. Levi's head spun.

"That's . . . that's a lot of pressure." He forced a laugh, which helped him find some air. "A lot for one man to live up to."

"Yeah, I know. You ever heard that saying that you shouldn't meet your idols?" Carter was speaking so softly, Levi had to lean in to hear him. "That you'll suddenly find out they're human, and you'll be disappointed?"

"Yeah. I've heard that."

Carter's shoe scuffed softly on the board beneath their feet. "Turns out that's a load of bullshit."

You don't say.

Levi swallowed hard. "Is that right?"

"Yeah." *Oh God, he's* really *close.* "It is."

Levi could feel Carter breathing now—there was only one way this moment could go, but neither of them closed that sliver of space. One move, and this dream would be over. One touch, and he'd wake up alone and frustrated.

Carter brushed Levi's lip with his. The world didn't suddenly shift back to Levi's empty bedroom, so he let himself do the same, just grazing Carter's mouth. The contact was brief but deliberate, each silently daring the other to be the decisive one. The one to take this from *almost* to *finally.*

Carter pulled in a breath, rearranging the air between their lips. He started to draw away as if he were about to say something. Panic jolted Levi—*come back!*

He grabbed the front of Carter's shirt.

Forgot all his nerves.

And kissed him.

They both froze. For a second—a minute? an hour?—they were completely still, lips pressed together but unmoving.

Then Carter put a hand on Levi's waist and tilted his head. As they came together again, they both parted their lips, opening to each other. Levi hadn't realized how long it had been since he'd touched a man until right then, as Carter wrapped his arms around him and they let the kiss deepen at glacial speed.

Levi ran his fingers through Carter's hair, and he couldn't say for certain who shivered, only that it drew their bodies closer together. They were both obviously aroused, only a few layers of clothing separating their erections, but there was something oddly chaste about the way they kissed. By all rights, they should've been tearing at each other's clothes by now. One of them should've been on his knees. There should've been gasps and groans and orgasms.

But Levi was only distantly aware of the way they were touching below the belt. All his attention was centered on the tender motions of their lips and tongues, of the way Carter's hair felt between his fingers—cool, but warm on the edges from the overhead lights.

They pulled back almost as slowly as they'd come together. The stage lights picked out the beautiful blue of Carter's heavy-lidded eyes. His cheeks were flushed—Levi had no doubt his were too.

Then Carter gulped. "I'm, uh . . ." He drew back a little and stared down at their feet. "I'm . . ."

Levi tipped Carter's chin up with his finger. "What's wrong?"

Carter still resisted looking right at him. "I'm not gonna lie," he whispered. "I've been fantasizing about you forever. But I don't . . . I'm not one of those guys who . . ."

"You don't jump into bed with someone right away?"

"Exactly." Carter's gaze flicked up, but only for a second. "I used to, but not anymore. It just gets too complicated, you know? I meet a guy, and suddenly we're—"

Levi silenced him with a gentle kiss. "It's all right. I'm kind of the same way, to be honest."

Carter finally met his eyes. "Really?"

"Yeah. Like you said, it tends to complicate things."

Carter nodded. "It does." He drew back a little more. "So, uh, should we head down to that diner?"

Levi swallowed. If they went anywhere now, they'd either be shyly avoiding eye contact, or gazing longingly into each other's eyes until they had a private moment. With the rumor mill already grinding, and the powers that be watching for any reason to believe he was gay enough to fire, maybe they were better off staying behind closed doors. Even if behind closed doors meant too many opportunities to negate their resolution against going too far, too fast.

"You probably have to be back on set early tomorrow, don't you?"

Carter scowled, but then sighed. "Unfortunately, yeah." Expression softening, he met Levi's eyes. "Damn it. I could've gone for a movie or two tonight."

"Yeah, me too." *But we never would've made it down to the theater like this, and we both know it.* "Tomorrow night."

Carter nodded. "Tomorrow night."

Levi couldn't resist running his fingers through Carter's hot and cool hair once more. "Sorry things went so late. I didn't mean to have you come here for nothing."

"Nothing?" Carter smiled, wrapping his arms around Levi again. "I don't think this counts as nothing."

Levi didn't argue.

He just let Carter pull him into another long, gentle kiss.

CHAPTER TEN

Did that really happen?

Carter couldn't sleep. He still wasn't sure how he'd made it home in one piece, and now he alternated between dreamily reliving that long center stage kiss—and the shorter one in the lobby right before they'd gone their separate ways—and wondering where they went from here.

Why the hell didn't I bring him home?

He sighed. Right this very minute, he could've been lying beside Levi. They could've been dead asleep, or maybe working their way back to hot and heavy so they could go another round.

Goddamn it. I could've made Levi come by now.

He shivered.

You had *to tell him you don't fuck right away.*

It was true, though. After a few too many hookups had become a little too complicated overnight, he'd backed away from the bedroom. He didn't fuck guys he'd just met.

Except he hadn't just met Levi tonight. They'd been hanging out, talking, clicking. This wasn't some guy he'd swapped numbers with in a club. This was the guy who'd been his faraway idol forever and was suddenly the guy taking up all of his downtime. Carter wouldn't exactly be jumping into bed with a stranger.

So . . . why am I here alone?

Because I fucking choked.

Damn it.

On the other hand, it wasn't as simple as kiss, fuck, and see where it goes. They were both very public figures—in spite of Levi's best efforts to the contrary—and even if they wound up dating, they couldn't date *publicly*. Not with the studio threatening Levi. Maybe after the first Max Fuhrman episodes aired, but they wouldn't be shown for at least a year.

Carter rubbed his eyes and groaned. Dating someone on the sly as a teenager had been too damned much stress. He'd promised himself after that relationship that he'd never play the secrecy game—and hiding it from dozens of cameras and millions of people would be a little tougher than hiding it from a boyfriend's parents.

And he loathed the idea of *being* a secret. Not just in relationships; he'd also been the reason his parents dreaded conversations with friends who might know what he was. Nothing in the world made him feel dirtier than being someone else's taboo subject, and he refused to put himself in that position again.

He wasn't ashamed of his sexuality anymore. For God's sake, he'd spent enough time in his own closet. He wasn't volunteering for a stint in someone else's.

Not even Levi's.

By the next morning, he could no longer feel the tingle of Levi's kiss on his lips, and the fluttery feeling in his stomach was long gone too. Though one look at Levi and he'd be back to that giddiness that had carried him home last night.

But all the way to the set, as he sipped his coffee and tried like hell to keep his eyes open, he couldn't conjure up the feelings he'd had while they'd been onstage together. Where there'd been nothing but excitement a few hours ago, there was only regret and worry. God help them if they'd slept together—he suspected this would've been the most awkward morning after in the history of sex.

But they *hadn't* slept together. They'd shared an impulsive kiss before making quick escapes. Funny how they'd been all set to get a late cup of coffee, but then it had suddenly been *too* late and they'd needed to get the hell out of there. Yeah, *that* was promising.

As he pulled into the parking lot outside the warehouse/soundstage where the crew would be shooting today, Carter took a long swallow of coffee and promised himself he'd stop obsessing over all this shit. He went inside and topped off his coffee cup. Focus. Just focus. He could sort things out with Levi later on. Might as well get used to concentrating on lines and directions now while Levi was on his mind as opposed to standing in front of him.

His stomach dropped. Oh God. They were going to be working together soon, weren't they?

Shit. Shit, shit, shit.

What was I thinking last night?

So what if the stage lights had made Levi even more irresistible? It had been a stupid, stupid thing to do. It wasn't like they could date, and he'd known it. He'd run through every possible scenario in his mind well before his lips had ever touched Levi's, and as long as Levi was closeted, and his role in *Wolf's Landing* hinged on him staying that way . . . no.

Carter swallowed a few more gulps of coffee, and then made himself concentrate on getting ready for his scenes. Usually, changing into Gabriel's clothes—shirt and tie, sometimes a duster—was enough to put his mind into Gabriel's head. He wasn't one of those actors who stayed in character the entire time, but once he was here and dressed, once makeup had finished with him, he could slip into character at the drop of a hat.

Today, he could barely stay in his own head, never mind Gabriel's.

It was just a kiss. Get a grip.

Just a kiss? Yeah, right.

After he'd dressed and visited the makeup department, he perused today's script. Not a lot of scenes for him today, fortunately. The longest and most complicated was in the morgue. Well, at least then Anna wouldn't be surprised if he flubbed his lines a few times. It was a running joke on the set that Carter would've made the world's worst doctor because he couldn't cope with big words. Oh, he was fine with big words in general, but he never had gotten the hang of effortlessly reciting medical jargon. Even when they were written out in big Sharpie printing on whatever file folder or clipboard his character was holding, he always managed to fuck up at least one. Which then meant he and Tina, who played the coroner, would be screwed for the next few takes while they kept bursting out laughing.

Carter chuckled to himself. Those scenes were frustrating, but they were fun. Perfect thing for him to focus on today. Especially whatever the fuck he was supposed to say while turning a disembodied human heart over and over in his gloved hands. That was going to be—

Goddamn it, he should've left his phone in the car.

A mix of excitement and nerves swelled in his chest as he pulled the vibrating phone from his pocket and looked at the screen.

Movie night?

Oh Christ. That meant going to Levi's house. So much temptation. Then again, it also meant they could talk candidly a few miles away from anyone who might care enough to write an article about it. Or take a picture of it.

He typed back, *I'm on set till 4. Meet you at 6?*

To talk, he reminded himself. To clear the air.

His phone buzzed.

6 works. See you then.

On his way to Levi's that afternoon, Carter didn't have any trouble remembering exactly where to turn. Sometimes when he was going to a newish place, he'd stress over "Was it that left?" and "Did I just miss it?" and "Shit, am I on the wrong road?" He usually had to switch off the radio so he could concentrate.

But he'd been down this road so many times, he knew every bend and landmark. He didn't even have to look for a particular tree or mailbox to know when he needed to slow down or turn anymore. Radio thumping with some Europop track, he started down Levi's driveway without a second thought, and pulled up in front of the amber cedar house.

He turned the key, and as the radio and engine went silent, he couldn't ignore his thundering heartbeat.

Chill. There's no reason we can't just be friends.

If Levi disagrees, then maybe we don't need to be friends.

Carter was halfway up the walk when Levi opened the front door. Their eyes met, Levi's betraying absolutely nothing. Carter's stomach flipped. The queasy feeling didn't disappear in favor of that intoxicating giddiness. If anything, it worsened.

He slowly continued up the walk and stopped an arm's-length away from Levi, realizing a second too late they'd been just this far apart last night. Right before they'd gotten too close.

Levi pulled in a deep breath. "Hey."

"Hey."

Well, at least he hadn't imagined how weird this would make things between them. If Levi had thought everything was fine, they would've been kissing by now.

Fuck you, goose bumps. Fuck every last one of you.

Eye contact. Dropped gazes. Eye contact again.

What the hell? They were grown men. They'd kissed. So what?

"Um." Levi cleared his throat. "Come on in."

Carter managed a slight smile, and then followed Levi.

Link and Zelda were on the back of the couch, paws curled under them as they balanced their wide bodies over their narrow perch. They both raised their heads when Carter came in, but neither approached. In fact, as Levi and Carter made their way into the kitchen, Zelda hopped off the couch and trotted down the hall. After a moment, Link followed.

Levi watched them leave, lips pulled tight. Carter's stomach turned into a ball of lead. Jesus. Even the cats could feel how tense the air was between them.

He slid onto one of the barstools at the kitchen island while Levi pulled his customary bottle of Coke from the fridge. He poured them each a glass, and for a moment, they drank in uncomfortable silence.

And it's not going to get any better until we do something about it.

"So." Carter swallowed. "Last night."

Levi stared into his glass. "Yeah. That was . . ."

"Unexpected?"

"Just a bit."

"Sorry."

"Don't be." Levi's smile was still tense, but genuine. "I'm not."

You should be. So should I.

"I'm not either, but . . ."

Levi watched him, eyebrows up.

"Look, I . . ." Carter exhaled. "You've got the studio putting demands on you, and if we . . ." His heart pounded. They'd kissed.

That's all. It wasn't like anybody had broken out a ring and pledged their lifelong love or anything. "I don't know how to word this, so just bear with me. You're not in a position to come out, and I don't even know if you want to anyway, but I can't . . . I've been someone's secret boyfriend before."

Levi stiffened.

Carter gulped. "And I'm not saying last night means we're committed or that this is going to turn into anything, but . . ." *Could I ramble any more?*

"No, no, I understand." Levi moistened his lips.

"You do?"

"Yeah." Levi broke eye contact and scratched the back of his neck. "And I guess since the studio and the fucking paparazzi are watching me like a hawk, this probably isn't a good idea."

Carter's heart sank, but he wasn't surprised. If anything, he was relieved Levi had said it first. "Yeah. Much as I'd like to . . ."

Levi chewed his lip. "That, and with the way the media's been sniffing around my personal life for years, if this comes out, it's going to put you right in the middle of it." He shook his head. "I don't want to do that you."

"I don't want to do it to you, either. I mean, give the media reason to dig into your personal life." Carter fought the urge to put a reassuring hand on Levi's arm. "You've got a lot on the line. If they're holding your contract and future gigs over your head, what choice do you have?"

Nodding, Levi avoided his eyes. "You know what's funny? I told myself when I first sat down with Finn that I wasn't going to play their games. I left Hollywood for a reason, and . . . fuck, now I'm right back where I was before. Bowing and scraping for the powers that be."

Carter winced. "It's bullshit, isn't it?"

"Yeah. The thing is, I've never regretted getting away from the business side of things, but I've missed acting so much. I've been doing it since I was a kid, and I . . . It was like I'd lost a huge part of who I am, you know?"

Carter nodded. "I can't even imagine what that would be like."

"Bad enough to make me play their fucking games." Levi groaned and rubbed a hand over his face. "I want one piece of my identity back, so I'm hiding another. Yep, right back to where I was before I ditched LA."

Guilt twisted beneath Carter's ribs. He hated that he was contributing to this, but what else could he do?

"Anyway." Levi took a swallow of Coke and set the glass down with a *clink* on the granite. "Guess this is the game we play when we work in showbiz. Sorry it's—"

"Don't sweat it. It's not your fault, and it's not mine." Carter forced a smile. "It's just shitty timing, you know? You're trying to get your foot back in the door. I get it."

Levi studied him for a moment, and finally relaxed a little. "Thanks for understanding."

"Don't worry about it." Carter paused. "I would still like to be friends, though."

"Me too." Levi cracked a hesitant smile. "Besides, who else am I going to watch obscure foreign films with?"

"Exactly. You know people are still going to speculate, right?"

"Of course." Levi laughed bitterly. "We didn't go into this business to lead private lives, did we?"

Scowling, Carter shook his head. "Didn't realize how small the damned fishbowl would be, though."

"Tell me about it. But let them speculate."

As if we could stop them.

Levi looked past Carter. "You know, it's a nice night. Why don't I throw together some dinner? We could eat out on the deck."

"Sure. Sounds good. Can I help with anything?"

"No, you're fine." Levi smiled again, and Carter thought he *almost* winked as he added, "Just provide conversation."

Carter laughed. "That I can do."

CHAPTER ELEVEN

A s Levi pulled everything out to make some burgers, the cats emerged from their hiding places. The second Zelda padded into the kitchen, Levi hoisted her up and draped her over his shoulder. She held on, back paws braced against his shoulder blade with the front clamped down on his chest. As he leaned over to get a frying pan out of a cabinet, he paused, grabbing the counter as she threw his balance off.

"Good God, cat. You're getting heavy."

She just purred and started kneading.

Behind him, Carter laughed. "Does she always sit there like that?"

"Yep." Levi rose slowly, Zelda still perched comfortably. "Keeps her out of trouble and keeps my hands free."

"And she doesn't scratch?"

"Well"—Levi gingerly plucked one of her claws off his shirt—"she doesn't scratch *much*." He turned his head toward her. "Do you, baby?"

She bumped the top of her head against his face, catching him right in the mouth. As he sputtered and tried to brush the fur off his lip and nose, Carter laughed. And of course, Zelda started kneading harder.

"Do you regularly cook like that?" Carter asked. "With a cat riding shotgun?"

"More often than I care to admit. As long as she's on my shoulder, she stays out of everything else."

"Looks like she's got you trained."

She purred even louder.

"Yeah, she does." Levi patted her paw. "She was not happy when my physical therapist wouldn't let me carry her at all."

"You couldn't carry your cat?"

"She's twenty-two pounds. I couldn't lift more than fifteen for almost six months."

Carter's eyes widened. "Really? Why?"

"Neck and shoulder." Levi adjusted Zelda slightly, then started putting together a salad. "After the accident."

"Oh. Right."

Heat rushed into Levi's cheeks. It was still weird to think people who hadn't known him back then knew about the wreck. Not that it should have been a surprise. The accident had been all over the goddamned news and internet—he was thankful as hell he'd been doped up and hospitalized for most of that. Carter had probably seen all the speculation about Levi's blood alcohol content, the extent of his injuries, and his prognosis.

And why the hell did I bring it up?

"Anyway." He nuzzled the cat on his shoulder. "She wasn't happy for a while, but she was thrilled when I could finally carry her like this again."

"I can imagine." Carter laughed, meeting Levi's eyes and making his heart jump. "Sounds like you made a full recovery."

Levi shifted a little, hoping it looked like he was adapting to Zelda's weight instead of fidgeting. "Took a while, but . . . yeah. Aside from some stiff muscles now and then, I do all right."

"Good." Carter smiled, and it didn't strike Levi as patronizing or fake. It wasn't that tight-lipped expression some people gave him, the one that was a mix of pity and "you brought it on yourself, idiot." Carter knew what had happened—what the media had reported anyway—but he was still . . .

Damn it, Carter. It'd be a lot easier to switch back to 'just friends' if you weren't such a good friend.

Levi managed to cook without much trouble in spite of his twenty-plus-pound passenger and the incredibly distracting man on the other side of the counter. When the food was just about ready, he pulled some fixings out of the refrigerator, and then leaned down to let Zelda jump to the floor.

As he stood, rolling his shoulder, he gestured at everything he'd put on the counter. "I don't know what condiments you like, so help yourself."

"Great, thanks."

Once they'd assembled their burgers, they moved out onto the deck. As Levi was setting his glass and plate on the table, Carter suddenly gasped behind him.

"Shit! Cats!"

Levi turned around as Zelda and Link trotted out onto the deck. "Oh, it's okay. They're allowed out here."

Carter's eyebrows jumped. "Are you sure?"

"Yep, it's fine."

Carter shut the sliding glass door and came over to the table. "I thought they were indoor cats."

"They are, but there's no way for them to get to the ground and take off, and I doubt they'd try anyway." Levi reached down and scratched behind Link's ears. "They're a little too spoiled to go running off into the woods."

"Good point."

As Levi and Carter settled at the table with their food, Zelda clawed her way up onto the railing and Link occupied one of the two empty chairs.

Levi wagged a finger at Link. "No begging."

The cat just eyed him like he'd lost his mind. Link sat up in his chair, and at his size, had no trouble seeing over the edge of the table. His eyes flicked back and forth from Carter's plate to Levi's.

Carter laughed. "Somehow I don't think he's listening."

"He never does." Levi tore off two tiny pieces of hamburger. He set one on the chair in front of Link and put the other on the railing for Zelda.

Carter smirked. "Gee, I can't imagine why they don't listen to you when you tell them not to beg."

"Hey. *Hey.* Don't judge me."

"Oh, I'm judging you." Carter took a bite of his burger and watched Link and Zelda going to town on their morsels of meat.

"Fine. Judge." Levi jerked his chin toward the cats. "You don't have to live with them when they don't get their way."

Carter chuckled.

They ate in silence for a little while, both gazing out at the forest and the Olympic Mountains. Levi tried not to steal glances—especially lingering ones—at Carter, but damn, it was a challenge.

Subtly admiring a gorgeous man from a distance was one thing. Keeping himself from staring at one he'd *almost* had? Jesus.

Carter seemed to have made the shift back to "just friends" with ease. He was obviously more relaxed now—his features weren't so taut, and he laughed at the cats' antics in between nibbling his burger as if he didn't have a worry in the world. He and Levi could talk and hang out. They could casually brush against the subject of Levi's wreck, and they could eat together in comfortable—well, relatively comfortable—silence. They enjoyed each other's company.

Basically, they were a few kisses and a hot sex life away from the kind of relationship Levi hadn't had in ages. Damn. It would've been perfect too. But they couldn't go there.

Levi gritted his teeth and picked at his salad. Trust Hollywood and his family to fuck up something else in his life.

"You okay?"

Levi realized Carter was watching him, and his brow was furrowed with concern.

"Oh. Yeah. I'm . . ." Levi reached for his drink. "I'm good. Just spacing out."

Carter eyed him skeptically, but didn't press the issue. He turned his head back toward the scenery. "Man, I can see why you bought a place out here. Everyone shits on Bluewater Bay, but I love it, and this . . ." He gestured at the trees and mountains. "It's amazing."

"Right? I love it. And it was definitely a switch from SoCal."

"That's what I like about it. I never did get used to living in the desert." Carter paused. "What about you? Where'd you live before LA?"

"Maryland. Grew up out on the Eastern Shore. It's a bit warmer than it is here, but it's greener than LA, which is why I liked this area so much."

"Everything is greener than LA." Carter set his burger down and wiped his fingers on his napkin. "That was one of the selling points for this role, to be honest."

"Living here versus there?"

"Yep."

"I don't blame you. And at least if you want to travel from here, you just have to deal with Sea-Tac, not LAX."

Carter groaned. "God, that is such a lifesaver. I'd rather eat glass than deal with LAX."

"You and everyone else."

He laughed. "And the ironic thing is, I haven't had to use Sea-Tac much. Most of the traveling I do is for conventions and the occasional talk show or awards shindig."

"No vacations?"

Carter shook his head. "I haven't gotten to travel as much as I'd like. For pleasure, I mean. You know, aside from the occasional cruise, and I've goofed off when I've gone to some exotic locations for films, but . . ." He shrugged. "Just haven't done a lot as a tourist."

"You're missing out. Have you at least done some traveling around here? Canada? Seattle?"

"Oh yeah. I go to Seattle a few times a year, and I've been up to Victoria two or three times. Some of the guys from the show go out fishing every chance they get, but I haven't been."

Levi blinked. "You've lived here for how long?"

He shrugged. "Coming on two years now, I think."

"And you've never been out fishing? Not once?"

"Not even once."

"How in the . . . You know what? Let's fix that. I've been itching to get back out on the water, and the weather's supposed to be perfect for the next week." Levi smiled. "You want to go?"

Carter didn't answer immediately. He took a drink and rolled it around on his tongue as he looked out at the trees, likely oblivious to the way Levi's gut had clenched. Maybe the idea of an afternoon with him on a boat, completely alone, was too weird. Okay, so they were alone now, and far from Bluewater Bay, but a boat would—

"Sounds like fun." Carter turned to him at last and smiled. "So you have your own boat and everything?"

Oh, thank God. Levi returned the smile. "Of course. Bought her before I'd even closed on the house. I wanted to make up for lost time." He sipped his Coke. "When is good for you?"

Carter's eyes lost focus for a moment. "Well, I'm on set tomorrow, but unless something changes, I'm off the next day."

"Works for me. Just meet me down at the marina. Only one in town. My boat's in slip twenty-two. Say, eight?"

"I'll be there." Carter met Levi's gaze.

"Great. You'll love it." *And I'll try not to be too . . .* Levi cleared his throat, his spine tingling from simply looking at Carter. "Especially if the weather holds out. And this time of year, we might even see some gray whales."

"Whales? Really?"

"Yeah." Levi smirked. "It *is* the ocean, you know."

Carter rubbed his eye with his middle finger.

Levi chuckled. "Oh, and sometimes the porpoises come out. They're a lot of fun. They'll jump alongside the boat and across the bow."

"Wow, cool. Sounds like you could make a killing doing whale-watching tours."

"Yeah, but the companies in Port Townsend and Port Angeles already have that market pretty well cornered. And besides, I'm not crazy about taking a big group out there."

"You don't mind taking me out, though?"

Levi smiled. "You're not a big group. And it's fishing. I'm not going to say no to fishing."

And I definitely *won't mind being out on a boat with you.*

They never did make it down to the theater. When the bugs started coming out, Levi herded the cats back inside, and he and Carter sat in the living room with their drinks until it was almost eleven.

"Wow, it's late again." Carter sat up and stretched. "I guess I should get out of your hair. I have to be on the set early tomorrow anyway. Again."

"Occupational hazard?"

"Yep."

Before he left, Carter helped bring in the dishes from dinner. They didn't talk much—maybe Carter knew as well as Levi that if they fell into another conversation, they'd be here all night. The silence wasn't uncomfortable, though. Not like it had been when he'd arrived tonight. That lack of conversation had been fraught with uncertainty and awkwardness. Now it was the complete opposite, which was a bigger relief than he dared let on.

Levi glanced at Carter. And his pulse shifted. Up. Down. Up again. Just looking at him threw Levi off.

Yeah, they'd settled their issues from last night, which was a relief, but who was he kidding? He was beyond frustrated now. One moment of touching onstage, a few kisses, and suddenly it drove him crazy not to be able to touch Carter at all.

Just need to get used to the idea. That's all. Last night shook things up. Give it time.

They still didn't say much even as Carter headed out for the evening, but on his way down the walk, he turned around, eyebrows raised. "We're still on for fishing, right?"

"I'm looking forward to it."

"Me too. I'll see you then."

They held each other's gazes for a few seconds longer than they probably should have, but finally Carter continued toward his car while Levi went back into the house.

He shut the door and leaned against it, closing his eyes and letting out a long breath. The evening had gone better than he'd expected. Though he still wanted Carter, and he didn't see that changing anytime soon, he could get used to this. It was simply an adjustment. And he *did* feel a hell of a lot better than he had after leaving the theater last night.

Now they were going fishing together. As friends. Nothing more.

Maybe they could pull this off after all.

CHAPTER TWELVE

I t was a perfect day to spend on a boat. Clear skies, calm seas—not a cloud or a whitecap in sight as Carter gazed out at the ocean from his second-floor balcony. He had learned real quick that the constant grayness of the Pacific Northwest was largely a myth. There were lots of drizzly, depressing days, especially around Seattle on the other side of Puget Sound, but out here on the Olympic Peninsula? It was fucking gorgeous. And he'd also learned the hard way that putting makeup over a sunburn *sucked*, so he was bringing plenty of sunscreen with him today.

Carter usually drove the Porsche, but when he wanted to lay low, he brought out the piece-of-shit Taurus he'd been driving since before he'd signed his first contract. It was dusty with bald tires and chipped paint, and the perpetually dirty windshield still had his junior college parking permits and a crack from two winters ago. Perfect for disappearing into the crowd.

The house he rented was a couple of miles outside of Bluewater Bay, tucked back in a tiny cul-de-sac not far from the main road. Not as secluded as Levi's place, but not out in the open either, so when he left in his "urban camouflage" car, very few people were around to notice.

Not far from the marina, Carter circled a block a few times to make sure no one was following him. There wasn't a camera lens in sight, and he decided if anyone was subtle enough to go unnoticed—and had recognized him in spite of the car—then they deserved to get a few shots.

Of me. Of Levi. Of us together.

Oh God.

No, they won't see anything incriminating, because we're not doing *anything incriminating.* He held the wheel tighter. *We're friends. We've got this.*

Right?

Only one way to find out . . .

He parked, glanced around again out of habit, and then continued to the marina. Each row of boats was labeled with the slip numbers, so he found the row marked "Slips 15-30," and walked down the weathered pier between the bobbing bows of everything from tiny fishing boats and sailboats to massive yachts.

"Right on time."

Levi's voice came from behind him, and spun him on his heel. And there he was, a red-and-white plastic cooler balanced on his hip and a pair of sunglasses pushed up onto the top of his head.

"Oh. Hey." Carter laughed. "I didn't know you were there."

"It's all right. I was just a few boats down." Levi tilted his head back in the direction he'd come from. "Grabbing something from a buddy of mine."

Carter stiffened. It hadn't occurred to him that someone might see them here, once they'd made it past the marina's gate. "Is your friend . . ." As guarded as Levi was about his privacy, this would have to be one hell of a trusted friend. Carter hoped, anyway.

"Relax." Levi continued toward his own slip. "There's no one else here. He just borrowed my cooler and left it for me to pick up."

"Oh. Okay."

"Come on."

Levi's boat turned out to be a midsized one. Not as big as the yachts, but definitely more impressive than the fishing boats. Maybe thirty feet long or so, complete with a small living space belowdecks.

"Wow, this is really nice."

"Thanks." Levi smiled. "She's kind of my second home."

Carter snickered. "So you really *did* come to Bluewater Bay and buy a mobile home."

Levi rolled his eyes. "Very funny."

Before long, they were out on the water, Levi steering while Carter watched the scenery go by. He'd been a little afraid he'd get seasick, but so far, so good. Even when the seas got rougher, when he had to hold on to the railing to keep his balance, his stomach stayed put.

Levi glanced at him, eyes hidden by dark lenses. "Not getting sick on me, are you?"

"No, no, I'm good." Carter loosened his grip on the railing. "Still getting my legs under me, I guess."

"You'll get your sea legs after a while. Everyone's a little unsteady the first time out." Either Levi had spent a lot of time on the water, or he had naturally perfect balance, because he moved around on the deck so easily, it looked effortless. Even when a large swell lifted the boat and dropped it unceremoniously, throwing Carter into the railing, Levi just casually braced himself with an arm against the cabin. It was like he didn't even notice. Obviously *someone* had obtained his sea legs a long time ago.

Carter's head was light now, and his balance was all fucked up. He tried to blame the boat's rocking—that was bullshit. The rocking didn't help, but the seas were only part of the problem. If they'd been on solid, dry land, he would've been just as unsteady.

Because . . . Levi.

It was no wonder someone had thought to cast the man in an action role—he sure had the body for it. Though he didn't have the bronze tan he'd had back then; a few years in the Pacific Northwest had that effect on everybody. Still, he obviously spent time out in the sun whenever he could, and he had some color on his powerful back and shoulders.

Standing at the helm of his boat in a pair of low-slung shorts and dark sunglasses without a shirt in sight, he was every inch Chad Eastwick. The only thing that set Levi apart from his character was that eagle tattoo on his upper right arm. And the lack of blood, since Chad usually spent most of a film getting battered within an inch of his life.

And as Carter stared, he couldn't decide who was hotter—the mythical Chad Eastwick, or the man who played him.

He looked away before he started openly swooning, and took a few slow breaths as he studied the rolling seas. He focused on the internal lecture that was rapidly becoming a mantra—*we're just friends, we're just friends, we're just friends*—and didn't let himself look at Levi for a moment.

Carter held on to the railing and closed his eyes as the wind played with his hair. He was having a harder and harder time convincing himself he and Levi were, and could remain, friends. It wasn't even because they'd kissed, or because of the tabloid rumors, or because he wanted so badly to tumble into bed with him.

It was because he could *breathe* around Levi. Not always literally—Levi could make his breath catch like no one else—but when he was with Levi, Carter never felt like he needed to put on an act. No being on his best behavior like everyone was in the beginning of a relationship. No pressure. No stress. Here he was, hanging out with his longtime crush and idol, and he could just *be*. And wasn't that exactly what he'd always craved in a boyfriend?

But having Levi as just a friend was the next best thing. Better than not being around him at all.

Right?

A swell hit the boat, and Carter stumbled.

Levi, of course, didn't. "You okay?"

"I'm good. Sea legs and all that." *Good enough excuse as any.* "I feel like a clumsy idiot. It's not like I've never been out on the water."

"Let me guess." Levi's eyebrows rose above his sunglasses. "Cruise ships?"

"Yep."

"Totally different. You feel it more in smaller boats." He faced forward again, fingers resting lightly on the wheel as he steered. "You'll actually get sicker on a big ship. The rocking is more subtle, and when you're inside, you can't see the horizon, so your brain can't find its equilibrium."

Carter smirked. "So you're saying size does matter?"

Levi opened his mouth to reply, but stopped. "I . . ."

"Sorry," Carter snickered. "I couldn't resist."

Shaking his head, Levi laughed too. "I kind of walked into that one, didn't I?"

"Right smack into it."

Levi glared playfully at him, and they both laughed again. "Well, you're doing better than Anna ever did."

"Yeah? She isn't much for the water?"

Levi whistled and shook his head. "*No*. Girl gets seasick just walking down the pier."

Carter laughed. "Anna? Seriously? She's always seemed like the type who can handle anything."

"Well, her Achilles' heel is the ocean." Levi grimaced. "Boy, she tried, though. We rented a boat one weekend when we were kids, and she was practically mainlining Dramamine, but she was still miserable. After the third time, she gave up."

Levi? And Anna? Boating together?

Carter studied him. "Three times?"

"Yeah, we . . ." Levi hesitated.

Carter's stomach flipped. Right. He'd mentioned a history with Anna. "You, uh, don't have to elaborate."

"No, it's okay." Levi tapped his fingers on the wheel. "When we were younger, Anna and I . . . we dated for a little while."

Carter stared at him. "Anna? Dated a *guy*?"

Levi nodded, gazing out at the water. "Back in our student film days. That was, um . . ." His fingers tapped faster, and he turned toward Carter again. "That was when she figured out she was a lesbian."

Carter winced. "Oh, ouch. That must've been rough."

"Yes and no." Levi shrugged. "The worst part was it almost ruined our friendship. But once we patched things up, it didn't really bother me that she wasn't into men. If anything, it explained a lot of the problems we'd been having, and putting that behind us meant we could be friends again."

"Oh. That makes sense, I guess."

"I, um . . ." Levi swallowed. "I haven't told anyone about that in a long time."

"It stays between us," Carter said softly, as if someone might overhear them even this far from shore.

"Thanks." A smile finally worked itself onto Levi's lips. "I figured you wouldn't broadcast it to anyone."

"No, definitely not. I mean, there's always Twitter, but . . ."

They both laughed, and Levi kept driving.

After an hour or so, when the town was long gone but the coastline was still visible, Levi slowed the boat and brought it to a stop. He cut the motor, and just like that, the world around them grew silent.

When they'd left the marina, there'd been the distant noise from the town and the highway, but out here, there was nothing. Even the squawking seagulls had stayed near the shore.

Though the water was relatively calm, the waves continued to gently rock the boat. Carter's sea legs remained questionable, but as long as he kept a hand on the railing, he was able to move around without much trouble.

And still, Levi moved effortlessly, as if he was barely even aware they were on the water at all. Jerk.

Levi took two fishing rods from behind the door. He eyed both of them for a moment, then selected one and handed it to Carter. "Here you go."

With anyone else on the planet, Carter would've been making jokes about using another guy's rod. He suspected Levi would've done the same—the man had a wicked sense of humor, and appreciated juvenile jokes as much as Carter did.

Neither of them made any comments, lewd or otherwise.

"So, um." Carter quirked his lips. "At the risk of sounding like a complete idiot, how do I do this?"

"You're not an idiot. You've just never done it before." Levi toed the cooler over to the side of the deck where a couple of weathered folding chairs were tied. "First things first, a place to sit." He untied the chairs and unfolded them on either side of the cooler. "And then . . . bait."

While Carter watched, Levi pulled what looked like a couple of herring filets from the cooler, and put them on the hooks at the ends of their lines.

"So, we're catching fish with other fish?"

"Just showing 'em who's where on the food chain."

"Right. Got it. And we're fishing for what?"

"Ideally, salmon."

Carter's mouth watered. "Please tell me you know how to cook a salmon."

Levi snorted. "Know how to? Pfft. My salmon would make Gordon Ramsay weep."

"Awesome. Then let's catch some."

"That's the plan. Have a seat."

They both sat in the folding chairs, and Levi handed over the baited fishing line. "Casting is easy. Just tilt it back like this, throw it forward, and cast the line out as far as you can." He demonstrated with his own, though he didn't let the line go. "Try it."

Carter did a few mock casts to get the hang of the motion, and then under Levi's watchful eye, he cast the line. The red-and-white bob landed with a plop in the water, and he reeled in some of the line to pick up the slack.

Levi grinned. "You're a natural at this."

Carter chuckled. "Doesn't seem that complicated."

"You'd be surprised." Levi cast his own line, which went about ten feet farther than Carter's had.

"Show-off," Carter muttered.

Levi laughed. "Now comes the fun part." He lounged in his chair. "We sit back, enjoy the sun, and wait for the fish to bite."

"I like the sound of that." Carter leaned back as well. "You usually catch much?"

"Sometimes. Once in a while, you get lucky and snag a lingcod. They're kind of terrifying the first time you pull one out of the water, but goddamn, they are good eating."

"Terrifying?" Carter glanced at him. "How so?"

"You'll know when you see one. They're . . ." He made a face. "They're big, and they're fucking hideous."

"But . . . they look so good when they're breaded and fried."

"Right? Not so much when they're still alive, though."

Carter thought for a moment. "Now I'm not sure if I hope we catch one, or I hope we don't."

"Let's just keep our fingers crossed for a salmon."

"Good idea."

Levi reached into the cooler again. No surprise, he withdrew a can of Coke. "Drink?"

Carter craned his neck to look in the cooler. "What? No beer? I thought that was a requirement for fishing trips."

Levi laughed, but there was a note of discomfort. "I, uh, don't drink. I guess I should've asked if you wanted anything, though."

"Nah, it's okay." Carter freed a Coke from the bed of ice. After he'd popped the tab, he glanced at Levi again. "It doesn't bother you that I drink sometimes, does it?"

"No, no. Not at all. Besides, I've never seen you have more than one or two, so . . ." He shrugged.

"Still. Some people who don't drink have, you know, an aversion to people who do."

"I don't like being around people who drink to excess." Levi turned to him, and his smile fucked with Carter's body temperature. "You don't do that. Which is nice. It's kind of refreshing, actually."

"Yeah, never been a big drinker." Carter took a swig of Coke because he needed something cold right then. "Are you just not a fan of alcohol or—" He snapped his teeth shut. Hadn't there been rumors about Levi being drunk when he'd wrecked his Vette? Levi had insisted that wasn't the case, but the subject clearly touched a raw nerve. Shit. Way to make the conversation awkward. Again.

"I was raised by alcoholics," Levi said quietly. "Trust me, it was enough to put my siblings and me off drinking forever."

"Oh." And didn't *that* raise some questions about the car accident, but Carter didn't go there. "You're not missing much anyway. I like a beer now and then, but anything more than that . . ."

"Eh, the odd beer never hurt anybody." Levi picked up his Coke can and gestured with it. "Hell, this shit will probably kill me eventually."

"With as much as you drink? Probably."

Levi shrugged. "YOLO."

Carter just laughed. For the longest time, they sat there and fished, occasionally reeling in their lines and casting them again, and relaxed. Though this wasn't the most exciting pastime in the world—Carter hadn't imagined it would be—he could see the attraction. Sitting back, soaking up the sun, listening to the waves slosh against the gently rocking boat. What wasn't to love?

And as a bonus, his sunglasses let him steal a few surreptitious glances at Levi, especially when he was leaning over to pull some bait out of the cooler, or when he smoothed on more sunscreen.

Thank God for those tinted lenses. After all, even if Carter couldn't touch, he could still look. Right?

He shifted his attention back out to the water. *Get a grip, Samuels. Jesus.*

Goddamn it. There were so many reasons why they couldn't be more than friends, and no amount of wanting would change that, but Carter couldn't help fantasizing about him. About what it would be like to take him to bed and see what else he could do with his mouth.

Or, for that matter, what it would be like to be here with him, just like this—fishing and soaking up the sun—but knowing that when the sun went down, they'd be tangled together. He loved that point in a relationship, when the novelty of sex had worn off enough that they didn't have to be fucking *all* the time. He'd never specifically fantasized about being in that state before, but envisioning himself and Levi like that simply . . . made sense. It was like everything between them was perfect except this artificial distance. They wanted each other, and they both knew it.

But they wouldn't go there. They couldn't.

Damn it. I want us to be—

Friends. We're just friends.

Carter had been so distracted by the man beside him, he almost lost his grip when something yanked at his fishing pole. "Holy fuck!"

"Hang on to it." Levi attached his own to the railing and then stood up. "I'll get the net."

"What do I do? Just hold it?"

"Start reeling it in slowly. *Slowly.*"

Carter did as he was told. It had never occurred to him how difficult it was to reel in a fish. Either this was a big fish, or it was putting up a hell of a fight. Maybe both. "Holy crap, that's heavy."

"I can see that. Whatever it is, it's definitely not small. Reel it in nice and slow so the line doesn't break."

Not that he had much choice. Turning the reel was surprisingly difficult, and "nice and slow" was the best he could do.

Levi leaned on the railing and craned his neck. "Ah, there he is."

Below the surface, a slender white shape appeared, maybe two feet long and squirming and fighting against the hook. With another tug at the line and some splashing, the fish was out of the water.

Carter did a double take at its distinctive sharp dorsal fin. "Is that . . . is that a *shark*?"

"Just a dogfish."

"It looks like a shark."

"Well, it is, but—here, bring it in close."

Carter pulled the rod back and the fish swung toward the boat. Levi leaned over the railing and caught the wriggling fish—*holy shit, it really* is *a shark*—like it was nothing. While Carter would've cut the thing away and thrown it back as quickly as possible, Levi grabbed it and tucked it under his arm. And reached for its mouth.

Carter blinked. The shark-thing squirmed.

Then Levi swore, and a second later, the dogfish flew back into the water and quickly disappeared beneath the surface.

"Damn it," Levi muttered. He let go of the line—hook and bob still attached—and stepped away, cradling his hand.

Carter's heart jumped into his throat. "You okay?"

"I'm good. Be right back." Levi returned a moment later with a rag, a roll of tape, and a couple of gauze pads.

"Did you . . ." Carter eyed the small but distinct bloodstain on the rag. "Did you just get bitten by a shark?"

"Well, a little one."

"Yeah, but still. A shark fucking bit you!"

Dabbing at his hand, Levi chuckled. "It's not that bad. He got me while I was getting the hook out."

"So I shouldn't tweet that Chad Eastwick just got—"

"Do it, and you're swimming home."

Carter laughed. "And people say fishing is boring."

"It is when you're sitting in a lake catching bass. Just be glad that wasn't one of those damned lingcod."

"But we could've *eaten* that."

"And the lingcod would've thought the same about us."

"Good point." Carter watched Levi trying to arrange the gauze pads on his hand. "Do you need some help with that?"

Levi shook his head. "No, no. I've got it. It's . . . damn it."

Carter propped the fishing pole against the railing. "Here. It's easier with two hands."

Sighing, Levi gave him the roll of tape and gauze pads. Carter tore off a few strips, then set the roll aside. He steadied Levi's wrist and quickly arranged the gauze so it would cover the wound without getting in the way more than necessary, and taped them down.

"You really know what you're doing," Levi said.

Carter shrugged as he carefully wound a piece of tape between Levi's thumb and forefinger to his palm. "I'm the oldest, and my mom faints at the sight of blood." He turned Levi's hand slightly and taped the other end of the gauze. "Someone had to put my younger siblings back together."

"Practice makes perfect?"

"Basically." Carter met Levi's eyes, and whatever he was about to say was gone as fast as the dogfish had disappeared beneath the waves. He hadn't realized how close they'd been standing. And he hadn't noticed that Levi had taken off his sunglasses.

Just friends. We're . . .

We're just . . .

Didn't you say this boat has living quarters? Like, with a bed?

Levi looked down. Then Carter did.

And realized he still had his hand around Levi's wrist.

He quickly drew it back. "Uh. Sorry."

"Don't worry about it." Levi laughed quietly and examined the bandage. "Nice job, Dr. House."

Carter chuckled. "Thanks."

"Thank you."

Their eyes met again, but Levi didn't let it linger. "Let's. Um." He gestured at the fishing poles. "Let's put some bait on that line and see if we can catch something that won't try to eat us first."

"Right. Good idea."

They sat back and cast their lines, and Carter wondered if Levi was still thinking about that moment with the bandages and the contact. Or if he regretted pulling away as quickly as they had.

Maybe one of them would catch another mouthy creature. Another bite, another opportunity to patch the other up.

Jesus, Carter. What's wrong with you? There are easier ways to get a man to touch you than getting bitten by a goddamned fish.

To get *a* man to touch him, maybe.

This one? Not so much.

But damn it, nothing was biting today.

CHAPTER THIRTEEN

L evi parked the boat in its slip, and quickly secured the lines. As he did, Carter stepped onto the pier, and paused, wobbling a bit. "You okay?" Levi asked.

Carter nodded. "Just a little weird to be back on solid ground."

"Wait until tonight." Levi grinned. "You'll feel the waves when you try to go to sleep."

"Oh great."

"It's not so bad. Kind of cool, actually. Just, uh, don't be surprised."

Silence elbowed its way in. Levi could feel the *I'll see you later* and *When do you want to get together again?* coming from a mile away. If he was honest with himself, he needed to get away from Carter for a little while. Catch his breath. Gather his thoughts. But something about Carter's eyes fucked with his senses, which in turn fucked with his good sense. Maybe he needed to put some space between him and Carter, but . . .

"You want to come by the house tonight? We've still got a fuck-load of DVDs to watch."

Carter laughed. "We could live to be a hundred and never make it through all your DVDs."

"But we can sure try."

"Yeah, we can. Just, uh . . ." He gestured down at himself. "Let me run home and get cleaned up. We didn't catch anything, but I smell like we did."

"Me too," Levi said with a laugh, not sure why he was so relieved Carter had taken him up on the invite. "Any preference for food?"

"Whatever you're in the mood for."

"All right. Come on over whenever you're ready."

"Great. I'll see around"—Carter glanced at his phone—
"probably six?"

"Perfect. See you then."

The cats met him at the door—tails up, eyes wide, noses twitching
as they searched the air.

"Sorry, guys." He nudged them back into the house, taking care
not to shut a tail in the door or set the cooler down on a paw. "Didn't
catch anything today."

They immediately descended on the cooler, sniffing it all over. He
took off the lid, revealing nothing but a few unopened sodas and a
couple of just-in-case ice packs.

Zelda turned up her nose and stalked off. Link, ever the optimist,
kept sniffing around.

Levi chuckled. "Good luck with that, kitty." While Link
continued inspecting the cooler—that would keep him busy for quite
a while—Levi headed downstairs. He already needed to grab a shower
thanks to the sweat and sunscreen, so he went to his home gym for a
short session of weight lifting. He usually worked out in the evening,
but knowing him and Carter, this would be a late night.

Pity it can't be that *kind of late night.*

Levi pushed that thought right out of his mind. Well, he tried
to. As he loaded plates onto the bar, he had to stop three times
to remember how much weight he'd intended to stack on the
damned thing. Twice he had to pull off a plate and replace it with
the correct one.

He had to focus on his lifting, though. One fuck-up, and he'd be
in physical therapy, and he wasn't going through that again. As long as
he kept in the best shape possible, his neck and shoulder didn't hurt
much. Even a distraction like Carter wasn't going to put his ability to
move in jeopardy. Not after two excruciating years of getting it back.

But focusing was definitely a challenge. All day long with Carter?
Putting on the "just friends" face and hanging out like they weren't a
lingering glance and a touch away from more?

Come on, Levi. Focus. Weights.

He took a deep breath and wrapped his fingers around the bar. It didn't help in the slightest that every time he grabbed a weight or even moved his hand a little, the cuts burned. The wound was minor, but still fresh enough to be aggravated by pressure or movement. And every time he aggravated it, he was reminded of how it had happened, and where he'd been, and who he'd been with.

Who'd bandaged his hand and let that platonic, absolutely nonsexual contact continue well past the point of platonic and nonsexual.

After a set of dead lifts, he put the barbell down and stared at himself in the mirror he'd been using to monitor his form. He'd said himself they couldn't pull off a relationship. Not now. Not with so much hanging over his head.

Holding his own gaze, he sighed. Was he being selfish? Maybe. Maybe not. But Carter had seemed relieved when he'd said this wouldn't work, so it was possible that, regardless of the reasons on his part, this was the best thing. And they were still friends, so if something developed in the future—

No, don't think about that. Wishful thinking is pointless.

He went back to lifting, carefully avoiding his own eyes and watching his form. Pushing through when he struggled with the weight. Gritting his teeth and finishing the set even when the last couple of reps had his arms shaking.

As he headed upstairs for a quick shower, his muscles burned pleasantly from exertion, and the ache in his upper back was annoying but mild. By the time he was out, dressed, and presentable, it was almost five, so Carter would be along soon.

He fed the cats. Checked the time. Checked his email. Took an Aleve for his back and neck. Glanced out the window. Glanced at the clock. Took another Aleve.

The purr of an engine grazed his nerve endings, and when he looked out the window, the candy-apple-red Porsche emerged from the trees, light and shadows playing on its windshield and sleek curves.

Levi's heart quickened.

As Carter parked, Levi went to the front door. Hand on the doorknob, he paused to collect himself. They were friends. They'd spent the afternoon fishing, and now they'd spend the evening in, just hanging out and watching movies.

The fact that they'd kissed one time—one amazing time—didn't mean anything.

Get over it. Like, now.

He took a deep breath and opened the door.

And tried not to notice the way his heart fluttered when Carter smiled at him on his way up the walk.

"Hey," Carter said.

"Hey." He stood aside to let Carter come in. "So what are you in the mood for tonight?" He cringed. "Noir? Something foreign?" *Good save, Pritchard.*

Carter shrugged. "I'm game for anything." He paused and cleared his throat. "Any genre."

Right then, before the awkwardness could really set in, the cats thundered into the foyer, tails up and eyes wide.

"Hey guys!" Carter knelt to pet them. After a moment, he glanced up at Levi. "What about you? Genres, I mean?"

"Pretty much anything."

Carter smirked. "How about *Jaws*?"

"Oh, ha-ha."

"How's your hand, anyway?"

"Just feels like a bad cat bite." He held it up, revealing a few small pieces of gauze still taped to his palm. "It'll be fine."

"I can't say I've ever known anyone who's been bitten by a shark before."

"Yeah, well. Telling someone that gets a little less impressive when you mention the shark wasn't even two feet long."

Carter laughed, scratching under Link's chin. "You can always leave that part out."

"Uh-huh. Until they ask to see the scar, right?"

"Hmm, yeah, that would make things difficult. Okay, so show them the scar first, *then* tell them it was a shark bite."

"Right. That'll work."

Carter took a breath like he was about to reply, but right then, Zelda pushed Link out of the way. Of course, Link slunk back because he was a big wuss.

"Oh, come on." Carter gently nudged Zelda aside. "There's enough attention for both of you. C'mere, Link." He scooped Link up off the floor and stood. "There. Better?"

Link climbed onto Carter's shoulder and purred loudly as Carter petted him.

And Levi's heart melted. Most people gave him the side eye for treating his cats like they were his kids—he did spend more time with them than anyone else, after all—but Carter adored them. He didn't mind a few long hairs on his shirt, and when Link kneaded too enthusiastically, Carter just gently popped the claws free and kept right on petting him.

There were few things in the world that endeared someone to Levi like being cuddly with animals. As if he didn't already swoon a little every time he looked at Carter.

Come on. Stop torturing yourself.

At his feet, Zelda meowed at him, so Levi picked her up. Each holding one of the content—and rather smug—cats, he and Carter went into the kitchen.

"Drink?" Levi asked over Zelda.

"I'll take a Coke if you're having one." Carter grinned. "Which I assume you are."

"I'm getting predictable."

"Just consistent." As Levi poured their drinks, Carter added, "What was it you said about that stuff killing you sooner or later?"

"You're drinking it too. I don't want to hear it."

"Fair enough." Carter adjusted Link on his shoulder and picked up his glass. Link craned his neck, peering into the cup. "What? You want some?" Carter offered it to the cat, who squinted and recoiled. "Didn't think so."

"Put some booze in it, he'll drink it."

Carter blinked. "Seriously?"

"Yep." Levi picked Zelda up again, then his own glass. "I left a Crown and Coke unattended once, and he had a few licks of it."

"Wow."

"Yeah, I think that's what *he* thought."

Carter just laughed.

With Cokes and cats in hand, they headed downstairs.

"So." Levi set Zelda on one of the recliners. "What are we watching?"

"You pick tonight. I think I picked the last few."

"Fair enough." Levi flipped through one of his binders, and finally selected an old Italian film that was, on the surface, about the Mafia, but was really a grim metaphor for sons rebelling against fathers.

As Levi started the movie, Link curled up in Carter's lap and Zelda parked herself on the broad armrest between the two recliners, a furry, purring reminder of the leather-wrapped barrier keeping them a foot apart. If she hadn't been sitting there, and things between him and Carter had been different, he could've lifted the armrest and tucked it into the back of the couch, effectively turning the bucket seats into a bench.

So much for ignoring what *wasn't* going on between him and Carter. Levi knew all too well how comfortably two people fit together on this couch without the armrest in between. He'd fallen asleep here with one of his ex-girlfriends as many times as he'd fucked her on it.

He missed the way an arm around the shoulders during the opening credits evolved into a warm, full-body embrace by the end credits. It didn't even have to be sex. Or making out. Arms around each other, maybe one person's leg hooked over the other's—he hadn't realized how much he'd missed that until now, when it took every ounce of self-control he had not to move Zelda, get the armrest out of the way, and reach for Carter. He'd been going crazy like that since day one, but it was a hell of a lot worse now that he knew what Carter's kiss tasted like.

Goddamn it.

His favorite part of the film came and went—the scene with the Don's daughter and his enemy's son on a Mediterranean beach—and he barely noticed. Before he knew it, the credits were rolling.

And he was still trying to get the hang of sitting this close to Carter again.

He cleared his throat. "We never did eat. You want to take a break? I've got some frozen pizzas upstairs."

"Sure, that sounds great." Carter gently lifted Link off his lap and dusted the hair off his jeans as he stood.

On the way up from the theater, Levi said, "I'd call for delivery, but no one delivers here."

"I'd be surprised if they *did* deliver all the way out here."

"No kidding. Anyway, let's get some food, and then I'll show you *Croupier.*"

"Sweet. I've been dying to watch that one."

In the kitchen, Levi preheated the oven, and while they waited for it to beep, they sat in the living room, talking about the movie they'd just watched. The cats didn't mind—Zelda sprawled out on the cushion between them while Link cuddled up next to Carter.

The pizza came and went, and they still didn't head down to the theater. With a plate full of crumbs and two glasses of melting ice cubes, they kept right on talking. Link fell asleep. Zelda got bored and wandered off. Levi refilled their Cokes. Again.

And they talked. The whole time. About their film careers. About the cats. About *Wolf's Landing.*

Before Levi knew it, it was dark outside, and even the caffeine from his soda wasn't keeping him fully awake. Big surprise—according to his watch, it was after midnight.

"Holy crap," he said. "It's twelve fifteen."

Carter laughed. "You know, I can't say I'm surprised. I think your house was built in a time vortex or something."

"What do you mean?"

"I mean every time I come over here, I blink and it's been hours." Carter eyed his empty glass. "You drugging my drink, or what?"

Levi laughed and put up his hands. "It's not me, I swear."

"Uh-huh."

They both stretched, joints cracking and popping from sitting for so long.

Carter sighed. "I guess I should go. I still have to do a load of laundry before bed."

Levi grimaced. "Damn, sorry I kept you this late."

"Nah, it's okay. I'd rather spend my day off fishing and watching movies than doing laundry."

"Yeah, who wouldn't?" Levi pushed himself up and took the glasses and plates from the table. "I should call it a night myself. I'll see you soon, though?"

"Definitely. I'm on set late tomorrow night, but the day after?"

"Sounds good. Just come on by when you're free. I'll be here."

Carter smiled, throwing Levi's pulse out of whack all over again. "I will. See you then."

On the way to the door, Carter stopped to pet both the cats again—and subtly kept Zelda from pushing Link aside.

Then he headed out, and as the Porsche's engine faded into the distance, Levi went back to the kitchen. The clock on the stove said it was indeed after midnight. Carter had been here for hours.

And they never had gotten around to watching that second movie.

CHAPTER FOURTEEN

C arter returned to the set the next night, and it was hard to believe he'd only had one day off. Wandering amongst the equipment and crew that had become as familiar as his own house, he felt like he hadn't been here in . . . in a long time. Or like everything had changed, though he couldn't put his finger on exactly how. He wasn't *about* to admit that it had anything to do with seeing the world through Levi-tinted glasses.

He shook the thoughts away and tried to get his head in the game. He had scenes to shoot. A character to play. The fact that his concentration was shot—probably because Levi had been getting so much mental screen time lately—didn't negate the fact that he had a job to do.

Though it was a comfortable evening—not hot, but definitely not cold either—Carter clung to his coffee cup the way he did during winter shoots. He was irrationally sure that the second he let go of that cup, he'd fall asleep. The coffee was only about half-gone, and he'd already begged one of the production assistants to bring him another.

A few more hours. I can do this.

It was just as well tonight's scenes were outdoors. He was away from the stuffiness of the soundstages, and the salty ocean wind was brisk enough to keep him from dozing off.

They were shooting on location, cameras and lighting equipment set up in an alien-looking semicircle around a beat-up car parked beneath a fire escape behind an abandoned motel. It was a series of intense, violent scenes—*that* would keep him awake if the cool wind failed.

"Your coffee, Mr. Samuels." The production assistant handed him an extra-large and steaming-hot cup.

"Thank you so much." He smiled and took the cup, which he poured into the one he'd already been nursing.

He wandered around to keep himself moving, and found his stunt double getting ready for an upcoming scene.

"Hey," Carter said. "You need a hand with that?"

Ginsberg shook his head and tugged at a strap that was meant to secure some pads to his rib cage. "No, I've got it. It's just being . . . ah, there it is." He fastened the buckle, then pulled his black leather jacket—identical to the one Carter was wearing—over it. "Much better."

"Good." Carter grinned. "So you're ready to get the shit kicked out of you on my behalf?"

"That's what they pay me the big bucks for." Ginsberg arched an eyebrow. "Are you ever going to talk to your character about maybe not getting his ass handed to him on a regular basis? For my sake?"

Carter laughed. "I've tried, man. He just won't listen."

"Hmph. And Hunter Easton hasn't responded to any of my emails either."

"Guess you're stuck." He jerked his head toward the building. "Ready to go out there and take one for the team, whipping boy?"

"Fucker."

Carter gave another laugh, but it was halfhearted this time. He sipped his coffee, wondering when the caffeine would finally kick in.

Ginsberg put his foot on a chair and rolled up his pant leg. As he strapped on a shin guard, he glanced at Carter. "You okay tonight? You look like you're half-dead, and I can't tell if it's the makeup, lighting, or what."

"I'm fine." Carter waved a hand. "Just tired."

Ginsberg's eyebrow rose again. "Mm-hmm."

"What?"

"Nothing. Nothing."

"Yeah, sure. C'mon." Carter brought his coffee up to his lips. "Out with it."

Ginsberg shrugged. "The name Levi ring a bell?"

Carter managed to swallow his coffee without choking, but just barely. And the playful smirk told him Ginsberg had seen how close he'd come to a damning sputter. So much for Ginsberg distracting him, the bastard.

Ginsberg smirked. "Thought so."

"What? Why?"

"You mean besides your sudden inability to drink your—"

"Yes. Besides that."

"You've been a tired, spacy mess since the day he showed up on set." Ginsberg glanced around, and then lowered his voice even more. "Come on, level with me. You have a thing for him or something?"

Carter narrowed his eyes. "Are you telling me you don't?"

"Please. Who *wouldn't* be into Levi Pritchard?"

"Exactly. So, yes, I have a thing for him."

Ginsberg studied Carter. "A thing for him? Or a thing *with* him?"

"For." Carter gritted his teeth. "He's straight, remember?"

"So they say."

"We're friends. That's all."

"You're—" Ginsberg straightened. "So you guys *have* been hanging out? I thought that was just a rumor."

Carter bit back a groan. So much for being discreet. "Yeah, we have."

"Seriously?" Ginsberg's eyeballs damn near fell out of his skull. "You've been hanging out with—"

"*Yes.*"

"Nice, man. Nice."

"And yes, I'd love to have more with him, but . . ." Carter shook his head. "He's straight."

"Wow. How in the world did you guys even meet?"

Carter shrugged. "You said he was working at that theater in town, so I went there to see if I could pick his brain about a few things." The stuntman's skepticism was palpable, and Carter barely kept himself from rolling his eyes. "Look, I've admired the guy as an *actor* for years. Turns out we both dig the same kinds of movies, so we've been swapping indie film DVDs back and forth." He gave another shrug. "We're *friends*."

Ginsberg put up his hands. "Hey, I'm not judging. I'm just curious."

Carter swallowed some more coffee, even though he suddenly didn't need the caffeine. He thought Ginsberg might press, but then someone called out, "Stuntmen on set!"

"Looks like I'm up." Ginsberg flashed a toothy grin. "Or as you so delicately put it, time for me to get my ass kicked on your behalf."

Usually, that would've made Carter laugh, but today he only managed a small chuckle. Ginsberg's grin faded, concern creasing his brow. His eyes said, "We'll talk more," and then he walked toward the set.

The stunt coordinator helped Ginsberg adjust his safety equipment, and then Ginsberg and the other stuntman for this scene took their places.

Watching them do take after take distracted him for a little while. The stunt was a painful one—tumbling off a fire escape onto the hood of a car just before another character landed on top of him—and it took seven takes to satisfy Anna.

"All right, I think we've got it," she called out. "Nicely done, gentlemen. Everyone take a break."

"Thanks." Ginsberg swore as the other stuntman got off him and the car, and then he eased himself upright. On his way off the set, he grimaced and rubbed his hip.

Carter grinned. "You okay?"

"Yep, I'm good. Just need some ice." With his other hand, Ginsberg clapped Carter's shoulder. "Can't say the same about your character, I'm afraid."

"He'll be fine. Nice job, Gins. You have this gravity thing down pat."

Ginsberg flipped him the bird, and then started removing his padding, wincing as he moved.

"Didn't I see something in the script where Gabriel gets hit by a car?" Carter tried to suppress a smirk. "That's coming up soon, isn't it?"

"Oh for fuck's sake." Ginsberg groaned. "Seriously, dude. Gabriel *really* needs to go back to kindergarten and learn to look both fucking ways before crossing the street."

Carter patted his arm. "Yeah, but if I did that, you'd be out of a job."

"True. But I'll also be out of a job if I hurt myself and can't do more of your reckless stunts."

"Well, then don't hurt yourself."

"Bite me."

A crew member came up and handed him an ice pack, which he gingerly pressed to his hip. Ginsberg winced. "Please, God, tell me Anna's actually happy with the shot."

"Fingers crossed," Carter muttered, and they both watched as Anna reviewed the footage on a laptop screen.

Carter recognized that tightness in her lips from a mile away. Judging by the groan, so did Ginsberg.

And sure enough, a moment later, Anna shook her head.

"Fuck." Ginsberg dropped his ice pack on a chair and picked up the pads he'd taken off. "Here we go again."

After four hours of shooting, Carter was almost as sore as his stunt double. He and Brian were supposed to brawl on top of the car Ginsberg had fallen onto, and tumble off the hood to the pavement. Though he wore as much padding as Ginsberg did, the shot took six takes to get right. That meant hitting the pavement on his back six times with Brian coming down on top of him. Three of those times, his elbow clipped the bumper on the way down. Twice a punch landed harder than it was supposed to. At least it only took him one take to realize there was no need to keep his gun on his hip during those shots. He'd have a Beretta-shaped bruise tomorrow, though.

The entire cast and crew had stopped for a dinner break, and he sat in a metal folding chair with a bunch of ice packs while he threw back his billionth cup of coffee for the evening.

He checked his phone for the new production schedule, which was supposed to be updated tonight. Nothing yet. Damn.

He turned to Brian, who was working his way through another cup of coffee too. "Hey, have you seen Anna?"

Brian gestured at the parking lot. "She was on the phone with Leigh, and . . ." He grimaced.

So did Carter. Maybe he'd talk to Anna later, when she wasn't on the outs with her girlfriend. Again. The woman was a consummate professional, but when things got ugly with Leigh, she struggled to hide the toll it took on her. She didn't need to deal with his crap on top of it.

Instead, he grabbed another cup of coffee and a couple of the rolls someone had brought in. While he nibbled in between swigs of coffee, one of the guys said, "Oh, hey, the production schedule just updated."

"Did it?" Carter pulled out his phone again. "Sweet. Guess I won't have to bug Anna after all." He set the app to update, and when it was finished, he scrolled through the new schedule, which detailed all the shoots and production meetings for the next six weeks or so.

About three weeks out, a single line jolted the world under his feet.

Ep. 3.8, Scene 6 – Fuhrman, Hanford.

He gulped. Oh, fuck.

There it was. Right there in black and white. In three weeks, Levi would be working here. They'd be face-to-face. Shit. Maybe hanging out hadn't been a good idea after all. Though he was fooling himself if he thought he'd have been able to keep his shit together opposite Levi if they hadn't gotten to know each other. If he hadn't had a chance to get used to being around him.

He'd be fine. He could focus.

He just wouldn't think about the fact that watching Levi on-screen, watching him slip effortlessly into character, did things to his mind. And that was before they'd spent all this time together, with Carter pretending all along that there was *nothing* simmering between them, beneath the surface or otherwise. With a kiss in the recent past and a hunger that kept Carter awake more nights than not, he was pretty damned sure seeing him act in the flesh would destroy any concentration he had left.

Fuck.

Anna came back to the set a half hour or so later, and called an informal meeting. Brian must've been right—she looked stressed, though she put on her best smile as she told her cast and crew about some location changes, and a heads-up that the main cast would be getting information soon regarding Comic-Con.

"And with all that out of the way, I don't know how many of you have looked at the shooting schedule, but you may have noticed a new name on the roster." She grinned. "So let me be the first to confirm the rumors—Levi Pritchard will be joining us for the end of season three, and into the remaining seasons as Max Fuhrman."

A few murmurs rippled through the group, some of surprise and some of excitement, but Carter just gulped. A second too late, he realized Ginsberg was watching him.

So it was no surprise that, when the meeting adjourned, the stuntman pulled him aside. "Hey, are you sure you're okay with this?"

Carter shrugged. "Doesn't matter if I am or not."

"No, but I'm still curious. Are you gonna be all right with him here all the time?"

"Of course." Carter swallowed. "Why wouldn't I be?"

"Because like I said before, you've been exhausted and spaced out. How are you going to handle it when he's here on the set with us?"

Carter's shoulders fell, and he avoided Ginsberg's eyes. He desperately wanted to believe he'd be all right when they were on set together just like he wanted to believe they could pull off this "just friends" thing. But goddamn it, the attraction was there.

That kiss had happened, and no matter how hard he tried, he couldn't convince himself he wasn't attracted to Levi, or that he didn't know that it was mutual. He couldn't pretend they hadn't been—or at least Carter hadn't been—attracted since before they'd started getting to know each other. Before the movie nights that had gone on until two in the morning, sometimes without even firing up the DVD player or going down to Levi's home theater at all.

"Hey." Ginsberg touched his arm. "I'm not judging, okay? And I'm not going to say anything to anyone. I'm concerned about you, that's all."

"Concerned about who I'm seeing?"

"Well, with as tense as you've been lately, either it's *only* the fact that you're into someone, which I know you are, or there's something else wrong too." The stuntman shrugged. "I'm just hoping for option A over option B."

What about a little of both?

"Okay, here's the thing. Yes, I'm into Levi. And yes, we've been hanging out." Carter sighed. "And yeah, that's as far as it's going to go."

Ginsberg grimaced. "Ouch. Sucks having a crush on a straight guy, doesn't it?"

Almost as bad as having a crush on a closeted gay guy.

"Yeah, it does. Ah well. There are worse things than hanging out with Levi."

Like trying to work with him. Oh God.

"Well, that's good." Ginsberg patted his arm. "Because in three weeks, it's *on*."

Carter gulped. "Yep." He hadn't even cracked the scripts for Levi's first two episodes yet. Though he was vaguely familiar with the story arc, he was afraid to see how much the two of them would actually be interacting. Gabriel would go to the ends of the Earth to find his partner, Detective Julia Morris, and Max Fuhrman was somehow involved in her disappearance. From what Carter had heard, there was at least one super intensive confrontation between Fuhrman and Gabriel.

Between Levi and Carter.

Fuck. Good thing he enjoyed a challenge.

CHAPTER FIFTEEN

L evi pulled yet another bag of vegetables—peas this time—from the freezer, wrapped them in a towel, and pressed them against the side of his neck. He went into the living room and settled into a chair, using the back of it to hold the makeshift ice pack in place so he could use his iPad with both hands.

Nothing held his attention. No games. No websites. Not even a backlog of emails he really needed to take care of. Finally, he put the iPad away and focused on holding the bag of vegetables against his painfully stiff neck.

Beside him, his phone buzzed.

Ran a bit late. Be there ASAP.

Some of the cable-taut tension in his neck melted away, and he smiled as he typed back, *See you soon.*

Well, at least the day would *end* on a positive note.

Less than an hour later, Zelda's head snapped up and turned toward the window. Then Link's did the same. And after a moment, the familiar sports car engine rumbled in the distance.

As he got up to greet Carter, he debated leaving the cold pack in the kitchen, but it was finally offering some much-needed relief, so he took it with him.

As soon as Levi opened the door, Carter saw the ice pack, and his eyes widened. "Whoa, are you okay?"

"Yeah." Levi adjusted the bag of peas. "Just that old injury that likes to come back to haunt me."

"You sure it's not old age catching up with you?"

Levi rolled his eyes. "Kiss my ass."

Carter laughed, and as Levi shut the door behind them, added, "If it's any consolation, I can barely move today myself. Anna beat the shit out of us last night."

"Oh yeah?" Levi chuckled and led him into the kitchen, where both cats eagerly jumped up on chairs to greet Carter. "Rough shoot?"

"It was pretty intense." Carter stroked Link and scratched Zelda's chin. "I don't know who has more bruises today—me or my stunt double."

"Ouch." Levi gestured with the cold pack. "You want one?"

"Nah, I'm good. I iced it all earlier, so it's not as bad."

"Good to hear."

Carter smiled, but faltered a bit. "So, uh, we made the news again."

Levi groaned. "God. What now?"

"See for yourself." Carter pulled up the article and handed him his phone.

Carter Samuels: Wolf's Landing *Star Keeping Low Profile*

Usually a visible face around Bluewater Bay, Samuels rarely seen since being photographed with Levi Pritchard.

Levi snorted. "Wow, you made the news for not doing anything newsworthy? Must be a slow day."

Carter laughed humorlessly. "Right?"

Levi kept reading. In the sidebar, under "Articles That Might Also Interest You," a name in a headline caught Levi's eye and hit him right in the gut. It had been years, but simply seeing Dylan's name still hurt like hell. And reminded him just how fragile the fishbowl he lived in really was—he could be discreet until he was blue in the face, downplay any incriminating photo that surfaced, and everything could still fall apart in the blink of an eye. It almost had when that particular ex-boyfriend had tried to out him.

Against his better judgment he tapped on the headline.

Dylan Masters & Fiancé Wed After Whirlwind Courtship

Below that, *Actor & singer, both 37, have only been together six weeks.*

And then the image loaded. Levi stared at it, his heart thudding against his rib cage.

Carter craned his neck. "What?"

"Hmm? Oh. Just an article about—" *My ex-boyfriend* stopped at the tip of his tongue. He tilted the phone to show Carter.

"Oh." Carter's eyes flicked up to meet his. "He's the one who . . ."

"Tried to out me." Levi absently thumbed through the article, curious to see if they still insisted on including that one damning line that always seemed to show up in articles about him or Dylan.

Sure enough, it was there.

Masters has also maintained that he and action film star Levi Pritchard, now 38, dated briefly several years ago. Pritchard, who has dated some of Hollywood's leading women, steadfastly denies the claim.

But this time, they didn't stop there.

Those rumors were reignited recently when Pritchard was spotted cozying up with Wolf's Landing *star—*

He closed the browser and cleared his throat. "Fucking vultures." As he returned the phone, he met Carter's eyes, and the question was definitely there. Carter's eyebrows lifted slightly, and he pressed his lips together like he was literally biting it back.

Levi sighed. "Let me guess, you're curious if anything really happened between me and Dylan."

Color bloomed in Carter's cheeks, but he nodded. "I've always wondered, to be honest."

"You and everyone else," Levi muttered.

Carter hesitated, watching Levi. "So . . . *did* you guys really date?"

It was Levi's turn for a long, silent hesitation, but then he nodded slowly. "Yeah. We did."

Carter's eyes widened. "Damn. Why the hell did he out you like that?"

Levi shook his head. "Who knows? We hit the rocks pretty hard, and I think he was just being vindictive."

"I'd have thought he was less of an asshole if he'd been making it up like everyone said." Carter scowled. "But someone who actually dated you and knew you? Outing you? That's messed up."

"Tell me about it." Levi eyed Carter's phone. "You know, as crazy as it is, I still feel guilty about that to this day. About denying that we'd dated." He sighed. "I know it hurt him. It had to."

"Why did you deny it?"

Levi swallowed. "I didn't want anyone to know about me. I guess I freaked out, and I didn't know what else to do. So I pretended I didn't know him, never mind that we'd dated for the better part of six months."

"That long? Really?"

"Yeah. It's . . . kind of a long story." He pulled the ice pack off his neck. "Damn it, these are starting to thaw. Be right back." Levi retreated to the kitchen, tossed the melting bag of peas into the freezer and took out a fresh one. There, he paused, letting the images of Dylan run through his mind. He might've had a shot at putting that relationship—and Dylan's vindictive attempt to out him—in the past if the media would let it fucking drop.

Fat chance.

He took a deep breath, set his shoulders back as much as the muscle tension would allow, and returned to the living room. As he sat on the couch, he said, "Sorry about that."

"Don't worry about it. So you said that's an old injury?"

Levi nodded gingerly.

"What'd you do?" Carter smirked. "One of those times when you regretted doing your own stunts?"

Levi laughed halfheartedly, adjusting the cold pack. "Not . . . not exactly."

Carter's amusement vanished. "Shit. Sorry. If it's a sore spot, you don't have to tell me. I was just curious."

"It's okay. It's . . . not something I talk about much." He swallowed, shifting on the sofa. "It's from the wreck. When I totaled the Vette."

Carter chewed the inside of his cheek, but didn't speak.

"I'm guessing you heard that I was shitfaced and driving too fast?"

Carter nodded.

"The story wasn't . . . it wasn't entirely accurate."

"How so?"

Levi ran his tongue along the inside of his lower lip. "I was going too fast, I'll admit that. But like I said before, I was *not* drunk." He adjusted the cold pack, letting that occupy his attention rather than looking at Carter's expression. "I, uh, hit kind of a bad patch."

"Ice?"

"No, no, I mean a bad patch in my life." He tapped his temple with a fingertip. "Up here."

"Oh." Carter studied him for a moment. "Were . . . were you trying to kill yourself?"

Heat flooded Levi's cheeks, but he nodded. "Yeah. I was a mess. Bad shit with my family, having a bit of an identity crisis and . . . Anyway, I went out one night, and I was flying down the 101, just trying to work up the nerve to let go of the wheel." Goose bumps prickled to life at the memory of the painted stripes whipping past his high beams way faster than they should've, and the deep shadows in the gaps between guardrails that had seemed so incredibly inviting in that cold, black moment. "I went around this curve, and I was going too fucking fast. I only went maybe a foot over the center line, but . . ." Closing his eyes, he shuddered, stiffening the already painful muscles in his neck. "Man, I almost hit that minivan. *Almost*."

"Oh, shit," Carter whispered.

"They swerved, I swerved, and we missed each other, but I was fucking rattled. I never set out to hurt anyone but myself, and that near miss, it shook me up good. And I guess it just made me realize I was being an idiot. So I started slowing down." Levi gnawed his lip for a second. "The road was wet, though, and next curve was slicker than snot. Next thing I knew, I was waking up in the hospital."

"Oh my God." Carter shook his head. "Sounds like you got seriously lucky."

"That's what they tell me. Thank God for those old-growth trees, or the car and I would've gone right into the Pacific. As it is, someone told me the cops almost didn't bother calling an ambulance because they didn't think anyone could've survived the crash."

"Yeah, I saw the pictures. The fact that you're still walking is unbelievable."

Levi shuddered again, and winced. "I never saw the pictures. I very carefully avoided those stories. I didn't want to see what my car looked like, and I really, really didn't want to see how close I came to doing what I'd set out to do that night."

"I don't blame you," Carter whispered hollowly. "So that"—he gestured at the pack of cold peas on Levi's neck—"is left over from the accident?"

"Yep. This too." He touched the scar on his temple. "All the cuts and gashes healed pretty quick, but the muscles took two solid years to recover and get back to normal. Well, this degree of normal, anyway." He rubbed his steel-tight neck. "I'm a lot better than my doctors ever predicted, so I can't complain if it still comes back to haunt me sometimes." He tried to roll his shoulders, but, Jesus, the muscles were stiff as fuck today. "When I get stressed out, this is the first place I feel it."

Carter's eyebrow arched. "What're you stressed about? The show?"

"No." Levi exhaled. "My parents called this morning. To confirm the details for their visit next week."

The eyebrow rose a little higher. "Doesn't sound like your muscles want them to come visit."

Levi laughed softly. "Hell, even my cats aren't going to be happy."

"Really?" Carter looked down at Link, who was sleeping peacefully in his lap. "I thought they liked people."

"Yeah, but they don't care for people who stress me out."

"Oh." Carter slowly petted Link. "They're that bad, huh?"

Levi nodded. "That bad. But we've been making progress. My family's never exactly been, uh, functional, but we've all been trying to patch things up for the last ten years."

"Sounds like you still have a ways to go."

"We do." Levi lowered the ice pack, tilted his head from one side to the other, and then put it back, grimacing at the ache in his elbow from holding his arm up. "But it takes a while to undo that much shit."

As he continued petting Link, Carter met Levi's eyes. "Stop me if it's too personal, but . . . how much shit do you all have to undo?"

Levi blew out a breath. "Both my parents are as-of-recently recovering alcoholics. And they've got some pretty outdated ideas. Hell, they disowned my sister for a while after she got a divorce. There's some . . . uh, well, typical things that go along with having two raging drunks for parents, even when they *aren't* stuck in the Dark Ages." The muscles in his neck definitely didn't like the direction of this conversation. "It's just kind of messy all the way around."

"Sounds like it."

Levi laughed self-consciously. "God, I'm sorry. You came over to watch movies, and now I'm telling you my lifelong sob story."

Carter waved a hand. "It's all right." Then he dropped his gaze. "Listen, uh . . ."

"Hmm?"

Carter hesitated for a few awkward seconds, but then met Levi's eyes again. "If it's not too weird, I, uh, know some techniques." He gestured at Levi's neck. "For working out muscle tension."

"Techniques? What kind of techniques?"

"Uh, well . . ." Carter swallowed. "Massage."

Levi's heart skipped.

"I won't be offended if you say no." Carter laughed uncomfortably. "If it'll make things weird, I'm—"

"No, it won't. Not for me, anyway." Levi raised his eyebrows.

"Not for me either. As long as you're . . ."

"Honestly? If it'll get rid of this stiffness—" Levi winced, heat rushing into his face. "I mean . . . goddamn it."

Carter laughed again. "I know what you mean."

Levi lowered the ice pack. "Well, it's worth a shot. The ice and Aleve aren't touching it."

"Okay. At the risk of making another double entendre, turn around."

Levi did as he was told, facing the other end of the couch, and his skin prickled as Carter shifted behind him.

Then Carter's hands materialized on his shoulders. Gentle at first, then more firmly. "I'd say this might hurt, but it's pretty much a guarantee. It's gonna hurt."

Levi exhaled slowly. "It already does."

"I can tell. It's going to get worse for a minute, but this'll help. Promise."

"Go for it. Can't be any worse than anything my physical— Oh, *fuck!*"

"Sorry." Carter let off a little, but kept working at the painful spot. He pressed his thumbs into the tender center of a knotted muscle, and Levi held his breath, hoping the tension would just release and be done with it.

"Breathe."

Levi did, and the knot slowly started to unravel. He focused on breathing slowly, and on Carter's fingers, which expertly unwound the knots. Before long, the pain faded into the background. It was still present, of course, still red and angry beneath his skin, but the spotlight had shifted to Carter's hands. This wasn't how he'd fantasized about having Carter touch him, but beggars couldn't be choosers. The fact was, Carter's hands were on him.

And then, abruptly, they weren't.

"Did that help?" Carter asked.

"Yeah." Levi tugged at his shirt, which gave his own hands something to do, and pulled the material over his lap. "Yeah, it helped a lot. Thanks."

"Good. Glad to hear it."

Levi hesitated, but then turned around again. At least his jeans made a cursory attempt to hide his hard-on, but if Carter looked, there'd be no pretending it wasn't there.

"So, um." Levi cleared his throat. "Still want to watch some movies?"

Carter shifted in his seat. "Absolutely."

"Great. Great. Let me get, uh . . ." He reached for the ice pack. "Another of these. Something to drink?"

Carter grinned. "I'm assuming you have Coke."

"Of course." Levi got up—*please, God, don't let him notice that massage turned me on*—and went into the kitchen. He spent a moment longer than necessary putting ice in their glasses and finding a fresh pack of frozen peas, letting the cold calm him down a little.

As Levi filled the glasses, Carter came in, Zelda in his arms and Link hot on his heels. They must've demanded his attention before letting him go into the kitchen.

Levi slid Carter's glass toward him. "Pity they don't like you."

"I know, right?" Carter laughed and took a drink, still balancing Zelda on his arm. "So what are we watching today?"

Levi gestured for him to follow, and as they started down the hall, he said, "I'm thinking *La Disposición?*"

"Oh, I haven't seen that one. Cool!"

They settled in the theater, arranging cats and drinks until everyone was comfortable—as comfortable as Levi could get, anyway—and clicked on the movie.

And the second it started, Levi regretted choosing that one.

It was an amazing film. Like *Romeo and Juliet*, if the Montagues and Capulets had been involved in Mexican drug cartels. Absolutely glorious piece of work with spectacular cinematography, amazing dialogue, and a few incredibly poignant scenes.

And some *scorching* hot sex.

It wasn't the first time they'd watched a movie with explicit scenes—indie directors, especially foreign ones, were notorious for going all out with sex and nudity. And Levi had seen this film at least a dozen times before.

But tonight, he wasn't as comfortable with it as he should have been. While the tastefully covered but fully nude bodies tangled together on the screen, he was hyperaware of Carter one seat over. Of how different he'd felt since Carter had shown up.

His parents had called this morning to confirm their flights and the dates they were coming out to visit, and Levi had been a sore, locked-up mess ever since. Same thing that happened every time.

And then Carter had texted him. *Be there ASAP.*

And then he'd pulled into the driveway.

And then he'd knocked.

And . . . Levi had relaxed. Little by little, minute by minute, he'd returned to a better state of mind and his body had reflected that. The skillful—if painful—massage had helped too. Carter obviously knew what he was doing, but there was also something about having those strong but gentle hands on him. There'd been nothing suggestive aside from their ill-timed, badly judged comments beforehand, but from the moment Carter had touched him, Levi had been off-balance. Even now he was still reeling: his muscles felt better, but his mind was all over the place and he had no idea what to make of anything.

He'd confessed a couple of his most shameful secrets—the accident, the power his family held over him even at this age—and Carter hadn't shied away. No judgment, no "What the fuck is wrong with you?" Nothing more than an offer to do what he could to help, even if it meant crossing that blurry boundary between platonic and not.

Sitting here now in the theater, without a soul around besides Carter, as they both watched two naked bodies moving on the screen, his mouth was dry. The actors and cameras had been expertly angled so the images *just* toed the line between explicit content and pornography, but with the way his heart was pounding and sweat was beginning to cool his hairline, they may as well have been watching a hard-core porno. His head was spinning. He couldn't—and didn't really want to—shake away the phantom fingers still kneading his stiff neck. What he wanted was the real thing touching him now. Touching him all over.

He suppressed a shiver and let his gaze slide toward Carter, turning his head as much as he could without being obvious about it.

The flickering, silvery light from the screen illuminated Carter's features, highlighting his eyes and playing on his carefully arranged blond hair. Jesus, it was no wonder the kid was in demand by fans and casting directors alike.

And Levi had kissed him. And he'd had Carter's hands on him tonight. And he wanted more of both.

Facing the movie again, he tried to hear the dialogue over his thumping heart. He could change this. The attraction was obviously mutual, and the only thing keeping them apart were Levi's issues.

All he had to do was bite the bullet and come out. It wouldn't be a big deal, would it? He'd only lose the role of his dreams and turn back a decade's worth of progress with his family.

He rubbed his neck, which was tensing up again, and tried not to notice the sideways glance from Carter.

Yes, it hurts again.

Yes, I'd love it if you offered to rub my neck again.

Yes, I know it'll turn into more.

But Carter didn't offer. Levi didn't ask.

And the movie played on.

CHAPTER SIXTEEN

A s his Porsche's engine roared to life in Levi's driveway, Carter let his head fall back against the seat.

What the hell was he thinking, offering a massage? Okay, fine, Levi had been in obvious pain, and Carter had a little experience in relieving that kind of pain, and . . .

And he shouldn't have been surprised his fingers had taken his mind to places it had no business going, and that the evening had turned into an exercise in unbearable frustration. A massage he'd meant innocently enough. A movie he hadn't heard a word of. A man he wanted but couldn't have. Jesus Christ.

God, he wanted Levi. After tonight, though, he was a breath away from coming completely unglued. Or turning around and burning rubber back down that driveway to tell Levi that he'd seen the way he'd looked at him during the movie, and yes, he'd noticed that Levi had been hard after the massage, and yes, he'd been hard as hell too.

Just like he was hard as hell now. As he turned onto the dirt road at the end of the driveway, he could barely manipulate the damned steering wheel, never mind the gearshift. He was beyond wound up, too turned on and fucking frustrated to see straight. Ever since they'd agreed to just be friends, he'd forbidden himself from jerking off to thoughts of Levi. Giving those fantasies even a second to take shape in his mind would only make things worse.

But tonight . . . tonight he couldn't resist.

He didn't make it home before he gave in and pulled over. He hadn't even made it a half mile down that long secluded road between Levi's place and the highway, but to hell with it. With the engine still rumbling, he killed the lights, reducing the world around him to total darkness except for the faint glow from the dashboard. His heart pounded. The click of his seat belt seemed to echo through the forest, and when the belt snapped back against the door, he almost jumped out of his skin

This was crazy. This was absolutely insane. Levi could come down the road at any time, heading into town for whatever reason at this hour. Someone else could drive past. And a Porsche on the side of a dirt road was hardly inconspicuous.

Oh fucking well. With shaking hands, he unzipped his pants. He didn't care if he got caught as long as he got off before he lost his goddamned mind.

All concern—hell, any awareness of the outside world at all—vanished as soon as he wrapped his fingers around his rock-hard cock. He gripped the steering wheel with one hand, jerked his dick with the other, and the close confines amplified every sound—leather protesting, skin rubbing over skin, sharp breaths, throaty groans.

A million images flashed through his mind of remembered moments and what they could've been. The kiss on the stage turning into a desperate fuck against the wall. The completely platonic shoulder massage becoming something hot and heavy and long overdue. Their bodies tangled up on the boat and keeping perfect time with the proverbial motion of the ocean. Levi fucking him, Levi taking him . . .

Even though it was fake, an expression and a sound manufactured for the camera, Carter had seen and heard Levi come. God, how many times had he watched that scene in *Broken Day*? How many times had he watched it with his hand on his dick, mesmerized by everything Levi did, just like right now as that scene played and played and played in his mind?

He knew it by heart, and he saw and felt every nuance of it. Levi and the actress, their bodies had been so close, their pounding hearts almost audible, and Carter had wondered a time or two if that sex scene hadn't been fake after all. If Levi had really been inside her, and if the way her eyes had flown open hadn't been because the script had told her to, but because he'd moved just right, touched her just right, and she'd been his and only his for those few seconds of screen time.

And then Levi had thrown his head back, eyes squeezed shut and features taut, and every shudder and tremor had looked real, and Carter had imagined it was his nails scratching Levi's chest and making him groan like that and—

"Fuck!" He gasped for breath and shook as semen coated his fingers. The fantasies in his mind exploded into white light, and he heard himself swear again, heard the leather protest and the steering wheel creak as he tensed and trembled.

Then everything was still and silent.

Panting, he rested his forehead on the hand still gripping the wheel. He couldn't remember the last time he'd come that hard. It wasn't the first time he'd ever jerked off thinking about Levi, but it was definitely the most intense. Jesus, if that fantasy ever became reality, he didn't know if he could handle it.

His heart rate slowly came down. The rest of the world faded in around him. He caught his breath. Found some napkins in the glove box to clean off his hand.

And felt like shit.

It wasn't shame. Just the feeling he'd gotten a taste of something he desperately wanted, and once that taste was gone, he remembered how far out of reach that thing really was, and no amount of denial or wishful thinking would change that.

He couldn't pretend he hadn't been holding on to a glimmer of hope that he and Levi might turn into more.

But . . . there was always a "but." Always a reason they couldn't do this.

Or, more to the point, reasons why they *wouldn't* do this. Carter wouldn't be a secret. Levi wouldn't go public. With no middle ground . . .

Carter blew out a breath. He could never imagine sympathizing with Dylan Masters for outing Levi, and God knew he'd never dream of outing anyone, but a weird feeling knotted in his gut now that he knew what had happened between them. He couldn't imagine being in Masters's shoes—being such a deep, dark, dirty secret in Levi's closet that the man wouldn't even cop to it when asked point-blank about it years later.

Carter ran a hand through his hair. These feelings he had for Levi—whatever the fuck they were these days—weren't going away anytime soon. He couldn't just turn them off, and he couldn't stop them from getting stronger the more time he spent around Levi.

But he could tear himself away. Find someone who wouldn't be afraid to be seen in public with him.

They could still be friends, but he needed to pull back. Spend a little less time with Levi and a little more finding someone he could connect with the way he wished they could connect.

He needed to move on.

CHAPTER SEVENTEEN

'm in hell.

Holy fuck. I am in hell.

Levi was stuck in a car. In line for the ferry. Three hours from home.

With his parents.

And they hadn't wasted any time: Couldn't he have parked closer to the terminal? Wasn't he aware that the speed limit was sixty? The sign said the ferries were off *that* off-ramp—shouldn't he have taken that off-ramp?

He was convinced the biggest downside to the two of them sobering up was they were even *more* aware of everything he and his siblings did wrong.

"Just be glad they don't live near you," his sister had reminded him on the phone this morning.

Oh, I am. Every fucking day, I am.

In the passenger seat, his mother played with the strap of her purse while she watched the ferry slowly approaching. "So, when do you start with this new television show?"

"I start shooting a couple of days after you and Dad take off." He tried not to think about how little time and energy he'd have to prepare—at least his first scenes were fairly short and without too many lines.

"I don't get what's so big about that show." His mother clicked her tongue. "Just sounds like *The X-Files* with werewolves."

"It's a little more in-depth than that." Levi tried to keep his tone light. "It's work, though."

She scowled, but didn't say anything. He forced himself not to roll his eyes. They'd both been after him for the last few years to get out of the house and do something. Neither approved of him sitting idle, even if money wasn't an issue.

And I care about their approval, why?

Yeah. *That* wasn't an argument he'd had with himself seven hundred times just since breakfast.

He cleared his throat. "It might open some doors. For other roles."

"I see."

His dad leaned forward in the backseat. "I thought you were giving up all this acting business."

"I was, but I really like the series and the role they offered me, so . . ."

"Mm-hmm."

His mother shifted in her seat. "I don't know if I like your name being on a program that's always got 'gay this' and 'gay that' attached to it."

Levi's gut tightened with both aggravation and nerves, but he forced a laugh and shook his head. "It's just the press, Mom. They latch on to anything they can, and turn it into something it's not. You've seen all the stuff they've said about me."

"I have." She eyed him. "And the last thing you need to do is give them more ammunition."

"It'll be fine," he said dryly, and stared out the windshield as if he needed to focus straight ahead even though they were parked in a long row of waiting cars. "Even if the tabloids talk, they'll eventually get bored and go find something else to sell their magazines." *I hope.*

"Damn vultures," his dad muttered.

Levi chuckled. He couldn't agree more.

"When does your play open? We're going to see it, right?"

"Of course." *Oh God.* "It opens Friday night." That was one of the reasons they'd chosen to come visit now, to see the play he was directing, but the thought of them in the audience—and in the car after the show—made his skin crawl.

They wouldn't come to all six showings, which was a plus. They'd stay back at the house, and he'd embrace his break from them.

"Will we be meeting any of your . . . friends this time?"

The mildly condescending and not so mildly suspicious edge to her voice almost brought a groan out of him.

Oh Christ. Here we go.

"Just the cast and crew at the play, if you'd like."

"I see."

He cringed. Damn their therapist—especially his willingness to do group sessions via Skype—and his insistence that they all communicate more. Because knowing his mother, that meant some "communication" in three . . . two . . .

"Levi, I want you to be honest with me."

Damn it.

"About?"

"Honey, please. I know we've been through this, but I—"

"Are you gay?" his father broke in.

"No." Levi had done this so many times, he could *almost* do it without cringing inside—he looked his mother in the eye and said, "Mom, I'm not gay."

Technically, he wasn't lying, but who was he kidding? She wasn't asking if he was exclusively into men. She was asking if he was into men at all. In her eyes, that meant he was gay, and he wasn't about to argue with her about the finer points of homosexuality versus bisexuality.

She pursed her lips, but didn't respond.

Levi rested his elbow on the steering wheel and ran a hand through his hair. "I don't know what more I can say to convince you."

"Well, if you dated a woman . . ."

He laughed, hoping he didn't sound as bitter as he felt. "Bluewater Bay's a small town. There's only so many—"

"You're a movie star, Levi." She glared at him. "I don't buy for a second that you can't find someone there or anywhere else."

He ground his teeth and stared at the back window of the car parked in front of him. Christ, she hadn't waited long. He supposed he could defuse some of the tension if he told her about Laura, the cop he'd gone out with a few months ago, or Casey, the park ranger he'd briefly dated last summer. But that would only bring on the interrogation about why it hadn't worked out and why he hadn't married either of them. It was easier to let his folks maintain their suspicions than it was to admit that he and Laura had been ridiculously incompatible in the bedroom or that Casey had been too much like his mom—complete with the alcoholism and estranged son.

Before Levi could divert the conversation, engines started coming on. He glanced at the end of the dock, and sure enough, the ferry had pulled in and was beginning to unload. He turned the key, adding the Jeep's idle to the collective rumble, and waited for the guys in orange vests to direct him onto the boat.

Once he was parked, he set the brake. "I'm going to go up and use the restroom. Do you two want to stay down here?"

His mother craned his neck to check with his dad in the backseat. "What do you think?"

"We can stay down here. Just leave the motor going so there's some air."

"Can't do that. Coast Guard regs." Levi opened the windows and then killed the engine. "I'll be back shortly."

He left the Jeep and headed above decks as the ferry lurched into motion. He walked right past the restrooms and out to the bow. Hands on the railing, he gazed out at the water and breathed in the cool, salty breeze.

Thank God the boat had arrived when it did. Those conversations were inevitable, and there would be more before his folks flew out in ten days.

As the ferry slowly made its way across the water, Levi relaxed as much as he could expect to anytime soon. His parents meant well, but as their therapist had pointed out, they'd spent two and a half decades of their lives in an alcohol-induced blur. For all intents and purposes, they'd hit the pause button on their personal growth, and were twenty-five years behind on maturing. It was like they'd gone to sleep at twenty and woken up with three grown—and deeply resentful—kids. With all the shit the family had been through, it was a wonder anyone was still on speaking terms. Making it this far was nothing short of a miracle.

He closed his eyes and let the wind rush against his face.

This visit wouldn't be all sunshine and roses, but it was good that they were here. Much as they stressed him out, this *was* a step forward. The frustration he felt in their presence today was nothing compared to what it would've been like five years ago. One visit and one conversation at a time, the Pritchard family was coming together, and there was nothing in the world he'd ever wanted more than a solid, functional family.

"It'll get better," the therapist had reminded him during their last Skype session.

It would. It already had.

He just hated—*hated*—the fact that a huge piece of his identity was the equivalent of a rambunctious dog running around a table with a house of cards on it. One bump, and the whole thing would come down.

Part of him wanted to believe he was exaggerating to himself. So what if they found out he wasn't straight?

The other part of him had watched them side with his ex-brother-in-law because apparently putting Levi's sister in the hospital was less of a disgrace than her divorcing his sorry ass.

He sighed, shaking his head, and then turned around to head back down to the car deck. In his pocket, his phone vibrated, and when he looked, he realized there was a text from Carter. He must not have felt it in the car.

Your parents make it into town?

He almost wrote *Unfortunately*, but that seemed like bad karma.

They're here. We're on the ferry to Bainbridge.

He sent the text and continued down to the car deck. Ten feet away from his Jeep, his phone buzzed again.

Good luck. Feel free to text if you need someone to keep you sane.

Levi smiled. *Much appreciated.*

Within hours, Carter's electronic presence became a lifeline. If not for their sporadic texts, Levi would have blown a fucking gasket. Of course he didn't spend all his time staring at his phone, but they snagged a conversation here and there after Levi's parents had turned in for the night and when Carter had a break on the set.

They drive you crazy yet?

Getting there.

How's your neck? Stress = pain?

Going through frozen peas like they're going out of style, but it's not too bad.

Got a number for a massage therapist in town. She's a miracle worker. And she'll give you a break for an hour.

May just do that. Could use a break.

Too bad you can't slip away – just got a DVD of Canberra High.

OMG. You're killing me.

LOL. I'll bring it over after your folks leave.

Looking forward to it. :-)

Whew. Opening night is over.

Nice! How did it go?

Went great! Parents loved it too, which is a plus.

Definitely a plus. Tried to get tickets – working every showing. :-(

It's ok. Maybe the next show.

When does that one start?

Ask me again once this one's over.

LOL.

Heading out?

Yep. Taking them to Victoria today.

Dude, check out Craigdarroch Castle while you're there.

Yeah?

It's awesome. They'll love it.

Good to know. Thanks.

NP. Visit going good?

Up & down. They're excited to see Canada, so today's promising.

Sweet. Gotta run – Director wants to reshoot a scene AGAIN.

LOL. Have fun.

Taking them out again today?

Yep. Mom wants to shop in Sequim.

Levi sent the message, and then set his phone on the empty weight bench. Carter must've been shooting early today—he usually didn't text until well after ten, and it was only eight o'clock. Perfect timing as far as Levi was concerned. He'd been getting out of bed a little early himself to hit the weights before his folks woke up. It was nice to have some company, even if it was via text messages.

While he waited for the reply to come through, Levi sat on the other weight bench, rested his elbow on his knee, and started doing curls.

Halfway through his set, he heard footsteps, and he looked up as his dad appeared in the doorway. "Oh. Morning, Dad."

"Mornin'." His father sipped his cup of coffee. "Your doctor know you're doing all this?"

Levi set the dumbbell at his feet. "She encourages it, actually."

"Does she?"

"Keeps the muscles from getting weak and keeps everything stable." Levi stood, rolling the fatigue and stiffness out of his shoulders. "As long as I don't overdo it, I feel a lot better this way."

"I see." His dad crossed the room and stood at the sliding glass door, gazing at the scenery. The view from here wasn't nearly as spectacular as it was from upstairs, but the property was high up on a hill, and the thick forest wasn't tall enough to hide the snowcapped Olympics entirely.

Levi toweled the sweat off his face and surreptitiously watched his father, wondering what had brought him down here. Boredom? Curiosity? A mission from Mom?

Without facing Levi, his dad asked, "You ever thought about selling this place? Coming back east?"

Levi suppressed a shudder. "I like it here, Dad." He braced for the criticism. The guilt. The "your mother misses you" and "we're all trying to smooth things over, but it'd be easier if you weren't three thousand miles away."

Almost a full minute passed before his dad spoke. "Maybe this place has done you good."

Levi blinked. "What?"

His dad shrugged. "Well, I was concerned when you said you were leaving your career behind and coming clear out here, and again when you said you were picking up with this TV show, but . . ." He paused for a few long seconds. "You seem happier than you have in a long time."

Levi nodded. "I am. I'm really happy here."

"Good." His dad nodded and murmured to himself, "Good, good." Then he turned toward Levi. "Didn't you say you had better chances in this business if you moved back to LA?"

"Yeah, and that's still true. But for now, I've got work here."

"So you do." His father sipped his coffee. "If I recall from when you lived in Hollywood, your schedule is going to be very full. Will you, uh, still have time to attend our sessions?"

"I can work something out with the director."

"Good. It means a lot to your mother."

What about you?

"I'll do what I can. I . . . want to keep going with the sessions too." He hesitated. "Seems like it's doing us all some good."

"It is."

Levi regarded him for a moment. "So you really don't have any objections? To me working again and staying here?" He hardly needed his parents' permission, but if he knew where they stood, maybe they could talk about things openly and honestly.

"Of course." His dad held his gaze and must've seen the skepticism in Levi's eyes. "Your mom and I aren't perfect parents, son. We never have been, and we never will be." He put a hand on Levi's shoulder. "But we want you kids to be happy. And if you're happy here, and you like what you're doing, I'm not going to try to talk you out of it."

Wow. That was definitely new.

"Thanks," Levi said softly.

Silence set in, and an all-too-familiar sensation tightened in Levi's chest. Whenever he and his dad had one of these close moments, where he was more like a son talking to his father than someone negotiating a tense peace with an adversary, he felt like this. Like courage was building up, his heart beating faster and faster. Should he take advantage of this moment to finally get this secret out of his mind and onto the table, or keep this tentative closeness alive?

Dad, I'm gay.

His mouth went dry.

I need you to know.

This is who I am. He looked up at his father. *Do you still love me?*

Right then, his dad smiled, and Levi instantly lost his nerve. They had too few of these moments—he wasn't ready to ruin this one.

Coward . . .

"Well. Anyway." His father cleared his throat and gestured at the door with his coffee cup. "I'll go make sure your mother's awake so we can get going."

"Sure. Right."

They locked eyes again, and then his dad left the room.

Levi released a breath, rolling his shoulders as renewed tension tried to tighten his muscles. Funny how conversations like this were almost more stressful than the arguments. These calm, honest discussions carried with them pressure he still wasn't sure how to cope with—that pressure to say the right thing, or at least not say the wrong thing, so the fragile peace didn't come apart.

He rolled his shoulders again and then sat back down on the weight bench to finish his set. Before he could pick up the dumbbell, though, his phone buzzed.

As he picked up the phone, his father's words echoed in his mind: *"You seem happier than you have in a long time."*

His heart fluttered at the sight of Carter's name. The message was fairly benign—*Oh cool, I've never been there*—but nevertheless brought a smile to Levi's face. It didn't even matter that it was silly to be so thrilled by a simple text message.

And as he typed a response—*Gorgeous hiking. You should check it out*—it occurred to him that it wasn't just the distraction from his parents that he looked forward to between messages. Texts from anyone else would've been a welcome distraction, but these were another thing entirely.

Because they came from Carter.

His thumbs stopped abruptly, midmessage.

"You seem happier than you have in a long time."

You might be onto something, Dad.

Sorry for the radio silence. Just got home.
Long day on set?
OMG yes. Might need some frozen peas myself.
Thought you had a stunt double.
He's going to need more than frozen peas.
Oh shit! Is he ok?
Yep. Just sore. Being Gabriel Hanford is not for the faint of heart.
LOL. Apparently not.
Just wait. Have you seen what happens to Max?
God, I don't even want to know.
LOL. No, you don't.
Crap.

2 more days. 2 more days.
Hang in there. It's almost over.
Thank God. It's going better than I thought it would, but I'm ready
for them to go.
We'll celebrate w/movies when they leave.
Hell yes.
Will have to be after this weekend, though. Heading to RainCon.
Oh that's right. Forgot it was this weekend. Looking forward to it?
You bet. This con's small, but it's even better than Comic-Con.
Awesome. Have a good time!
Will do. And will text as much as I can, but it'll be busy.
Don't worry about it. You should be enjoying the con. I'll be here
when you get back.

Pulling away from the airport after a visit from his parents was always a liberating experience. It hadn't been a bad visit, considering some of their previous ones, but there was no such thing as easy where they were concerned. Progress, though. Progress.

Of course, he hadn't managed to come out to them in spite of *almost* working up the nerve more than once. He hated himself for caring so much about how they'd react. For being so damned afraid of their disapproval and disappointment.

As Sea-Tac International faded behind him, he was tempted to send an *I'm free!* text as soon as he stopped. He didn't, though. The convention had started this morning, and the last thing Carter would want to do was look at his phone. If he was anything like Levi, he probably didn't even have his cell on him. So much easier to enjoy a con without that constant distraction.

I-5 took Levi north into Seattle so he could grab a ferry and head back to Bluewater Bay. On the way into the city, a thought occurred to him.

The convention was in Seattle.

As his stomach somersaulted, he drove right past the exit for the Bremerton ferry, making a half-assed attempt to rationalize that he was going farther north to take the Kingston ferry instead. Any excuse to drive past the con, right?

Especially since there was no avoiding the venue—the Washington State Convention Center was situated in the heart of downtown Seattle, in plain sight right over the top of Interstate 5. As he flew up the freeway, that huge building dead ahead, Levi rapidly drummed his fingers on the wheel.

He could drop in. Day passes weren't sold out. The *Wolf's Landing* panel was this afternoon. Probably standing room only, as they always were, but he was pretty sure he could get Anna or someone to squeeze him in. Even if he didn't make it to the panel, he could say hello to Carter.

No. He'd wait until next week when Carter was back in Bluewater Bay. Showing up at a con—even if he had a following of his own at these things, not to mention an upcoming role on *Wolf's Landing*—smacked of being a bit more clingy than a friend should be. It felt too much like changing the rules.

I know we're supposed to be just friends, but . . .

Yeah, that wouldn't fuel any rumors.

They were friends, and they would stay friends, and Levi would wait until they saw each other in Bluewater Bay rather than crashing the con. No sense giving Carter—or anyone else—a reason to believe he wanted more than their comfortable, platonic friendship.

Just walking down the sidewalk together had been enough to spark rumors. Rumors that had gotten him and Carter talking, which had led to—

Yeah, this probably isn't a good idea.

He drove under the convention center's overpass, and kept right on driving.

By Monday evening, Levi hadn't heard from Carter, but he wasn't worried. He'd been to enough conventions himself to understand the need to decompress. After a particularly crazy Comic-Con one year, he'd turned his phone off for three solid days. Maybe Carter handled them a little better than he had, but either way, Levi would leave the ball in Carter's court for now.

And even if he didn't call or text, they'd see each other soon enough—tomorrow was Levi's first day on the set. As he climbed the stairs with a script and his iPad under his arm, plus a pack of frozen peas in his hand, he had that nervous, queasy-but-excited feeling in his stomach that he always got before starting a new role. He'd had it the first time he'd gone onstage in high school, and he'd had it the night before he'd shown up to play Chad Eastwick for the last time. It had absolutely nothing to do with the man who'd be acting opposite him tomorrow. Nothing at all.

He set everything on the bed, and went into the bathroom to brush his teeth. Now that his folks were gone, the tension in his neck and shoulder was slowly dissipating, but they were definitely still tender, so he intended to ice them for a little while before he went to sleep.

When he came back from the bathroom, the cats had already settled onto as much of the bed as two twenty-pound cats could occupy. Link had sprawled out across one side, and Zelda was lying beside Levi's iPad on top of the frozen vegetables.

"What are you—" He nudged her out of the way. "Those are *cold*, you weirdo."

She batted at his hand as he took the pack, and he laughed. They played for a minute or so while Link watched, Zelda attacking Levi with her huge paws but keeping her claws in. He smiled—both cats had been MIA for the last week and a half, hiding under his bed or in unoccupied rooms, and it was good to have them out and about again.

After Zelda got bored chasing Levi's hand, he picked her up and moved her so there was room for him. Then he climbed into bed and stacked a few pillows behind his back so he could sit against the headboard. Once he had the frozen peas pressed comfortably—more or less—between his neck and the headboard, he propped his iPad up on his knee.

When he checked his email, he saw that Anna had sent out a message to the cast and crew with links to photos from the convention.

You all did great this weekend! Fans are raving about the entire Wolf's Landing *gang. Check out the pictures!*

Levi tapped the link, which brought up dozens of photos of the cast on their panel, posing with costumed fans and signing autographs. He tapped the first, and went through them one at a time.

Three photos in was a shot of Carter, and Levi's breath caught. They hadn't seen each other in a week and a half, and suddenly it seemed like longer. Goddamn, now he couldn't wait until tomorrow. Even if they were just friends.

He continued through the photos. He hadn't met the crew or even most of the cast, but he recognized the actors from the show. It would be interesting to meet them all—going from a fan of the show to a member of the cast would be cool and a little surreal.

He paused on a photo when a face in the background caught his eye. Why did that guy look familiar?

Oh hell. Who knew? These cons were crawling with actors— Levi must've seen him in a movie he couldn't remember off the top of his head. And he'd probably feel like an idiot once he figured out which movie—and actor—it was. Or maybe he'd just seen him in a few other shots.

The next set of photos looked like they'd been taken backstage at the panel, where some incredibly lucky and happy fans had had a chance to do a meet and greet with the cast. Several of them were beaming in photos with Carter, whose smile made Levi's spine tingle.

And in the background, there was that guy again.

A couple of shots later, there he was again. And again. And again.

The next shot was of some more cast members, but Carter wasn't in the foreground.

He was in the background.

With the other guy.

Levi's heart plummeted. They weren't posing, weren't interacting with anyone aside from each other, and though Levi couldn't see Carter's face, he could see that guy's hand resting conspicuously on Carter's hip.

Oh. Fuck.

Out of sheer curiosity—or because he was a fucking masochist—Levi kept looking through the photos, all the way to last night's after-party.

And there it was, the image that said it all.

Carter may not have even known they were being photographed. By the way he and the other guy were gazing at each other, arms around shoulders and a hand on Carter's thigh, he'd probably all but forgotten there was anyone else there.

Levi swallowed.

Good. Good for him.

CHAPTER EIGHTEEN

I *should be there by the time you're finished shooting.*

Carter smiled at the text from Marcus. Just a few more hours.

Can't wait. See you tonight.

He slipped his phone into his pocket and held still so the makeup artist could apply a fake gash to his temple. Ironic that he was being made to look like he'd just had the shit kicked out of him when he couldn't stop smiling.

They'd met after Marcus's panel with the other voice actors from a Seattle-based anime series, and from that point forward, they'd spent the entire con flirting. He didn't even care if the cameras saw them. Let the tabloids talk—he was having a great time.

By Sunday afternoon, they'd been slipping away every chance they had for a discreet kiss or two. If Marcus hadn't had to be at the studio early Monday morning, Carter was almost certain they would've spent Sunday night in one of their rooms at the Four Seasons, but with a few loaded comments and mouthwatering looks, they'd gone their separate ways.

All the way back to Bluewater Bay, Carter had been grinning like an idiot.

Just a few more hours . . .

The makeup artist finished with him, and Carter made his way to the set. The shooting schedule was light today. No major stunts, thank fuck—he and Ginsberg both needed a break after last week. He might even be out of here by the time Marcus showed up, and they could—

Carter stopped dead in his tracks.

His heart dropped.

Levi.

Standing with Anna while another makeup artist touched up his face, he was every inch Max Fuhrman—the green army jacket covered in tattered patches, faded camouflage pants, dark hair tousled just right to make him look a little unhinged—but he was all Levi to Carter.

You've moved on. You knew you were going to be working with him, but you've moved on. Get a grip.

Carter turned away and dug his phone out of his pocket, hoping for a text from Marcus, but none had come through. Out of desperation, he scrolled through their last few messages.

Think I should take the Bainbridge or Bremerton ferry?

I'd take the Kingston.

Really? OK.

Trust me.

I should be there by the time you're finished shooting.

Can't wait. See you tonight.

They couldn't have been any more mundane, but they were something to distract himself. What the hell was his problem, anyway? He'd made peace with the way things were with Levi. And besides, Marcus would be here in a few hours. Now that they'd have some time alone, without all the exhaustion and chaos of a convention, they could finally—

"Carter?"

Oh fuck.

He turned around. "Hey. How's it going?"

"Not bad." Levi smiled, but it looked halfhearted. "How are you doing?"

"I'm all right." Carter managed a smile too. "Welcome to the nuthouse."

Levi chuckled. "Thanks. It's, uh, great to see you again."

"Yeah. You too." *Really great. Christ.* "Recovering from the visit?"

"Slowly. Actually, it wasn't as bad as I thought it would be. Still stressful, but . . ." He shrugged. "So I, um, heard you had a good time at RainCon."

Heat rushed into Carter's cheeks. "You heard about that?"

"About—" Levi put up his hands and shook his head. "No, no, I meant the con. Itself. Not . . . uh . . ."

"You did hear, though." Carter shifted his weight. "About me and Marcus."

"I . . . well, I saw the pictures from the con. The ones Anna sent out."

"Oh. Right." Even when it was just pictures sent around to the cast and crew, this whole "living in a fishbowl" thing was never going to feel normal. "I was hoping to tell you myself. It's, uh—"

"Carter." Levi met his eyes. "It's okay. You don't owe me an explanation for what you do with your own life."

"Right. I know, but . . ." Carter shook his head. "Anyway. Maybe this weekend, we can catch up over some DVDs?"

"I'm free whenever you are. You're welcome to come by anytime this week."

"I would, but Marcus is . . ."

"Oh." Levi may have been a great actor, but when it was his own emotions and not a character's, he couldn't fake a smile to save his life. "Well, have a good time."

"I will. But this weekend? Definitely."

"Great. The play closed on Saturday, so my schedule's wide open." He gestured at the set. "At least until things pick up here, anyway."

Carter laughed. "Yeah. Enjoy that free time while you have it. Once you're a regular cast member . . ."

"I fully intend to enjoy it, believe me." Beat. "I mean . . ."

Their eyes locked. Carter's heart jumped. He swallowed, and was about to break the silence, but Anna's assistant appeared beside them. "You two are on in five."

Levi nodded. "Thanks." He turned to Carter. "Guess that's our cue."

"Yeah. Guess so. See you on the set."

"See you there."

It was an outdoor shoot today, using the end of the warehouse where the exterior had been converted to look like the front of the police station.

A crew member put a pair of handcuffs on Levi and helped him into the back of the squad car parked outside the "station." Paul took his place in the driver's seat, with Joe in the passenger seat, and Carter stood beside the entrance to the building with a smoldering cigarette in his hand.

"Quiet on the set," Anna barked, and all the activity ceased. "Action."

Paul and Joe got out of the car. As Paul went around to the back to open the door, Joe approached Carter.

Carter dropped his cigarette on the concrete.

Paul smirked. "Those things'll kill ya, you know."

Carter threw him a look as he crushed the cigarette under his heel. "This is the guy? Max Fuhrman?"

Paul nodded. "This is the guy." He turned around, and they both watched as Joe dragged a struggling Levi—Max—out of the back of the car.

"Where'd you find him?"

"Half a mile from where she ditched her vehicle."

Carter eyed Levi the way Gabriel was supposed to eye Max, pretending that didn't fuck up his ability to speak. "So he was nearby. Doesn't mean he knows anything."

"There wasn't another soul for miles." Paul shrugged. "Wasn't like anybody was just gonna happen by that car."

Still watching Levi, Carter scowled. "Circumstantial at best."

"Yeah, but we found this in that trailer he lives in." Paul handed Carter an evidence bag containing some photos. Sweet, merciful distraction.

For several seconds, Carter studied the images, thankful no one—not even the cameras—knew his mind was on Levi. Then he handed the bag back and faced Levi again. "Put him on ice. I've . . ." He gulped. Crap. "I've . . ."

"Cut!"

Fuck.

He turned to Anna and smiled sheepishly. "Sorry."

"It happens. Go back to right before Paul hands over the evidence."

Carter nodded. He handed back the evidence bag.

"Action!"

Carter shrugged. "Circumstantial at best."

"Yeah, but we found this in that trailer he lives in." Paul gave him the evidence again.

As scripted, Carter studied the photos, heart pounding as he chastised himself for letting Levi get to him like that. *What in the world is the matter with—*

Paul made a subtle throat-clearing sound.

"Put him on ice." Carter gave back the prop. "I've got another potential witness I need to talk to first." He started to walk away, adding over his shoulder, "*Nobody* talks to Fuhrman except for me."

Behind him, Paul sighed heavily. "You heard the man."

"And cut!"

Carter closed his eyes and released a breath. He needed to get a grip. Stat. Levi hadn't even had any lines yet. He'd only been dragged out of the car while Carter and Paul talked. If Carter couldn't handle that much, what the fuck was he going to do during tomorrow's interrogation scene?

Carter had just wrapped up the day's shooting—mercifully, most of his scenes had involved other actors besides Levi—when his phone buzzed.

Be there in 5.

Carter quickly finished removing the last of his makeup, grabbed his coat, and headed outside right as Marcus's Lexus pulled into the gravel parking area. Heart going a million miles an hour, he made his way from the warehouse door to the lot.

The engine shut off, and when Marcus stepped out of his car, he grinned at Carter. "Hey you. Long time no see."

"Much too long." Carter returned the grin, trying to push away the weird guilt that was taking up residence in his chest. *What the hell? I've been looking forward to this ever since I left Seattle.*

A few spaces down from Marcus's car, Levi's Jeep caught his eye. He quickly pulled his gaze away from it. This was stupid. He had nothing to feel guilty about.

Marcus put a hand on Carter's waist and kissed him gently, and the guilt was immediately replaced by the giddy fluttery feeling he'd had all weekend long.

He drew back and met Marcus's eyes. "It's good to see you."

"Likewise." Marcus kissed him again. "So, what's the plan for this evening?"

Carter's throat tightened. "Uh, well. We . . ." *Let's not beat around the bush. We both know why we wanted to see each other.*

Marcus ran his fingertips along Carter's cheek. "Relax. We have three days. Why don't we grab something to eat for now, and then see where the night takes us?"

As if either of us don't know where it's going to take us.

"Okay. Sure." Carter slipped his hand into Marcus's. "There's an awesome bar and grill in town. Want to try it?"

"Sounds great."

They climbed into Marcus's car and headed into town.

All the way back to Bluewater Bay, the butterflies in Carter's stomach refused to quit, and it wasn't just excitement. *Why the hell am I so nervous?* Sure, there was always a little performance anxiety the first time he was with someone new, especially when there'd been time to build up some anticipation, but this felt . . . different. Not quite nauseating, but almost.

Get a grip, Samuels. It's been a while. That's all.

"Wow, this really is a tiny town." Marcus chuckled as he checked out the buildings lined up along Main Street. "How do you stay sane here?"

Carter shrugged. "It's not a bad place. The fishing's good."

"You fish?"

A memory flickered through Carter's mind of Levi wrangling the squirming mini-shark onto the boat. He swallowed. "Sometimes."

"You didn't strike me as the type." Marcus put his hand on Carter's thigh. "You're full of surprises, aren't you?"

Carter laughed halfheartedly. "Guess so." He looked the other way as they passed the Bluewater Bay Theater Company. The marquee had changed to reflect an upcoming version of *Fiddler on the Roof.* Carter caught himself wondering if Levi would be directing that too.

"Oh wow." Marcus craned his neck to check out the theater. "Is that one of those old indie theaters?"

"No, just a playhouse now."

"Damn. Seattle's full of indie houses."

"You're lucky. We only have this and the first-run movie theater." Carter paused. "Speaking of which, I know it's mainstream Hollywood shit, but do you want to catch a movie after we eat?"

Marcus glanced at him, then shrugged. "Sure."

"Great. The restaurant is up that way. Turn left at the light."

For once in his life, Carter wasn't interested in what was on the screen. A few times he actually forgot what movie they were watching. He just needed a little time to collect his thoughts—ninety minutes plus previews seemed like enough.

In theory, anyway.

As the previews ended and the lights went down, Marcus rested his hand on Carter's leg. Carter put his hand on top. The gentle contact distracted him from the movie, but not in the way a date's touch should have. He should've been squirming, his pulse pounding as he thought of all the things they'd be doing when they eventually made their way back to his place. Or wondering who'd be the first to make the move to start making out like a couple of high school kids.

But his mind was about as focused on Marcus as it was on the movie, and his inability to concentrate drove him insane. He'd barely thought of Levi all weekend long, and he'd convinced himself that meant he'd really moved on.

Now, with Marcus sitting beside him and Levi someplace else, he knew damn well that wasn't the case. He'd managed to block out Levi's existence while his parents were in town. And at the con, he'd had Marcus to occupy his attention.

But then one damned look at the man on the set and now Carter couldn't get him off his mind.

Marcus. Concentrate on Marcus.

Levi's not available. There's no point.

Carter laced his fingers between Marcus's.

Marcus is here. Levi isn't.

And Marcus is willing to take this to places . . .

Carter squirmed in his seat. He and Marcus had both been itching for some privacy and some time together since they'd met at the con. Now that there was no one looking over their shoulder and no camera lenses pointed their way, every look they exchanged should've been nothing short of a green light. After all, Marcus hadn't come all the way out here for the weekend to sleep on the couch. Up until this afternoon, that thought had excited Carter so much, he could barely stand the idea of waiting a few hours.

Now . . .

Carter shivered.

Marcus turned his head and whispered, "You okay?"

Carter nodded. "Yeah. Sorry."

Marcus gently freed his hand. Carter was about to object, but then Marcus put an arm around his shoulders and drew him in close. Though the armrest bit into his ribs, Carter liked being against him like this. He looked up, and Marcus met his gaze, the movement from the screen dancing on his features and in his eyes.

Carter reached for Marcus's face, and they both pulled in breaths when his fingertips trailed along Marcus's jaw.

They were moving in, the distance shrinking, Carter's pulse soaring, and though a voice in the back of his mind screamed at him to back off, he didn't. Their lips met, and Carter immediately broke out in goose bumps. Marcus knew how to kiss. In fact, that thing he did with his tongue was just . . . *shiver.*

So why do I want to get the hell out of here?

Carter could barely summon up the energy to return the kiss with a shred of enthusiasm, manufactured or otherwise. Any other time, any other place, Marcus would've had him climbing the walls and begging to be fucked. Hell, they probably would've fucked by now.

Any other time.

Any other place.

But he couldn't focus. Couldn't keep his mind here, now, on Marcus.

Levi.

Levi.

Fuck, I want Levi.

"Maybe we should get out of here," Marcus murmured. "This armrest is digging into my side."

Carter forced a grin. "Damn bucket seats."

"Seriously. I lost track of the movie anyway." Marcus glanced up at the screen, then met Carter's eyes in the low light. "Shall we?"

"Definitely."

They made it through the front door, but Marcus didn't even give Carter a chance to turn the dead bolt before he grabbed him by the waist. He pinned him to the door and kissed him, and Carter was so damned turned on, he forgot everything that wasn't this hot, aggressive man pressing against him.

For a few seconds.

God, Carter. Get a grip.

Maybe getting laid will help. Maybe I just need to drag him to bed and stay there until I forget about—

Except that wasn't him. He didn't fuck one guy to forget another. He fucked him because he wanted him, or not at all.

Right?

Carter toed off his shoes and shrugged out of his jacket. Marcus's jacket landed at their feet, and Carter started pulling Marcus's shirt free.

What am I doing?

A tug at his own belt sent a surge of panic through Carter.

I can't do this.

Marcus's hands froze. He pulled back, forehead creased with concern. "You okay?"

"Um . . ."

Marcus loosened his embrace. "What's wrong?"

Carter held his gaze, and no matter how much he wanted to, he couldn't look Marcus in the eye and pretend his heart was in this. "Look, I'm . . . I'm sorry." His shoulders dropped and he rubbed a hand over his face. "I don't think I can do this right now."

"Oh. Well, we . . . It doesn't have to be tonight." Marcus took Carter's other hand. "We can take things slower if you want."

"No, it's not just tonight." Carter sighed. "To be honest, I don't think I'm in a good place to be seeing anyone."

Now that he'd said it, he felt even worse. Guilty. Depressed.

Marcus drew back a little more. "So, why am I here?"

Because I didn't realize it until I saw Levi today.

"I thought I . . . All weekend, I was . . ."

"This is about that Chad Eastwick guy, isn't it?" Marcus set his jaw. "The one they've been talking about you dating?"

"What? No!" Carter waved his hand. "No, I'm . . ." *So hung up on that Chad Eastwick guy, it isn't even funny.* "I'm . . ."

"Is this why you never wanted to go back to the hotel all weekend?"

Guilty.

"No, of course not. We were . . . It was a convention. We couldn't . . ."

Marcus raised a skeptical eyebrow.

Carter exhaled. "I'm sorry. I thought I was—"

"This is bullshit." Marcus turned away, shoving a hand through his hair. "And you couldn't bring this up while we were still in Seattle? You had to wait until—"

"Do you think I'm doing this for fun?"

"I don't know why you're doing it," Marcus snapped. "But you could've saved me a couple of tanks of gas and half a fucking day—"

"You want money to cover the gas?"

"No. That's not the point. The point is, I don't like having my time wasted to—"

"I'm sorry," Carter said again. "If I'd thought this would happen, I would have . . ."

Marcus watched him silently for a moment, then stooped to pick up his jacket. "Take care, Carter. I'm out of here."

Carter winced, and said the only thing he could say: "I'm sorry."

But there was no one around to hear him.

He pinched the bridge of his nose and swore under his breath. He had no business getting tangled up with Levi. There was no way he was going to be someone's dirty secret, especially not someone who was creeping up on forty. If Levi wasn't out now, he was never going to be. Not with Carter or anyone else.

But Marcus deserved to be more than a convenient warm body. He deserved a guy who wasn't thinking about someone else when they were getting hot and heavy.

And there was one and only one man on Carter's mind tonight.

CHAPTER NINETEEN

L evi didn't have to be on set until four the next afternoon, which meant he didn't need to show up until around three. Usually, he'd have arrived an hour or two early just in case makeup took longer than expected, or the director suddenly decided to shuffle the shooting schedule.

Today, he took his sweet time, pulling into the gravel parking lot outside the warehouse-turned-soundstage at a few minutes shy of three. All the way from his house to the set, he promised himself he'd focus on his scene and not Carter. Even if that scene was *with* Carter.

They'd get used to this new reality—with a flesh and blood confirmation that they really were just friends—eventually, but for now, he had to concentrate on nothing but being Max Fuhrman.

So, of course, the second he walked into the warehouse, without even thinking about it, he homed in on Carter, whose back was turned to him while he and Joe listened to Anna explain something.

As far as Levi could tell, that other guy wasn't here, and Levi felt guilty for his relief at the man's absence. Jesus Christ, it had hurt seeing Carter with someone else.

Levi wasn't jealous in a malicious way. He genuinely hoped things worked out and they were happy—Carter deserved nothing less.

But it fucking *hurt*.

In a few short weeks, he'd grown closer to Carter than he'd ever been to any of his exes, male or female. There were still plenty of things they didn't know about each other yet, but he was so at ease with Carter. Comfortable with him in a way he'd rarely been with another person.

Now that he'd seen Carter with someone else, now that he had confirmation that he'd pushed Carter out of reach, *now* he realized how much "just friends" didn't cut it.

This is what you wanted, Levi.

Wanted? Yeah, right.

But this was the way it needed to be. He'd made the decision a long time ago to stay closeted, and now this dream job, the very role he was getting ready to slip into, was on the line. There was no discreetly dating the most eligible gay man in showbiz, and anyway, Carter had found someone else. Levi had gotten over people before, and he'd get over this one.

Levi left the soundstage and got dressed before taking a seat in the makeup chair. While the artist worked her magic, Levi propped the script on his knee and busied himself going over the scene again, though he knew it by heart. It was something to do, even if it meant reading and rereading a scene that would involve prolonged eye contact with Carter.

You've got this. You're a professional and so is he.

Anna's assistant appeared in the doorway. "Levi, Anna needs you and Carter in ten."

"He's almost done," the makeup artist said. "Tell her five minutes, tops."

Five minutes. Levi closed his eyes. Five minutes until go time with Carter.

I've got this. I've done tougher scenes under more pressure. I've totally got this.

That mantra brought his pulse back down and kept him focused while the makeup artist finished with him. It kept him breathing. Kept him sane.

Until the moment Carter walked onto the set.

I've got— Fuck, I don't even know.

Carter came up, but couldn't seem to hold Levi's gaze. "Hey."

"Hey."

"So, um." Carter cleared his throat, and his smile was definitely forced. "You ready for this?"

Not a chance.

"I've got my lines down, if that's what you mean."

Carter laughed. "Well, that's good."

They locked eyes, and Levi scrambled for some sort of benign small talk. Carter broke away first, muffling a cough and staring at his feet. Levi glanced around in search of a distraction.

Mercifully, one came—Anna summoned Levi into the office.

"Good luck," Carter said.

"Thanks. Hopefully I didn't piss her off."

"Oh, you'd know it if you did."

"Mm-hmm."

Still, Levi was a little nervous as he stepped into Anna's office. She closed the door behind them and faced him.

"So." She folded her arms. "What do you think?"

"Of?"

"The show. The production. Everything."

"I like it." He smiled. "Did you think I wouldn't?"

"Well, no. But the thing is . . ." She bit her lip and dropped her gaze.

Levi tensed. "What? Something wrong?"

"No. But . . ." She met his eyes. "Cutting right to the chase, there was a lot of talk about you at the con this weekend. Word's gotten out that you may be joining the cast, and we had dozens of fans asking us to confirm it."

Levi swallowed. "Did you?"

Anna shook her head. "I wanted to talk to you first. The thing is, I've got some footage from yesterday that could be *conveniently* leaked." She held up her smartphone. "All I have to do is hit Post, and everyone in *Landing* fandom knows you're Max Fuhrman."

Levi stared at the phone. "And the studio would—"

"The fans will go batshit." She grinned. "There's no way in hell the studio will fire you when you're making the fans happy. And nobody knows this particular Twitter account is mine, so I'm safe too." She gestured with the phone again, and her expression turned serious. "But if I let it slip, it also means you're not going to be able to exercise that 'easy out' in your contract."

"Right. Which means I need to . . . behave."

Anna nodded. "I'm sorry about that part, Levi."

"I know." He blew out a breath. "The price of working in this business, am I right?"

"Yep."

"Though if it's out that I'm on *Wolf's Landing*, will they really fire me if—"

"Don't test the studio on this, baby." She shook her head. "Just . . . don't."

He chewed the inside of his cheek. "So I'm guessing you called me in here to ask for a green light to 'leak' the footage?"

Anna nodded. "You don't have to make any decisions now. It can—"

"No. Go ahead and post it."

"Really?"

"Yeah." He smiled again. "This is the role I've been itching for. If leaking the footage keeps the studio from finding a way to can me? Go for it."

Anna laughed. "Well, if you insist . . ." She winked and turned on her phone. "This should keep Twitter and Tumblr busy for a day or two."

"Yeah, probably." Levi chuckled.

"And . . . done." She set the phone aside. "Let the fireworks begin."

"Hopefully the fans will be happy."

"They will be, sweetie." She touched his arm. "Trust me, most of the fans who came up to ask if you were really going to be on the show were so excited, they couldn't see straight. This is going to make their collective day." She let go of his arm and gestured over her shoulder. "And now you're stuck on my show, so get out there on the set so we can shoot this scene."

"Yes, ma'am."

This particular set was one he'd seen a few times on the show, though it was strange to physically be here. The "room" was mostly bare concrete walls surrounding a metal table and a pair of folding chairs, plus the usual two-way mirror on the whitewashed wall beside the steel gray door. The cinematographer had painstakingly lit the room to be as bleak and soulless as possible on the screen, but while it appeared cold, it was actually quite hot. Just as well, since Levi's character was supposed to break into a sweat during his interrogation. That would be easy enough.

Levi took a seat in one of the folding chairs. A crew member put a pair of handcuffs on his wrists and Levi rested them in his lap.

Carter toed the other chair out from under the table and stood beside it, facing Levi. He tugged at his tie, disheveling it, and someone from the crew tweaked his hair slightly to give him a more frazzled look.

And then Levi and Carter were alone on the set. They were surrounded by at least two dozen people—the director, those manning cameras and equipment, makeup artists standing by for touch-ups—but everyone and everything behind the bright lights disappeared into heavy shadows. The two of them may as well have been isolated in a real interrogation room, staring each other down over the table without oversized lenses looking on like prying eyes.

"Action!"

The set was completely silent. Carter's character perused something in a file folder while Levi watched him. Without looking up, Carter said, "Tell me again where you were last night."

"At home."

"Doing?"

"I was asleep." In character, Levi tried to wring his hands, but the cuffs hindered him, so he dropped them in his lap again. "And no, there's nobody who can vouch for me. I live alone."

"Care to explain this?" Carter fanned a series of blurry black-and-white photos on the table.

Levi gave them a cursory look, then sat back and shook his head. "It's not me."

"Really?" Carter snorted and dropped the file folder on top of the pictures. "You know anyone else in this town who's got a jacket like that?" He gestured so sharply at Levi's patch-covered field jacket, he almost smacked him.

Levi glared up at him. *My God, you're fucking gorgeous.* "It's not me."

Carter—Gabriel—leaned over the table so they were almost face-to-face. "I'm done playing games, Max."

Levi fidgeted and squirmed under his scrutiny, cuffs rattling between his hands beneath the table. "Who's . . . who's playing games? I told you everything I know."

Gabriel slammed his fist down on the table, the bang nearly sending Levi toppling backward. Christ, it was a good thing Max was supposed to be ready to jump out of his skin during this scene.

"Quit lying to me!"

Levi shook his head and stared at the table. "You've got no proof. I"—*can't remember what the fuck I'm supposed to say*—"wasn't anywhere near there when—"

"Like hell you weren't." Carter snatched the front of Levi's shirt and dragged him halfway up out of his chair. Their faces were almost touching, Carter's eyes flashing with fury. "So help me, if anything happens to her, I'll—" He hesitated, the rage vanishing for a split second in favor of something Levi couldn't identify. "I will—"

"Cut."

Carter released Levi's shirt and swore under his breath. "Sorry." He laughed halfheartedly. "I know my lines, I promise."

"Sure you do." Anna laughed. "Start with 'I'm done playing games' and go from there."

Carter nodded. Levi eased himself back into his chair and straightened his clothes as much as he could in cuffs. He mentally ran through his lines while he pretended his heart wasn't racing.

They faced each other, and Carter took his place again, leaning over the table, though he kept his gaze down.

"Quiet on the set!" A second later, "Take two. Action!"

Carter lifted his gaze and that simmering fury was back—goddamn, he was good at this—boring into Levi as Carter glared down at him. "I'm done playing games, Max."

Levi shifted, wringing his cuffed hands under the table. "Who's . . . who's playing games? I told you everything I know."

Carter slammed his fist down on the table. "Quit lying to me!"

Levi shook his head and—thank God—broke eye contact. He stared at the table. "You've got no proof. I wasn't anywhere near there when—"

"Like hell you weren't." Carter dragged Levi up by his shirt, cuffs banging against the table's edge, and that momentary pain distracted Levi for a second before he was completely focused on Carter's face again.

"So help me," Carter snarled, "if anything happens to her, I'll break your damned neck."

Levi drew back as much as Carter's grip allowed. "I don't know where she is."

"Then who does?"

"How the hell am I supposed to—"

The door flew open, and Paul stepped in. "Detective Hanford, I've got something you need to see."

"This had better be important." Carter shoved Levi back into his chair, spun on his heel, and stormed out.

"Cut! Perfect, guys."

Levi pulled the quick release on the cuffs, dropped them on the table with a loud *clang*, and rubbed his wrists gingerly.

Carter came back through the door. "I felt your hands hit the table. Didn't hurt you, did I?"

"No, no." Levi forced a laugh. "The cuffs just got caught. It's fine."

"Oh. Good." Their eyes met, and they both quickly looked away.

"Nicely done, gentlemen," Anna broke in. "You two take a break, and the crew will set up for the next scene."

Carter and Levi left the set in opposite directions. Levi dabbed some sweat from his face before he hunted down a cup of coffee—as if he needed it—and found an out-of-the-way spot to go over the next scene while the crew moved cameras and lights around.

He took out his phone and pulled up the Twitter app. "Holy shit . . ."

There must have been five hundred tweets tagging him under the *Wolf's Landing* hashtag. He scrolled through them, not entirely sure what to expect.

OMG! Is that real? Please tell me that's real.

HOLY FUCK I KNEW IT.

Wolf's Landing just turned into the most awesome show ever.

Levi laughed and shook his head. Apparently Anna was right. Aside from some trollish tweets—

Chad Eastwick is going to ruin Wolf's Landing.

WTF. Way to fuck the series, assholes.

Levi Pritchard as Max Fuhrman? Noooooooooo

—the response was largely positive.

He continued reading as the crew rejiggered the set. There was nonstop activity on a soundstage, and he'd long ago learned to ignore it when someone brushed by him.

But then a presence right next to him sent a tingle up the length of his spine. When he turned, he wasn't at all surprised, but he still couldn't quite breathe.

"Hey." Carter hesitated. "Can we talk for a minute? In private?"

Levi's heart skipped. "Sure." He pocketed his phone. "What's up?"

Carter glanced around, then gestured for Levi to follow him.

They left the soundstage and went to the portable building between Anna's office and the storage shed.

The door was unlocked. Carter went in first.

Levi followed, and nudged the door shut behind him. "So what's—"

Carter kissed him.

One second, they were an arm's-length apart. The next, Carter had him pinned up against the door, crushing Levi's mouth with his. Levi was stunned, but his body didn't hesitate—he grabbed onto the back of Carter's neck and returned the breathless, hungry kiss.

The forcefulness melted away. They remained as passionate as the moment their lips had met, but the sheer violence faded, replaced by gentleness. Carter's fingers ran down Levi's face. Levi held him close and explored his mouth like they had the whole damned night instead of a few stolen minutes.

When they came up for air, they were both shaking.

"I . . ." Carter licked his lips. "We— Fuck it." He kissed Levi again, raking his fingers through Levi's hair and pressing him harder against the door.

"But I thought you . . ." Levi gasped for breath and struggled to form words between kisses. "I thought you were dating—"

"Didn't work out."

"Oh. I'm, uh, sorry to—"

Carter silenced him with a deep kiss. "I'm not." He drew back enough for their eyes to meet. "I . . . I had to let him go because I couldn't stop thinking about you."

Levi stared at him. "You . . . what?"

Carter swept his tongue across his lips. "You heard me. And I know we shouldn't. But I don't care." He cradled Levi's face in both hands and touched his feverish forehead to Levi's. "I don't want to keep fighting this. I want you."

Levi's spine melted.

Carter kissed him again. "I can't even think when I'm around you."

Levi stroked his hair. "I can't either. You've had me tripping over my own feet since day one."

"You too, huh?"

"Yeah."

Carter ran his thumb across Levi's cheekbone. "Then why do we keep doing this to ourselves?"

"Fuck, I don't even know anymore." Levi kissed him, drawing it out for a moment, savoring it, because he was sure they were seconds away from being interrupted by Anna or their own sense. "We can't do this here."

"Then where?" Carter was out of breath, panting hard against Levi's lips. "I can't . . . I can't fucking wait."

Jesus Christ. "Neither can I. And goddamn it, my place is so far."

"Mine is . . ." Carter shook his head. "There's too many people around. Who know who we are."

"We can't . . ." Levi licked his lips. "And we can't do this right now. We're still shooting."

"I know."

Levi brushed a few strands of blond hair out of Carter's face. "The marina."

Carter blinked. "What?"

"My place is too far, and yours isn't discreet." Levi trailed unsteady fingers along Carter's jaw. "But the marina's only ten or fifteen minutes from here. You remember which slip is mine, right?"

"I . . ."

"Twenty-two. Meet me there and we'll . . ."

Shivering, Carter closed his eyes. "I'll be there."

A mix of relief, excitement, and nerves rushed through Levi. "My scenes are done before yours. I'll . . . I'll make sure we've got everything we need."

Carter laughed softly. "You don't think buying condoms and lube at Walgreens will kick up more rumors?"

Levi grinned. "There are more discreet places in town. Trust me."

"I'll take your word for it." Carter swallowed. "We should get back to the set. Before someone figures out we're gone."

"Yeah, good idea." Levi paused. "One more thing before you go, though."

"Hmm?"

He didn't say a word. He just pulled Carter close and kissed him.

As luck would have it, Levi's character was supposed to be a jittery wreck who was half out of his mind in this episode. In later appearances, he'd be cold and calculating, but tonight, Max was shaking and stuttering, and Levi didn't even have to fake it.

"Great job!" Anna hugged him as he stepped off the set. "I *knew* you were perfect for this role."

Levi laughed. "I'm not sure if I should take that as a compliment or an insult."

"Hmm. Probably a little from column A—"

"Shut up."

"Hey. Don't talk to your boss like that." She nodded toward the set and turned serious. "I do want to get that last bit one more time from a different angle."

Levi saluted playfully. "You're the boss."

"I am. All right, places everyone. Camera three, I need you over here."

Once the cameras had been reconfigured, they ran through the scene once more, and Anna was finally pleased with it. After that, Levi's scenes wrapped up around nine, and as soon as he could escape, he slipped away from the set without a word or even a look at Carter. A shared glance would've given them away. A nervous good-bye would've put a spotlight on their quiet little scandal-in-progress. Worse, any interaction at all might remind them why they'd avoided this for so long and why they should keep avoiding it tonight.

Keeping his head down and his gait fast so no one could pull him aside and hold him up, he hurried out to the parking lot. There were some cast and crew out here smoking and chatting, but none of them said anything to him. Still, he didn't slow down until he made it to his Jeep.

In the driver's seat, he exhaled. Home free.

He headed across town, hands sweating on the steering wheel, and parked a few doors down from his destination—no sense giving the paparazzi a shot of his Jeep parked in front of Red Hot Bluewater.

The inside of the glass door was covered with black paper, as were all the windows, and it had "No One Under 18 Permitted" displayed in huge, red letters. He wondered if there should've been a restriction like "No One Who's This Close to 40 and Still Worries His Parents Will Find Out He's Gay."

Chuckling nervously to himself, he pulled open the papered door and stepped inside. Immediately, he was greeted by the heady scents of leather, incense, and about seven hundred types of massage oil.

Violet Hayes, the owner, peered out from between a display of LED cock rings and some novelty penis lollipops on the counter. Her eyes lit up. "Oh hey, sweetheart! Haven't seen you in here in a while."

And if he wasn't blushing before, he sure as hell was now. "Yeah, I haven't been around much."

"Well, glad to see you back." She winked at him, and his cheeks were on fire, but for all she teased, at least he knew she'd be discreet. Violet probably knew a lot of things about a lot of people in this town, but she wouldn't say a word to anyone. He was definitely safer buying what he needed here than at Walgreens.

Violet wouldn't say a word, and no one who came in here would either—that would mean admitting they'd been in here. Soon, Levi would be on the boat with Carter, and there'd be no one around to find out at all. No one would know but them.

Just this once, Hollywood didn't have him by the balls and his family didn't have him in a choke hold. He wanted Carter. Carter wanted him. And if only for tonight, what they did together would be nobody's goddamned business.

Levi pushed his shoulders back. No, he wasn't going to get cold feet and call this off. He came here to get what he and Carter needed, and he would, because tonight was happening.

He knew the shop's layout by heart, and went straight to the racks of every type of condom imaginable. He and Carter had no need for colored, flavored, or glow-in-the-dark, so he didn't find the huge selection the least bit daunting.

Still, pulling the box of condoms off the rack made his knees shake. Not out of nerves this time. Just knowing he was taking another step toward being in bed with Carter.

Finally.

CHAPTER TWENTY

*T*his is a bad idea. You know it's a bad idea.

Carter could barely hear his footsteps over his own heartbeat as he made his way across the gravel to the marina. Three times between his car and the edge of the pier, he stopped, rocking from his heels to the balls of his feet. Would a *Maybe we shouldn't do this* text be any less awkward than a *We probably shouldn't have done that* morning after?

One thing kept negating the million reasons he should've turned and run: he wanted this. Consequences be damned, Levi was waiting for him, and Carter wasn't turning back. Not this time.

He kept walking, disbelieving this was real. It wasn't what he'd had in mind when he'd pulled Levi aside earlier. He'd only meant to talk to him. About what, he couldn't even remember now, only that he'd needed a moment alone with him to step away someplace private and talk.

But the second that door had closed . . .

Carter shivered and started down the row of slips. His shoes clomped on the wooden pier, almost drowning out the blood pounding in his ears. What the hell was he doing?

Exactly what he'd done when he'd taken Levi aside—giving in to the inevitable before it drove him insane.

And Levi hadn't resisted. Quite the contrary.

Carter walked past slip sixteen.

The pier creaked beneath his feet, and he was sure the sound would turn every head in Bluewater Bay. Maybe even in Victoria, which glowed faintly on the other side of the water.

Slip seventeen.

Eighteen.

Nineteen.

Who cared if it was a bad idea? No one had to know but them.

Twenty.

Shit, this was definitely not something they should be doing. They were asking for problems. With the production company. With the press. With Levi's family. With Levi.

Carter stopped between slips twenty and twenty-one. He gulped.

It wasn't too late to turn around. That would probably make him a coward, but he'd pretty well established that when he'd bowed out of fooling around with Marcus. Shit, the rumors must be flying by now. Wolf's Landing *Star Single-handedly Dispels Promiscuous Gay Male Stereotype—Is Either Terrified of Sex or a Fucking Prude.*

Up ahead, beyond the sailboat in slip twenty-one, he could see the bow of Levi's boat bobbing in the tide.

This is it. Here we go.

When he'd passed the sailboat, he didn't even have to double-check the slip numbers. Every other boat was dark, but a soft light glowed in the windows of this one.

Then the cabin door opened, and Levi stepped out. The second their eyes met, Carter's head started spinning. He stopped in his tracks, just like when he'd seen Levi on the set yesterday, heart pounding and stomach fluttering.

Levi smiled, which didn't help at all. "I was almost afraid you'd reconsidered."

I should. God, I should.

"Had to wait for Anna to let me go." *Why am I here?* Carter held Levi's gaze, and those gorgeous eyes were filled with the same lust that had driven Carter here in spite of his nerves. *Oh, yeah. That's why I'm here.*

He glanced back down the pier. There wasn't a soul in sight—they were one hundred percent alone. No one to see them, hear them, or have any clue at all what they'd come here to do. The only question remaining . . .

Why the fuck am I still standing here?

Carter stepped from the pier onto the boat.

"You made it. That's all that matters." Levi slipped an arm around Carter's waist, and his kiss—his soft, unhurried kiss—canceled out every second thought Carter had had. The few times they'd done this before had been enough to weaken his knees, but there was something foundation rattling about this one. Maybe the fact that years' worth of fantasies were on the verge of becoming a reality.

Carter grinned against Levi's lips. "You have everything we need?"

"You'd better believe it." Levi gently freed himself and gestured over his shoulder. "Come on in."

They climbed down the ladder into the main part of the cabin, and Levi led him into the back. The living quarters were roomier than he'd expected on a boat this size, but still a tight fit. They both had barely enough clearance to stand, though if Levi stood on his toes, his head would touch the ceiling.

In the tiny room inside the boat, they faced each other.

Here we are. Oh my God, here we are.

Neither of them said a word. They inched together, eyes locked, and Carter wondered if Levi's heart was racing like his was.

Almost touching, they stopped, and Carter was more aware than ever of their height difference—Levi was a little taller, but this close together, Carter had to tilt his head up to meet his eyes.

Levi's fingertips brushed Carter's cheek, sending a shiver through both of them. "You sure about this?"

Carter swallowed. "Are you?"

Levi didn't answer. He just gathered Carter in his arms and kissed him, and everything about that kiss said that yes, yes, yes.

Carter pushed Levi's shirt up and off, and then he ran his fingers down the man's sculpted torso. Seeing Levi like this on-screen was nothing compared to seeing him in person. He was all lean muscle. Pure power.

He slid his hand up Levi's chest. Sure enough, Carter's heart wasn't the only one going a hundred miles an hour. He could feel Levi's thumping pulse. His body heat.

Carter had seen the scars on Levi's arm and the one on his face, but there were more on his biceps and shoulder, and a nasty one under his collarbone. They weren't unattractive—if anything, they were silvery-white reminders of how the odds had been stacked against this moment happening at all.

He tried to take a step, but wobbled a little.

Levi caught him. "You all right?"

"Yeah." Carter laughed, steadying himself. "Guess I still don't have my sea legs."

"It's okay." Levi wrapped his arm tighter around him. "We don't need to stay on our feet anyway." He drew Carter backward with him and they sank onto the bed.

The warmth of Levi's skin took Carter's breath away. "Oh my God."

Levi ran his hands down Carter's sides. "I want you so bad, I don't know where to start."

"I don't even . . ." Carter shivered, pressing his body against Levi's. "I don't even know if you're a top or a bottom or what."

Levi dragged his nails up Carter's spine. "I'm whatever you want me to be tonight."

Jesus. H. Christ.

He searched for Levi's lips, and right before he kissed him, he murmured, "Fuck me."

Levi moaned and pulled him into a deep, breathless kiss. They held each other tighter, scraping fingernails across flesh and kissing as hungrily as they had this afternoon.

"Don't move." Levi reached for a black plastic bag on the edge of the bed. Carter's heart beat faster as Levi tore a condom from the strip. It wasn't only arousal, either.

Levi's eyebrow arched. He paused, running a hand along Carter's thigh. "You okay?"

Shit. He must've tensed without even realizing it. "Yeah, I'm fine." He swallowed. "I, uh, just haven't done this in a while. Bottomed, I mean."

"It's okay. I'll go slow." Levi tipped Carter's chin up with two fingers and kissed him lightly. "I've wanted this for a long, long time. Believe me, I'm not in any hurry for it to be over."

Carter melted, and he wrapped his arms around Levi again. In between kissing and touching, they got the condom out of its wrapper, and with four hands and a lot of clumsiness, they finally rolled the condom onto Levi's cock. It wasn't like either of them were inexperienced, but they were too damned busy making out to concentrate on anything else.

Panting, Levi broke the kiss and pushed himself up. He reached for the lube, and once he'd put some on, he met Carter's eyes. "Turn around."

As Carter obeyed, Levi kept a hand on him, a light, warm touch that moved from his shoulder to his back and finally to his hip.

He couldn't tell if it was the boat's gentle rocking or his own fucked-up equilibrium, but he was sure the entire world was about to list violently beneath him. He gripped the sheets, breathing slowly as he tried to steady himself.

Then Levi's other hand materialized on his ass. Carter closed his eyes.

"I'll go slow," Levi said softly. "I promise."

Carter just nodded. It wasn't nerves now. All anticipation. And disbelief. And complete and total surrender.

Levi teased him gently, and he hadn't lied—he wasn't in any hurry. There was never pain. Never discomfort. At the first hint of resistance, Levi backed off, giving Carter a chance to relax completely before he continued. Maybe with any other guy, he'd have resented being slowly prepped like a scared virgin, but Levi made it feel so, so good. With a single finger, he had Carter trembling. When he added the second finger, Carter stopped caring about anything except how amazing he felt. How Levi knew exactly how to touch him, tease him, drive him slowly out of his mind.

He'd almost forgotten this was a step toward something else until Levi withdrew his fingers.

Oh. Oh God.

That's where this is going.

He opened his eyes, staring down at the comforter he was gathering in his fists.

Behind him, Levi released a ragged breath as he ran a hand up Carter's sides. "I can't even tell you how long I've wanted to do this."

Carter shivered. "Likewise."

Levi laughed softly, and then they both gasped as he pressed his cock against Carter's entrance.

Oh God. Oh my God . . .

Carter didn't move. He focused on breathing as Levi slowly pushed into him. Vision blurring, he reminded himself again and again to relax—it wasn't that he was worried that Levi would hurt him, this just felt so damned good, it was all he could do not to pass out and miss it. And, God, he didn't want to miss a second.

Levi withdrew and then slid in again, easing himself deeper inside Carter, and every slow, gentle stroke made Carter light-headed. If there was one perk to lengthy periods of celibacy, it was the intensity of that first fuck after so long without. As Levi carefully worked himself in, a shiver drove Carter onto his forearms. The angle now, leaning downward with his ass in the air, may not have been the most dignified position ever, but he didn't give a damn. How he looked was irrelevant because Levi felt so fucking good.

Somehow, Carter managed to lift himself up onto his arms again, and he rocked back against Levi, matching his rhythm.

"God, this is even better than I imagined," Levi murmured, and Carter's whole body broke out in goose bumps. Levi had imagined this too?

"This is . . ." Carter closed his eyes. Everything about this was amazing, so much better than *he'd* imagined it, but he couldn't speak.

Levi wrapped his arm around Carter and kissed the side of his neck. He used his body weight to guide Carter down onto his stomach, and once they'd landed gently on the firm mattress, he started moving again, slow, fluid strokes at the most incredible angle.

The only thing missing was Levi's addictive kiss.

He turned his head and finally managed to slur, "L-let me get on my back."

"I like the sound of that." Levi kissed beneath Carter's ear, and then he pulled out. They shifted position, Carter lying on his back and spreading his legs so Levi could guide himself in again. Levi watched himself take a few slow, deep strokes, whispering what sounded like curses.

Carter reached up, took Levi's face in both hands, and drew him down into a kiss. Levi slid his hands under him, hooking them over Carter's shoulders. A few times, Levi's hips all but stopped, as if he couldn't focus on fucking and kissing at the same time. Carter lost himself too, running his fingers through Levi's hair and letting the kiss consume him completely, and then Levi would start moving, and they'd both gasp as their bodies began rocking together.

A hard shudder went through Levi, and he broke the kiss again, letting his head fall beside Carter's for a moment before he pushed himself up. His slow, intermittent strokes became deep thrusts, and Carter was in heaven.

He put a hand on Levi's shoulder, and with the other, he started stroking himself. He didn't know if he was stroking in time with Levi's thrusts, or if it was the other way around, but that didn't change how fucking incredible it felt.

Carter heard himself groan. Then he realized it hadn't been him at all, and he forced his eyes open and met Levi's.

And this time, the groan was his.

Holy fuck, Levi looked amazing. This was Carter's hottest fantasy come to life—Levi on top like he'd been in *Broken Day*, eyes half-closed and lips apart, low light playing on the sheen of sweat as he moved like he intended to draw this out till dawn. And yet this wasn't Levi the action star, or Levi the man he'd idolized. This was the man he'd been getting to know all this time. The one who'd gone from his faraway idol to his closest friend.

From the one who'd inspired him to act and made him realize he was gay, to . . . to *this*.

In all his fantasies of getting Levi into bed, Carter had always imagined he'd be starstruck, but he was awestruck. The limelight had faded a long time ago, and Levi was just . . . Levi. And somehow that made him more than Carter had ever imagined.

Levi picked up speed until he was thrusting hard enough to push Carter back against the headboard, and Carter rocked his hips, encouraging him to fuck him even harder. His elbow ached from jerking his own cock, but he didn't care because Levi had him right on the edge, ready to lose it at any moment, ready to unravel completely at just the right touch, the right sound—

The right look.

Levi's eyes met his, lids heavy and pupils blown, and Carter lost it. His back arched off the bed. Semen coated his hand, his abs, Levi's abs, and Levi didn't stop. A low groan left his lips, and the cords stood out from his neck as his lips peeled back over his teeth and his eyes screwed shut, and then his eyes flew open. He gasped. Thrust all the way into Carter. Shuddered.

His weight shifted. Then his lips brushed Carter's, the kiss lazy and soft, and Carter held him close as they caught their breath.

Eventually, Levi pulled out, and they both shivered again. Levi kissed him once more before he sat up. "I'll be right back."

"I'll be right here."

Levi grinned, and then disappeared into the boat's tiny bathroom.

Carter grabbed some tissues from the shelf beside the bed, and after he'd cleaned himself up, he lay back on the pillows. He listened to his heartbeat slowly coming down. The boat continued rocking. The world was still turning. The dust was settling.

He couldn't believe he'd just lived his hottest fantasy, and it had been even better than he'd imagined. But as all things did, it eventually had to end and the smoke had to clear. Reality set back in, and an uncomfortable feeling knotted in Carter's gut.

Sooner or later, they'd have to leave this boat and return to a world where this—whatever it was—could affect their jobs, their reputations. Yeah, he'd wanted a night with Levi Pritchard, and he'd gotten his wish, but . . .

Now what?

CHAPTER TWENTY-ONE

L evi refused to meet his own eyes in the mirror as he took care of the condom and quickly washed his hands.

Excitement had kept his second thoughts at bay for hours, but now that he'd finally taken Carter to bed, he couldn't escape them. The voice that had been whispering from the back of his mind was shouting now. *What happens next?*

It wasn't as if one-night stands were below him. God knew he'd had his share. But sleeping with a friend and coworker, that could get complicated. Especially when that friend was Carter. The one person on the planet Levi couldn't convince himself he'd had—or would ever have—casual sex with. Especially since Carter wasn't into that, and had made that clear from the beginning.

Fuck. This was going to get complicated.

He dried off his hands, set his shoulders back, and returned to the tiny living area.

Carter hadn't moved. He gazed at Levi with heavy-lidded eyes, and his sleepy smile was almost enough to chase away those worries all over again.

"You're not gonna kick me out yet, are you?"

Levi laughed and joined Carter in bed. "Of course not."

"Good," Carter murmured as Levi pulled the sheet over both of them. "Because I don't know if I can stand up."

"I'll take that as a compliment."

"Oh, it is."

They fit perfectly together. Carter's body molded against his, head beneath Levi's chin with an arm slung over his stomach. Maybe they should've gotten up, but . . . *This feels so nice.* He could've stayed like that all night long.

I could stay like this for—

"Comfortable?"

"Mm-hmm." Carter raised his head. "Should we get out of here?"

Levi stroked Carter's hair. "We don't have to." *But we should.* "Isn't like we're paying by the hour for this place."

"Won't your cats get worried?"

"Oh, they don't mind having the house to themselves as long as they have food." Carter rested his head on Levi's shoulder again, and Levi kissed it. "To tell you the truth, after the last week and a half, they're probably happy to be on their own for a little while."

Carter chuckled. "I can imagine."

Levi trailed his fingers up and down Carter's arm. "And anyway, I'm not in any hurry."

"Neither am I."

It wasn't a dream.

As Levi slowly came around, the boat's gentle rocking trying to lull him back to sleep, he realized Carter was still beside him. The sleepy sex they'd had in the darkness at God knew what time, that might've been a dream—though the twinges in his hips suggested otherwise—but they'd definitely fucked a couple of times before that.

Some people didn't like the smallish beds on boats like this, but Levi wasn't complaining about it. Not when it forced him to stay this close to the man he'd slept with last night.

Carter. Jesus, he couldn't believe they were here. He closed his eyes and smiled. What was it Carter had said about meeting your idol? How people said it ruined the illusion? Oh, meeting Carter hadn't ruined anything. And sex with him? Amazing.

Those nagging worries still tried to pour cold water on him, but he ignored them for now.

Whatever comes next, just let me have this.

He kissed the back of Carter's shoulder. "Morning."

"Is it?" Carter lifted his head. "It's not even light out."

"No, but we both have to be at work soon."

Carter buried his face in the pillow and grumbled something.

Levi laughed and kissed his shoulder again. "We should get breakfast."

"Coffee," Carter muttered. "Need. Coffee."

"I have coffee on the boat."

"Thank God."

Levi got up, and after some stretching and cursing, so did Carter. They gathered their clothes off the deck. Dressing together in the tiny cabin wasn't quite as easy as undressing—probably because they'd been holding each other and stripping off their clothes with no regard for anything, while they needed a little elbow room now.

In spite of the tight confines, they managed to get dressed. As they moved into the kitchen/living area, Levi's stomach was quickly becoming a ball of nerves. Sooner or later, they were going to have to deal with last night.

While they waited for the coffeepot to do its thing, they faced each other, and Levi's ball of nerves grew.

"So, um." Carter fussed with his sleeves. "What now?"

Levi gulped. *Here goes.* "I've gotten about as far as getting off the boat. What about you?"

"Same." Carter gnawed his lip, staring at the deck between them. He laughed cautiously. "So much for being just friends, right?"

Guilt twisted beneath Levi's ribs. "Except I'm not sure what exactly we *are* now."

"Neither am I."

Levi studied him for a moment. "Things don't have to change just because we've slept together."

Carter's gaze slid toward Levi, something unreadable in his expression. "I . . . um . . ."

Levi raised his eyebrows.

Carter shifted his weight. "I didn't think anything had changed because of that." He avoided Levi's eyes, color blooming in his cheeks. "I guess I kind of thought we . . ." The color deepened, and he sighed.

"What?" Levi stepped a little closer, but stopped when Carter tensed. *Oh shit.* "Talk to me."

Carter swallowed, and then met Levi's eyes. "Maybe it's stupid and naïve of me, but I guess I thought we slept together because things had changed between us. Not . . . not the other way around."

Levi's heart fell into his feet. "We've both known for a long time we're attracted to each other. Ever since—" Just thinking about that kiss in the theater made his breath catch.

"I know. And . . ." Carter ran a hand through his hair. "Look, it's not that I only sleep with someone if I'm in love with them or anything like that, but we've been keeping each other at arm's length this whole time, and it . . ." He was quiet for a long moment, eyes unfocused and brow furrowed. Finally, he shook his head. "Okay, you know what? I'm just gonna say it. Everything that happened last night? It wasn't *only* because I wanted to sleep with you."

"Then, why—"

"Please don't make me spell it out," Carter pleaded, barely whispering.

Levi winced. *Damn it, Carter. You don't know how bad I want—* "That doesn't . . . It doesn't change our—my—circumstances."

Carter clenched his jaw and broke eye contact. "So anything we do has to stay on the down-low."

"Unfortunately. It doesn't mean we can't give it a shot. We've been laying low all this time, and—"

"And that didn't stop the paparazzi from seeing us and speculating." Carter met his eyes again. "You'd really want to do this, but keep it hidden?"

Levi had never struggled so hard to read Carter's face. Whether it was because he was afraid to find out what hid between the lines, or because Carter was really keeping his thoughts that far beneath the surface, he didn't know, but with a gun to his head, he couldn't have guessed what was running through Carter's mind.

He moistened his lips. "What do you want me to say, Carter?"

"I . . ." Carter sagged against the wall. "Damn it, I feel like such an idiot."

"Don't. You're not." Levi leaned on the counter, trying to ignore the beginnings of painful tension creeping into his neck and shoulder. "We've been friends this long without too many people catching on. There's no reason anyone has to know if we take it to the next—"

"It's not about how easy or difficult it is to keep it quiet. Fact is, I am not going to be your dirty secret." Carter's quiet but hard-edged words hit Levi in the gut.

He shook his head. "I don't *want* you to be my dirty secret. But I . . . You know why I can't go public with this."

Carter studied him. "Everyone knows you're playing Max Fuhrman now. The episodes haven't aired, but the word's out." He folded his arms loosely across his chest. "So you don't have your job hanging over your head anymore."

"No, I suppose I don't. Not like before."

"So . . ." Carter held his gaze. "It's not a problem, right?"

Levi exhaled. "It's not that simple. If it was, I wouldn't be this close to forty and still in the damned closet."

Carter's eyebrows slid upward. "Your family."

"Yeah."

"Do you actually hear yourself?" Carter's voice was gentle, but held a distinct note of frustration. "You're this close to forty and staying in the closet because of an industry that drove you all the way to Bluewater Bay, and a family that's so dysfunctional, even your *cats* can't cope with them."

"Those are the cards I was dealt." Levi gritted his teeth. "I'm not crazy about my family, but they *are* my family and I'm trying to fix everything with them. And if I want to act, then this is the industry I have to put up with."

Carter's lips tightened. Levi couldn't tell if he was frustrated with the situation, or with the way Levi handled it. Maybe both.

Finally, Carter released a breath. "When are you going to stop being what the world wants you to be, and be your damned self?" He threw up his hands. "Isn't that why you moved here in the first place? Because everyone in LA is so fucking fake? You're faking it as much as they are!"

Levi flinched. "So I'm fake because I'm trying to protect myself?"

"Protect yourself from *what*?" Carter snapped. "The people who want you to be straight are no better than the assholes who want to typecast you and pigeonhole you. I don't care if they're blood relatives or if they sign your fucking paychecks. You shouldn't have to hide who you are or who you're with because of people like that." He exhaled, and his shoulders sank. His voice was soft and unsteady as he continued. "You say you want to protect yourself, but what you're doing is being even more dishonest than all those phony assholes you left behind."

Levi drew back, eyes wide. "What do you want me to do? Do you want me to tweet that I'm gay and hope I don't spend the foreseeable future regretting it?"

"I don't know." Carter shook his head and threw up his hands again, but it looked like it took a lot more effort this time. "I don't believe that you're really happy keeping yourself a secret."

Levi inclined his head. "But you've only brought this up now that you're concerned about me keeping a relationship between us a secret?"

"It's bothered me all along, but I . . ." Carter hesitated. "Okay, maybe this is selfish of me. The fact is, I want to be with you, but not if I have to be something you keep hidden."

"So you're giving me an ultimatum?" Levi shifted, fighting a losing battle against defensiveness. "Come out or fuck off?"

"You're asking me to keep any relationship we have a secret." Carter gave a sharp half shrug. "Doesn't seem like that ultimatum's out of line, does it?"

Levi ground his teeth. "You knew where I stood before you came on to me yesterday."

"And I didn't see you trying to stop me." Before Levi could respond, Carter sighed and shook his head. "The thing is, I get what you're up against, Levi. I do. And I didn't think things would get this complicated. I came looking for you in the first place because I respected you as an actor, and yeah, I'd had a crush on you since forever." He swallowed. "But then things changed, and that's not who you are to me anymore. You haven't been Levi the actor to me in . . . in I don't even know how long. I got to know the real you, and all I want now is the real you. The Levi who loves his cats and can't watch a movie without a glass of Coke and likes to go out fishing like a regular guy."

Levi lowered his gaze.

"But that other Levi is calling the shots. And I . . . I want this. I want you." Carter exhaled hard. "But I *can't* be something you're afraid of other people finding out about. I can be a lot of things, but I can't be your secret."

Levi rubbed his forehead. "I don't know what else to do."

"Neither do I, but I *refuse* to be another Dylan Masters."

Levi blinked. "You know exactly why I did that. And he knew what it was when he went into it."

"Good for him. But I know what this is, and—"

"You knew I wasn't out and I didn't want to be out," Levi growled. "But you still came on to me last night. Did you think I'd suddenly change my—"

"I just wanted you, all right?" Carter's voice was suddenly shaky. "I didn't think this through, and I doubt you did either. All I knew was how much I wanted you. And to tell you the truth, if I'd known we'd be standing here doing this afterward, I still would've done it."

Levi wanted to say he still would've done it too, but he couldn't. Not with that bone-deep hurt in Carter's eyes. Nothing that had happened on this boat last night was worth the pain Levi was causing him now.

"What do you want me to do?" he asked finally. "I mean, my fucked-up family aside, I'm in a bad spot careerwise. I spent years pretending I didn't want to be an actor anymore, and when I finally couldn't deny that I did, the powers that be decided to hang my sexuality over my head from the start. Before I even signed. Stay in the closet, or lose that opportunity. Maybe they won't fire me from this gig, but they'll remember it, and after my character is killed off, I might be hard-pressed to land any role. You know damn well second chances don't come twice in this business."

"They don't come twice with people either," Carter said in a low growl.

"What's that supposed to mean?"

"It means we both know the suits will sign you again if they think you can make them money. And hey, if you'd still sign with them after all this crap they've held over your head?" He waved a hand dismissively. "That's on you. Some of us aren't keen on being used."

"Jesus Christ, Carter." Levi sighed. "I did *not* use you."

"That's up for interpretation."

"What? How did I use you? Because you kissed me, and I had sex with you? I didn't realize taking our clothes off meant I owed you a public relationship."

Carter blinked. Then his expression hardened as he folded his arms across his chest. "So it was just a roll in the hay for you? It didn't dawn on you once that it was more than that?"

Oh, it dawned on me more than once.

"It doesn't matter now." Levi gripped the edge of the counter, which was a challenge with his sweaty palms. "It's done. And no matter how I play this out in my head, the fact is, I can't give you more than a discreet relationship. You knew that from the beginning."

"Yeah, I did." Carter deflated a little. "I guess I thought things had changed."

Oh, they have . . .

"Some things haven't."

"Yeah, that's for sure." Carter's eyes narrowed. "You're still letting your life be dictated by bosses you hate and a family who drives you insane."

Levi rubbed the bridge of his nose. What the hell was he supposed to say to that? He lowered his hand. "This career, it's a piece of my identity that's been gone for too long. I just want to—"

"Yeah? Well, I hope all the money and awards keep you warm at night." Carter met his eyes, and the hostility vanished in favor of something even more painful. "You know, a few times, I actually considered going through with this even if it meant being your dirty little closeted secret. I seriously thought about agreeing to see you because I wanted to be with you that badly. You're the *only* man in the world I've thought about dating on the sly since I was a teenager." He set his jaw. "Because I wanted you *that* much, Levi. And maybe that's why it hurts so much that you'd ask me to *be* your secret."

Levi winced. "Except you knew from the get-go—"

"I know. I did." Carter nodded. "But I didn't think I'd feel this way about you."

Levi rubbed the stiffening muscles in his neck. "I'm a messed-up guy, Carter. I've got . . ." He paused, composing himself. "You deserve better than that."

"Yeah." Carter took a decisive step back toward the ladder, and the gap between them seemed too large to be contained inside this tiny cabin. "You're right. I do."

With that, he was gone.

Levi dropped into a chair.

As the silence set in, he replayed their conversation over and over again, the mental film clips interspersed with dimly lit memories of last night.

Hadn't Dylan told him ages ago that the longer he stayed in the closet, the harder it would come back to bite him in the ass? That the more he let other people, be they his family or his employer, dictate his personal life, the more deeply he'd regret it?

And Levi had believed it. He hadn't known when or how, but he'd always known his ex's prediction would eventually come true.

He just hadn't bargained for someone like Carter.

CHAPTER TWENTY-TWO

C arter didn't go home. He got on the highway and drove, flying past farms and forests en route to the coast because he didn't know what else to do.

Mile after mile, town after town, he berated himself for how this morning had played out.

Are you really surprised? What the fuck *did you expect?*

Carter rested his elbow below the window and rubbed his neck. Nothing about this morning should've surprised him. He never should've gotten his hopes up, but Levi had done things to his head that no other man had done. Normally, Carter could keep a platonic distance from a friend even when there was an obvious mutual attraction, but he'd lost all semblance of control with Levi. Looking back, he couldn't fathom how they'd made it this long without tumbling into bed together.

And now . . . now this.

It wasn't that he needed to be in love to have sex with someone. Sex didn't have to be special or meaningful—he'd just found the penis-go-round to be a little exhausting. Especially once his face had started landing on magazine covers and billboards, and his personal life had become public property. His sex life was the one thing he could keep to himself. The one place where he could decide who had access and who didn't.

And he understood why Levi guarded his privacy so jealously, but there was a difference between refusing to let the entire world know who was in your bed and demanding complete secrecy about a relationship. Assuming Levi even thought there was the potential for a relationship between them. Hell, maybe to him, last night had just been . . .

After all, he hadn't reciprocated when Carter had said he had feelings for him.

Carter groaned and rubbed his eyes. Letting his guard down for Levi hadn't been easy, and apparently it hadn't been smart either. What exactly had he expected? One night of boat-rocking sex didn't negate a lifetime in the closet. Especially not when Levi had legit reasons for staying in that closet.

He got it. He knew no amount of pleading with the universe would change anything.

But goddamn, sometimes the truth really did hurt.

Levi wasn't even sure how he got himself home. He vaguely remembered making the numb walk from the boat to the car, and if he worked at it, there were bits and pieces of the drive, but whatever. Somehow, he'd made it.

He let himself into the kitchen from the garage and tossed his keys onto the counter. A second later, the dull, rhythmic thump of heavy paws on hardwood brought a faint smile to his lips. He knelt as Link and Zelda came around the kitchen island.

"Hey guys." He scratched their chins. "Miss me?"

They just purred. When he stood, he expected them to trot off in the direction of their food dish—after all, now that he was home, it was time to make himself useful—but they stayed close. While he made himself some coffee, they were underfoot. The entire time he was in the shower, two dark blobs sat on the other side of the frosted-glass doors, and they "helped" him get dressed. And as he wandered around the house in search of something to do, they were hot on his heels.

For the better part of the last few years, he'd been the only one here more often than not. Just him, Link, and Zelda. When a friend or family member came by, the five-thousand-square-foot house had seemed almost crowded because he was so used to it being the three of them. When his parents were here, this may as well have been a studio apartment for all the breathing room he had.

But without Carter, this place was fucking empty.

Levi didn't have to be at the soundstage for a few hours, so for the time being, he pulled out an old radio and kept it playing in the living room to drown out the silence while he fucked around on his iPad. He briefly considered going downstairs and putting in a movie, but banished *that* thought in short order.

The cats didn't seem to understand what was going on. Link curled up right beside his leg and meowed pitifully whenever Levi went to refill his drink. Zelda perched beside Levi and kneaded his thigh, staring up at him. Every time he looked away, she made those weird little chirping noises she made during windstorms. That sound he'd long ago figured out meant she didn't understand what was going on, and needed him to remind her everything was okay.

He balanced his iPad on his other leg and petted her until she flopped down beside him, and he kept his hand on her while he continued playing a game on the tablet.

By noon, the walls were closing in. He needed to get out of here, but where could he go? An aimless drive was a means of escape he'd abandoned after the accident. He couldn't take the boat out, either. Not today. Not when it had become the scene of the crime. The place where they'd fucked and then fucked it all up.

And there was really no escape anyway. He could go out for a few hours, but then he'd have to make his way to the set where there'd be no avoiding anything.

Because they were shooting another scene together.

Carter couldn't sit still. He hadn't been on edge like this since he'd been waiting for his agent to call and tell him if he'd gotten the part on *Wolf's Landing*.

Levi was here. Carter had caught a glimpse of him heading to the makeup artist's chair, and Anna wanted them both on the set in twenty, which meant they'd be in the same room any minute.

He didn't even know how he'd feel once they were face-to-face. Right now, the pendulum swung between lashing out and breaking down.

Just let it go.

Easier said than done. He would get over it, of course, but it would take time. Last night hadn't happened overnight—it was weeks in the making, and damn Levi for getting that far under his skin.

Except I was the idiot who let him.

Carter had known from the get-go what this was and what it wasn't. The fact that they'd given in and slept together didn't change anything. For that matter, Levi had carefully cultivated a delicate balance in his world, keeping certain aspects of his life private in order to keep other aspects from falling to pieces, and Carter wasn't being fair by asking him to disrupt that on the off chance they could make this work.

Still, he couldn't help feeling hurt. And frustrated. And fucking pissed off. Whether his anger was directed at Levi or the incredibly unfair world they lived in, he didn't even know. All he knew now was how much he wanted to feel what he had during those few hours on Levi's boat.

A voice grazed the outer edges of his senses. He couldn't hear what was being said, only the presence of a familiar tone amidst all the chaos on the set.

He turned around, and the pendulum vanished.

There was no lashing out. There was no breaking down.

Their eyes met. Levi faltered midstep. Carter faltered midbreath.

It wasn't the first time he'd had trouble breathing with Levi in the same room, but it was definitely the first time he wished he could bolt for the door and get the fuck out of there.

Strange, he'd always imagined being starstruck and inarticulate in the presence of an actor he admired. He'd never imagined feeling hurt and humiliated.

Anna appeared between them. "Oh good, you guys are here. Let's get you in your places and—" Her gaze flicked back and forth from him to Levi, and little by little, the "what the fuck?" in her expression gradually shifted to "are you fucking kidding me?" Voice flat, she said, "Levi, can I talk to you for a minute?"

Without a word, Levi followed her into her office.

Carter exhaled. They weren't done shooting today, but at least he had a chance to catch his breath.

Funny how last night, they couldn't get close enough. Now he couldn't get far enough away from Levi.

Anna shut the office door and leaned on it, arms folded across her chest. "What the hell is going on?"

There was no point in playing stupid with her. She'd been working with Carter for a long time, and she knew Levi better than a lot of people—if she saw a reason to pull him aside, then she knew something was up.

He sat on the edge of her desk. "Carter and I just have some shit we need to work out."

She watched him silently for a good minute. Then she closed her eyes and let her head fall back against the door. "You slept with him, didn't you?"

Coming from anyone else, the accusation would've sent him into a defensive panic. From her, it wasn't much of a surprise.

He rubbed his neck. "Yeah."

"Jesus, Levi." She gave him one of her patented "you idiot" looks. "What were you thinking?"

He glared at her. She returned it, but after a moment, she sighed and pushed herself away from the door, stepping a little closer to him. "So what happened? I'm assuming there's more to this than just an awkward morning after."

"Yeah, you could say that."

"What's going on, then?"

Levi pinched the bridge of his nose and sighed. "Depending on who you ask, I'm either preserving my career and keeping the peace with my family, or I'm being a colossal idiot."

"Levi, look at me." When he did, she arched her eyebrow. "Are you telling me you're choosing showbiz and those fuckwits who raised you over Carter?"

He glared at her. "This from the woman who's warned me not to test the studio?"

She blew out a breath and rolled her eyes. "Levi. Sweetheart. I never said don't date anybody. Just keep it on the DL."

"So I guess you're in the 'you're being a colossal idiot' camp?"

"Oh, honey." She folded her arms. "I'm in *charge* of that camp." She sighed. "If you and Carter have a connection, are you really—"

"What do you want me to do, Anna?" Levi shook his head and sighed. "Carter doesn't want to be someone's dirty little secret, and I'm not going to force him into the closet for my benefit."

"I—" Anna deflated, letting her arms drop to her sides. "Okay, I guess it's not that easy."

"No, it's not."

"How do you feel about him?"

Levi winced.

"That's what I thought."

"What?" He laughed dryly. "He's not the first guy I've gotten hung up on."

"No, but I haven't seen you *this* hung up on anyone since Dylan."

Levi exhaled. "Well, I got over him."

"Barely."

He eyed her.

She put up her hands. "Honey, I'm just calling it like I see it."

"Yeah, it's really helpful." He rubbed his neck again. Tonight was definitely going to involve some frozen vegetables. "I don't know what to do."

"Maybe you need to let the dust settle first. Then you guys can talk things over."

"Which would be fine if we could avoid each other long enough to let it settle."

She grimaced. "At least it's only one episode, and then you both get a break for a few weeks until Fuhrman comes back."

"There is that."

Anna stepped closer and hugged him tight. "I'm sorry, sweetie. I wish these things were simpler."

"Me too."

Carter had never been so happy to hear "That's a wrap."

It was almost midnight when Anna finally dismissed the exhausted cast and crew, and Carter didn't hang around. He didn't even bother taking off his makeup, even the bruising around his eye. He could do that at home—he just needed to get the fuck out of here.

Driving way too fast down the highway, he relived the day's shoot over and over in his mind. It was probably one of his best shoots. He'd been hell-bent on getting every scene right in as few takes as possible to minimize the amount of time he'd had to spend being Gabriel and trying to drag information out of a jittery, strung-out Fuhrman. Either Levi was doing the same thing, or he was just that good at memorizing lines and directions—the only retakes they'd had to do were to correct lighting and camera angles.

In between takes, they'd barely looked at each other. They sure as fuck didn't talk to each other.

Levi was lucky as hell. Max was *supposed* to be volatile and edgy during this scene. His voice was supposed to be shaky, bordering on hysteria here and there. Whatever Levi might've been feeling had disappeared beneath the veneer of his character's madness.

Carter hadn't been so fortunate. Half the time, Gabriel had to keep a cool head. Calm, controlled, cold. The other half, he was in Max's face, shouting at him, demanding answers, barely keeping himself from kicking Max's ass. Carter had pulled it off, but goddamn, looking Levi in the eye and staying professional had been harder than stunt work.

He almost wished they'd parted ways in a shouting match. The kind of fight that could get the cops called on them. At least then he would have been able to channel all that anger into the scene.

And he was angry, but every time he'd tried to have Gabriel take that anger out on Max Fuhrman, it had taken every bit of energy he had. Lashing out at Levi hurt like hell. No matter how much he wanted to, he couldn't blame him. He couldn't hate him.

And he couldn't have him.

Carter pulled into his garage and turned off the engine, but didn't get out of the car yet.

They'd really made a mess of things, hadn't they? Damn it, Levi felt farther away from him than he had been when Carter had been watching him as an actor on the big screen. That was the part that hurt the most. Not that they'd finally fucked, but that they'd walked away afterward. Not that Levi had chosen the certainty of his family and career over a relationship that could flame out on a moment's notice.

As he sat in the garage, the engine clicking quietly as it cooled, the truth slowly settled in.

I don't care if we can't date.
I want my friend back.

CHAPTER TWENTY-THREE

L evi couldn't sleep. He couldn't get the conversations—with Carter, with Anna—out of his head. The tension in his neck wasn't helping, either. He needed to relax, physically and mentally, and that wasn't happening soon.

It was definitely getting bad—three times, he caught himself seriously considering a liquor store run. Levi had sworn off booze years ago after seeing what it had done to his family, but the thought of a night's oblivion was tempting. At least his tolerance was low—one or two drinks, and he wouldn't feel a thing until morning. And it wasn't like he'd be the first actor who showed up to work hungover.

But . . . no.

The whole reason he was in this was because of his constant need to avoid everything. Stress. His parents' disapproval. Hollywood's bullshit. The tabloids' scrutiny. And avoiding all that shit had served him *so* fucking well.

By two thirty, Zelda had gotten tired of his tossing and turning, and jumped off the bed. Half an hour later, Link left too.

At a quarter after four in the morning, Levi gave up. He carefully wove around the sleeping lumps on the floor and went downstairs to put on some coffee. Thank God he didn't have to work until tonight. Maybe he'd manage a nap so he didn't pass out on the set. Assuming he could sleep in the middle of the afternoon when he hadn't been able to all fucking night.

Wandering aimlessly around the house with a cup of coffee in his hand, his eyelids heavy, and his body exhausted, he decided this couldn't continue. He had to do something to fix this, or he and Carter were going to drive themselves insane.

There was one thing he could do. It had serious potential to blow up in his face, but there was a serious lack of alternatives.

He wasn't ready for that yet, though.

Instead, he dug through some old emails in search of a phone number he hadn't used in years. It was entirely possible the number was obsolete now, that this was a waste of time, but he had to give it a try.

Finally, deep in the archives of his inbox, he found a message he'd sent to himself detailing contacts he needed to move from one cell phone to another, back in the days before cellular kiosks could take care of it. With his heart in his throat, he entered the number, and didn't give himself a chance to think twice before he sent the call.

The phone rang on the other end. That was a good sign.

"Hello?" The sleepy voice almost knocked Levi out of his chair.

He swallowed. "Hey, Dylan. It's Levi. Please don't hang up."

The line went silent, and he was sure his ex-boyfriend had done exactly that, but then he heard some subtle movement. And finally, "Um. Okay."

"Can we talk? Just, uh, for a few minutes?"

A good ten seconds passed before Dylan said, "All right. What about?"

"I wanted to apologize. For . . . for everything." He rubbed his eyes with his thumb and forefinger. "Mostly for denying us."

More silence. "Really?"

"Yeah. I wanted you to know I never did it because I wanted to hurt you. That's the last thing I ever wanted to do."

Dylan slowly released a breath. "There's . . . there's a question that I've wanted to ask for a long time."

"Sure. Go ahead."

His ex went quiet again for a moment. "Were you ashamed of dating me?"

"*No.*" A lump formed in Levi's throat. "No, never." When Dylan didn't speak, Levi went on. "I was never ashamed of you. Ever. And I wasn't even ashamed of being gay, I was scared. And it took me until recently—very recently—to realize how much that fear has been running my life."

"What do you mean?"

"I mean I fucked things up with you, and . . ." The lump rose higher, and Levi struggled to force it back. "I just fucked things up with someone else."

"Oh, damn." Dylan sighed. "Sorry to hear it."

"God, what is wrong with me?" Levi rubbed his eyes again, telling himself it was simply to occupy his idle hand. "Hollywood doesn't give two flying fucks about me. My folks are always looking for a reason to disapprove of me. And I—" His voice cracked. "And I keep letting both of those scare me into pushing away people I love."

"Your family is still dicking you around?" Dylan's voice was surprisingly gentle. "After all these years?"

"Yeah." Levi laughed bitterly, and sniffed. "Stupid, isn't it?"

"No, I just think it proves what kind of assholes they are." He took a deep breath. "Listen, I don't know how things have changed since we last talked, but think about it. Look how much you've hidden from them. And how much you've lost because of them."

Levi closed his eyes, and when that squeezed out a tear, he quickly swiped it away.

"You're almost forty now, aren't you?"

"Close, yeah."

"Okay. So that's forty years you've given to being the son they don't deserve, which means not allowing yourself to be happy." Dylan's voice softened a little more. "When are you going to start living for you and not them?"

Levi wiped his eyes again. "Forty years. Goddamn it."

"And for that matter, you and your siblings have bent over backward for years to appease them. When have they ever given a little?"

"Well, they did stop drinking."

"Because a judge ordered them to."

"And their doctors, but . . . point taken." He swore under his breath.

"Levi, this is *your* life, not theirs. If they don't approve, then fuck 'em. Look, I know it's not easy, but enough is enough. You being afraid of them killed our relationship, and it—"

"Wait, you knew?" Levi's eyes widened. "I didn't—"

"Of course I knew. And I'll admit I hated you at the time for letting them push us apart, but now I want to smack both of them." His voice hardened. "And so help me, whoever this guy is you just broke up with? If you let them keep you away from him, I will smack *you*."

Levi couldn't even muster a humorless laugh. "I probably need it these days. And . . . Jesus, Dylan. I am so sorry. About everything." Levi leaned back in his chair and stared up at the ceiling. "I've been so fucking scared of people finding out I was gay, and about pissing off my parents, I completely lost sight of how much that hurt the people I loved. I can't . . . I can't even begin to apologize enough for that."

"No, I get it. I didn't really get it back then, but I do now." Dylan muffled a cough. "And I'm sorry for trying to out you like that. I was angry, and . . . I admit, I did want to hurt you then."

Levi winced. "I guess I kind of deserved it."

"No." Dylan exhaled hard. "We both fucked up pretty good, I think."

"Yeah. We did." Levi swallowed. "God, I'm sorry. And thank you. For everything you said. I just called because I needed to apologize, but that was . . ."

"It's all stuff I wanted to say to you back then. Guess I couldn't quite work up the nerve either."

"I wouldn't have listened back then. But I . . . I can't even tell you how much I appreciate it now."

"Don't mention it."

Levi drummed his fingers on the edge of the desk. "I, um, I saw in the news you got married."

"Yeah." He could hear the smile in Dylan's voice. "Still feels kind of weird, wearing the ring."

Levi laughed. "I'm sure it does. Congratulations. I'm really glad you found someone."

"Thanks." Dylan paused. "I'm glad you've found someone too."

That hit him in the gut. "Except I'm pretty sure I—"

"If he's got you shaken up like this, I don't think you're going to let him go quietly."

"It's not a question of what I'll let him do. It's a question of whether or not he'll take me back."

"Talk to him. Don't . . ." Dylan hesitated. "Look, can I be perfectly honest?"

Levi gulped, not sure how much more truth he could handle today. "Please."

"If . . ." Dylan cleared his throat. "When we split up and things were still ugly, if you had called, I . . ." He took a deep breath. "If you'd called, I would've taken you back in a heartbeat."

Levi's stomach flipped. "You could've called me."

"Yeah. You're right. But you didn't, and I didn't, and here we are."

Closing his eyes, Levi exhaled.

"I'm happy now, and you'll be happy when you get shit straight with him. Just don't let the window of opportunity pass you by, okay?"

"I won't." Levi wiped a hand over his face. "Thanks." He paused, chewing his lip. "Would it, um, be out of line to ask if there's a chance we could be friends again?"

"Not out of line." The smile was back. "Maybe one of these days we can do a double date."

Levi laughed. "Yeah. Maybe."

After they'd hung up, he set the phone down and sank against the back of the chair. His head was spinning, his heart beating a million miles an hour. The relief was so profound, he could physically feel the weight coming off his shoulders.

But another weight settled in its place. Fresh stiffness crept into his neck. He'd resolved things with Dylan, but the shit still remained with his parents. And Carter . . .

Levi rubbed his eyes.

A soft meow turned his head, and he lifted his arm so Link could jump into his lap. The cat climbed onto the desk so they were eye to eye. Reaching up to pet him took more energy than it should have. Even scratching Link's ears couldn't bring a smile to Levi—he was too fucked in the head for his purring, affectionate cat to cheer up.

Replaying the conversation with Dylan over and over in his mind, he decided his ex was right. This was bullshit. When petting his damned cat took this much energy and still couldn't make him feel better, it was bad, and he was done.

He knew what he had to do. And there would be no working up any nerve. None of that courage swelling in his chest right up until he backed down at the very last second.

It was now or never, because if this moment wasn't enough to make him do it, nothing ever would.

His hands were shaking and his stomach was sick, but he picked up his phone and made the call.

"Levi?" His mother's smile was palpable all the way from Maryland. "This is a surprise."

"Yeah." He gritted his teeth against the rising nausea. "I wanted to tell you and Dad that I've met someone."

"You— Oh, honey! That's wonderful! Tell me about her!"

Levi winced. "Um, well." *Here goes. Just do it.* "His name is Carter."

The coffee he'd drunk almost came back up. He clenched his jaw and held his breath, his heart going crazy as his own words echoed through his mind. He could never take it back. The words were out and the demon was exorcised, and yet somehow the world hadn't split open beneath him and he could still breathe. Sort of. He was dizzy with relief, but also with that crushing fear that reduced him to a fifteen-year-old who'd just admitted to swiping twenty bucks from Mom's purse or taking one of Dad's beers.

His mother broke the lengthy silence. "I beg your pardon?"

Levi petted Link, which centered and calmed him a little, as did the big blue eyes staring back at him *without* implying he was a horrible person.

"His name . . ." Levi rested his hand on top of Link's rump. "His name is Carter. And I love him."

For a split second, he wanted to drop to his knees and lose it because he realized he did love Carter, and now he'd quite possibly lost his shot with him.

But that was followed by a surge of anger.

Because in his mother's silence, he could hear the disgust that was likely widening her eyes and contorting her lips. He could feel the disapproval. The disappointment. And how many times in his life would that have reduced him to a prodigal son, begging for forgiveness and promising to change in order to please two people who could never *be* pleased? Especially not by their son living an honest, open life?

His mother took a breath. "I don't—"

"I'm gay, Mom." He didn't feel the need to split hairs over his bisexuality. Whether or not she could comprehend the difference between the two, he didn't care anymore. "I'm gay, and I'm in love with—"

"No, you are most certainly not," she snapped. "That's—"

"I really don't give a damn what you think about it." He clenched his teeth to keep from getting sick—who knew one statement could be so terrifying and so liberating at the same time?

"What? Levi, what has gotten into you?"

His hand trembled as he stroked Link's long fur just to keep himself sane. "What's gotten into me is I'm tired of lying to please you and Dad. It's cost me too damned much and that stops now." He'd never shaken this badly in his life.

"All those times you've looked me in the eye and promised me you were straight, you were—"

"I was lying. I was afraid of you and Dad rejecting me."

She laughed bitterly. "And you think we're going to accept . . . *this*?"

"Quite honestly, I don't care if you do or not. I've made my choice, and that's to be with Carter." *God, please . . .* "What happens between me and you guys, that's up to you, but Carter is nonnegotiable."

"Oh. I see. Well."

The only sound was Levi's thumping heart and Link's loud purring. He petted the cat to steady his hand.

"You're serious, aren't you?" his mother asked after a while.

"Yes."

"I see." She sighed heavily. "That's a shame, Levi."

And with that, the line went dead.

Levi dropped the phone on the desk beside the keyboard and let his face fall into his hands. He felt too many things right then—relieved, hurt, alone, sick—to even begin to deal with them. To get his thoughts in order or his emotions under control. There was just too much.

Link bumped his head against Levi's arm.

"Hey, buddy." Levi's voice cracked as he scratched behind the cat's ear. Link looked up at him with those huge blue eyes, and meowed softly.

Exhaling hard, Levi gathered the enormous cat up and buried his face against the thick fur.

And lost it.

CHAPTER TWENTY-FOUR

Damn Hunter Easton for refusing to allow any modifications to the story line. Gabriel Hanford was in it for the long haul. So was Max Fuhrman, at least until the seventh or eighth season. Unless someone from on high made a last minute recasting decision, Levi wasn't going anywhere.

Which meant they couldn't avoid each other.

Carter closed his eyes and took a deep breath.

Just focus on the script. The lines. The actions. Talk to Max Fuhrman, not Levi Pritchard.

It was an outdoor shoot again tonight, and the crew had set everything up down by the coast. The scene was relatively short, but Anna would make them run through it a million times; she wasn't easily satisfied with nighttime lighting. One odd-looking shadow in the background, and they'd start over.

So they'd probably be here until two or three in the morning. With Levi and Carter going through their lines again and again at close quarters—sometimes staring each other down, and sometimes, God help him, touching.

Levi arrived an hour or so later, and one glance at him sent Carter's stomach into his feet.

Levi looked like shit. He didn't talk to anyone. He kept his eyes down, whether he was perusing the script or not. The lights and makeup were certainly at play, but Carter was sure Levi really was that pale. The dark circles under his eyes didn't look fake, especially not with the way he kept trying to roll the visible stiffness out of his neck and shoulders.

Carter itched to ask if he was all right. Even if they'd gone their separate ways in a less than amicable manner, he still *cared* about him. Maybe more than he should have—Levi could go fuck himself, but Carter didn't wish any *actual* ill on him.

Anna summoned them both to the set. Carter paused, calling on every technique he'd ever learned so he could get into the character he'd been playing forever. Then he joined Levi, and they faced each other across a few feet of damp sand.

Levi-as-Max was bloody, battered and muddy, skin gleaming in the "moonlight" with sweat. He barely resembled Levi the actor at all. *Whatever helps you sleep at night, dude.*

"Action!"

You can do this.

Carter forced himself to focus on Max, not Levi, as he inched across the sand until they were an arm's-length apart. "No more games, Fuhrman."

"Who's playing games?" Max's wild eyes met his. "I've told you everything I know."

"Yeah?" Carter stopped, gesturing at Max's shirt and coat. "Then explain all that."

Max looked down at himself, touching the muddy bloodstains as if he hadn't realized they were there at all.

"You're one of them, aren't you? You're one of the wolves."

"So what if I am?" Max's eyes flicked up. An electric shock surged through Carter. He barely heard Max add, "You're one of us too, aren't you?"

Carter opened his mouth to speak, but he couldn't . . .

He couldn't see Max.

The smears of blood and mud, the grizzled hair, the torn-up clothes—none of that did a thing to mask the man standing in front of him. Max didn't exist. Only Levi. Where there should've been a sociopath with a secret, there was a gentle, soft-spoken man with cats and a boat and a thing for indie films and a slight addiction to Coke.

Carter's chest tightened. He tried to conjure up any rage and menace he could find, but the way his throat ached, his voice would crack the second he tried to speak.

On cue, he whipped the prop gun out and pointed it at Levi's— Max's—chest. "Enough games, Fuhrman. Just tell . . ." *Do you know how much it hurts to look at you?* "Just tell me where she is."

"Cut!"

Carter lowered the gun and put it back into its holster.

"I need less hesitation there, Carter," Anna said. "Hanford has the upper hand in this scene."

"I know. Sorry." He cleared his throat, and once Anna had directed them to start, he jabbed the gun into Max's chest and snarled, "Just tell me where she is."

Levi stepped forward, chest pressing against the muzzle of the gun. The pressure transferred through the weapon and into Carter's arm, pushing back as if Levi's entire body had him pinned to an invisible wall instead of pushing that single point of contact.

Their eyes locked because the scene demanded it, but Carter couldn't have looked anywhere else if he'd wanted to. Levi held his gaze, and as the seconds ground past, the scripted rage in his expression melted away. Carter's heart pounded. Where did Levi end and Max begin? How many of the emotions in those dark eyes were real and how many were scripted and how fucking many was he imagining?

As the script had ordered, Levi slowly shifted his eyes downward to focus on the gun between them. Then he put his hand—gloved, but still *his* hand—over Carter's, pinning it to the revolver and the trigger, holding the gun against his own chest. And slowly, exactly as the script dictated, Levi lifted his gaze again to meet Carter's.

There was supposed to be a beat of silence, and then Levi's line.

Beat.

Beat.

Beat.

Carter swallowed.

Beat.

Just say the line, Levi.

Eyes still locked on his, Levi took a breath. "I love you, Carter."

"You . . ." Carter's heart stopped. "What?"

Levi swept his tongue across his lips. "I . . . I love you."

He was distantly aware of the murmurs coming from behind the lights and cameras, but all he could do was stare at Levi and hear those words echoing through his mind.

"Levi, just . . ." Carter cleared his aching throat. "Just do the fucking scene."

"Uh, guys?" Anna said.

Levi kept his gaze fixed on Carter, not even glancing in Anna's direction. "I made a huge mistake."

Carter couldn't speak. Or move. Or think.

Anna coughed. "Levi? Carter?"

Levi shook his head. "I'm sorry. I . . . I can't do this." He pushed the gun and Carter's arm out from the space between them, but didn't move any closer. "I gave you up because I thought you were costing me too many important things, but I was so wrong."

Carter struggled to find his breath. "We need to shoot this scene."

"I know." Levi took a half step toward him. "But I need you."

Carter's balance almost gave out.

Anna cleared her throat again, louder this time. "Hey, guys?"

They both turned. She eyed them, then looked straight at Levi, eyebrows knitted together. They were silent for a long moment, as if having some sort of telepathic exchange while the crew watched and Carter stood there with his heart going crazy.

Then Anna stood. "Everybody take fifteen."

The set was instantly alive with activity. Equipment was turned off. Footsteps across sand and grass. Whispered voices.

Carter's pulse continued to ratchet up as everyone gave them room, leaving him alone with the man who'd just simultaneously knocked his world off its axis and put it back *on* that axis.

"Anna." Levi didn't look away from Carter.

One set of footsteps halted. The rest of the activity continued until the cast and crew were out of earshot.

Levi finally broke eye contact, lowering his gaze to the damp sand beneath their feet. After a moment, he turned his head toward Anna. "You might want to call Finn. Let the studio do whatever they're going to do."

Carter touched Levi's arm, the skin-to-fabric contact sending a shock through him. "Are you sure?"

"Yes." Levi glanced at him. "Yes, I'm one hundred percent sure." Levi turned to Anna again. Then soft footsteps told Carter that Anna was continuing after the others over the small bluff.

"Um." Carter coughed. "You're assuming we're getting together after—"

"I'm not assuming anything." Levi faced him. "I'm tired of hiding who I am, and I'm not going to do it anymore." He swallowed hard. "Especially since it cost me the best thing that's ever happened to me."

Carter blinked. "You're . . ."

"My parents know." Levi nodded in the direction the cast and crew had gone. "And now everyone does." He met Carter's eyes and swallowed again. "The only thing left was for you to know that I'm sorry, and I love you."

Carter turned toward the trail of footsteps in the sand, and then back at Levi. His heart still beat out of control. He desperately wanted to grab on to Levi and hold him as long as he could, but he was terrified to hope this was real. "You could lose your job. And your family . . ."

"If it costs me this job, then I'll . . ." Sighing, Levi shook his head. "I don't know. I've been trying to figure that one out all day. But I got so caught up in the idea of a second chance at my career, I let myself get sucked back into the bullshit that I left Hollywood to get away from in the first place. Yeah, I want to act, but not if it means losing myself." He took a cautious step closer, forcing all the air from Carter's lungs. "And not if it means losing you."

Carter's mouth went dry. "This is . . . First we were supposed to be just friends, and then . . ."

"I think that was the best thing we could have done."

Carter cocked his head. "What? I don't—"

"We were friends, so it was safe. You were safe." Levi touched Carter's cheek, sending a shiver right through him and making his chest tighten with a million emotions. "You were my closest friend, and that's exactly why I fell in love with you."

A lump rose in Carter's throat. He tried to force it back enough to speak.

Levi beat him to it, though. "I am so sorry," he whispered, drawing Carter closer. "I never should have let you go."

"Levi, I . . ." *I want to believe this is real.* "What about . . . what about your family?"

"I've wasted the last twenty years walking on eggshells because I knew they'd never accept me if they knew the truth. Why the fuck would I choose them over you?"

"They're your family."

"They don't deserve to be." Levi took a deep breath. "And maybe this is premature, since we haven't known each other all that long, but I'm pretty damn sure you're the love of my life."

He was afraid to speak because he'd fall apart. Just . . . fall apart.

Levi touched Carter's cheek again with a slightly unsteady hand. "I love you. And I don't fucking care who knows as long as *you* know."

"But this is your chance to have your career back." Carter couldn't look him in the eyes, especially as his vision blurred. "You can't give that up for me."

"I'm not giving it up. I'm just not giving you up, and wherever the chips fall after that . . ." He gave a taut half shrug.

Carter closed his eyes, fighting to keep his emotions even. "Levi . . ."

"If this means the rest of my career is nothing but bit roles in indie films that no one will ever see, fine. I've spent my whole goddamned life trying to be the person everyone else has wanted me to be." Levi paused, as if he needed a second to collect himself. "With you, I can *be* me."

Carter swallowed. "I'd never ask you to be anyone else."

"I know. And I was an idiot for wanting to keep you a secret." He cradled Carter's face and pressed a tender kiss to his forehead. "I want the whole world to know I'm with you." He pulled back, eyebrows lifting. "If you'll have me, I mean."

Sheer disbelief kept Carter from responding. He couldn't speak, not without choking on the words or losing it completely.

Levi drew a ragged breath and broke eye contact. "If you don't want to do this, I'll understand, but I—"

Carter kissed him.

This was better than the kiss on the stage. Or the night he'd shoved Levi up against the door before they'd dragged each other down into bed. Because there was no question in the back of his mind. He didn't have to ask himself if it was right to be pulling Levi closer. He didn't have any doubts as he ran his fingers through Levi's hair. He didn't hear that nagging voice telling him to stop as he opened to Levi's insistent tongue.

Carter broke the kiss just long enough to whisper, "I love you."

CHAPTER TWENTY-FIVE

Between Carter's whispered words and his kiss, Levi's knees almost buckled right out from under him. In every scenario he'd played out in his head, this had seemed like the least-likely version.

But here they were. Holding on to each other, kissing each other. *I love you.*

God, he did. He so did.

Levi rested his forehead against Carter's. "The cats will be happy to know you're coming over again."

"It'll be nice to see them again. I've missed them."

"So you're using me for my cats?"

Carter shrugged. "Them, your DVD collection, and your home theater."

Levi clicked his tongue. "I should've known."

They both laughed and drew each other into another long kiss.

After a moment, Carter pulled back and glanced at the bluff. "We should, um. I guess we should finish this scene."

"Yeah. We should. I'll, um . . ." Levi broke eye contact. "I'll go let Anna know we're good." He paused. "And we are, right? We're good?"

Carter smiled, caressing Levi's cheek. "We're definitely good."

Levi kissed him gently, and then followed the trail of footsteps to the other side of the bluff. Everyone was standing around or sitting on car bumpers, sipping coffee and playing on their phones. As Levi came closer, every head turned.

Anna rose from her perch on a van's bumper. "Everything all right?"

"Yeah." Levi smiled. "Yeah, everything's good."

"Good." Her smile was a little hesitant, though. "Okay, everybody, back to the set." As everyone obediently headed toward the beach, she gestured at Levi. "Except you."

Once they were alone, she locked eyes with him. "So, um. Your secret is pretty much out now."

"I know. And if they fire me, then . . ."

"I'd like to tell you they won't, but I can't make any promises. Finn's going to be pissed. The studio's not going to be happy, either." Three ceases formed on her forehead. "And what about your family?"

"They already know. Believe me, they're not happy."

Anna squeezed his arm. "But maybe you will be for once."

Levi smiled. "Maybe, yeah."

She returned the smile, and it seemed genuine this time. Then she turned toward the cluster of lighting, equipment, and crew members.

Levi cleared his throat. "I guess we should get back to work."

"You know what? We'll just shoot with the stunt doubles tonight." She grinned. "Why don't the two of you cut out early? Sounds like you could use a little time to decompress."

"Decompress?" He chuckled. "Is that what kids are calling it these days?"

"I can still change my mind, you know. If—"

"We're going, we're going."

Anna laughed. "Come here, you." She hugged him. "I'm glad things worked out."

"Even if it messed up your shooting schedule?"

"I mess that up more than everyone else, so . . ." She shrugged as she drew back. "Just promise me you guys can do this scene tomorrow night without eye-fucking each other the whole time."

"Deal."

"Good. Now get out of here."

"All right, I'm going."

She started toward the set. "I'll send Carter your way."

"Thanks, Anna."

"Anytime, sweetheart."

She disappeared over the bluff, and a moment later, Carter came into view, backlit by the glow of the set as he made his way to Levi. The closer he came, the more his features materialized in the low light, and his smile made Levi shiver.

"So I guess we have the night off." Carter put his arms around Levi's waist. "You didn't actually ask her for—"

"I swear to God, I didn't. She offered."

"Uh-huh."

"I'm serious. But as long as we *have* the night off . . ." He leaned in slowly, and didn't care who saw them.

Before their lips met, Carter stopped him with a hand on his cheek. "You know there's no turning back now, right?"

"Do you want to turn back?"

Carter let his hand slide off. "Fuck no."

"Neither do I." Levi pressed his lips to Carter's. He didn't know which was more liberating—finally coming out to God and everyone, or resolving things with Carter. All he knew was, he hadn't felt this good in a long, long time.

Carter met his eyes. "We should get out of here."

"Your place or mine?"

"Hmm . . ."

Levi grinned. "The marina's not far from here."

Carter returned the grin. "Meet you there."

They didn't even bother getting out of their costumes. Levi had shed his muddy, bloody jacket, but otherwise, they were still dressed as Gabriel and Max as they stepped from the pier onto the boat.

The second they were in the cabin, they were in each other's arms. There was no coyness like last time. No uncertainty. They tore at each other's clothes as they kissed hungrily, and more than once, Levi considered shoving Carter up against the counter, dropping to his knees, and sucking him off.

But the bed was only a few feet away, and there were condoms and lube there, and if he didn't fuck Carter soon, he was going to go out of his mind.

"Bed." He nudged Carter back. "Let's . . . bed . . ."

Carter got the message. He grabbed Levi's belt and pulled him the rest of the way. They tumbled onto the small bed, half-dressed and already out of breath.

Levi kissed his way down the side of Carter's neck. "Fuck, I was *crazy* for thinking I could stay away from you."

Carter sucked in a breath like he was about to speak, but then Levi gently bit his collarbone, and he shivered.

"I want to fuck you so bad right—"

"Yes, *please.*"

"I swear to God," Levi murmured, "I don't usually skip foreplay."

"It's been foreplay since the night we met." Carter squirmed under him, grinding their clothed erections together. "Just fuck me."

"Get out of those clothes—" Levi nipped his shoulder "—and I will."

They both got up and stripped away the last of their clothes. Carter grabbed the condoms and tore one off the strip, and as he tried to put it on, they came together in another breathless kiss. Like last time, it was a struggle to get the condom on while they made out, but they managed, and once it was in place, Carter murmured, "Want me on my knees?"

"I liked how we did it before," Levi said between kisses. "With you on your back."

Carter pulled in a breath and dragged Levi down on top of him. They ground together and kept making out, and Levi was in heaven, except he wasn't inside Carter yet.

Though it meant breaking the kiss, Levi sat up and pushed Carter's legs farther apart. He put on some lube, but as he started to put some on Carter, Carter grabbed his wrist. "C'mon. I don't . . . I can't wait."

Levi wasn't going to argue—Carter knew his own limits.

He guided himself in, and they both moaned as Levi found a slow, easy rhythm. Carter took him easily, and then Levi was fucking him good and hard and deep, and thank God they had more condoms because they weren't going to need this one for very long.

But then Carter drew him into a kiss. And Levi slowed down. And then he stopped. And just like the first time they were together, Levi was too overwhelmed to do two things at once. When he focused on kissing Carter, his rhythm fell apart, and when he focused on fucking him, he couldn't remember how to kiss at all. He didn't care. They were touching, they were moving together, and if they weren't multitasking like porn stars, then oh fucking well.

Carter broke the kiss with a gasp. He arched under Levi, eyes shut tight, and Levi moved faster, his own head spinning as Carter's face flushed and his whole body trembled.

"Oh . . . fuck . . ." His fingers dug into Levi's shoulders. He rolled his hips just like he'd done the other night, nearly driving Levi out of his mind.

Carter whimpered, and suddenly he was so fucking tight, Levi could barely move inside him, but he did keep moving, and it felt so good, so goddamned good, so perfect, he didn't even fight it as his orgasm took over. He kept thrusting until he couldn't move anymore, and then sank down on top of Carter.

"Jesus," Carter breathed, stroking Levi's hair.

"Uh-huh."

They got out of bed long enough to clean themselves up, and then collapsed onto the mattress again. Though it was a warm evening, Levi pulled the sheet up over both of them, and for a while, they just held each other.

This time, those worried voices in the back of his mind were silent. Though there would be fallout, especially once the studio caught wind of this, Levi didn't regret a thing. Lying in bed with Carter, their skin still hot from sex, was perfect. How the hell had he thought he could walk away from this?

Levi turned on his side, and Carter mirrored him so they faced each other.

"I'm sorry," Levi whispered. "I should've—"

Carter kissed him gently. "Don't. I understand why you did it."

"Still." Levi ran his fingers through Carter's hair. "I'm sorry."

"Everything's forgiven."

They both smiled, and Carter was just starting to draw Levi closer to him when a text message beep turned both their heads.

"Is that yours or mine?"

"Mine's on vibrate." Levi had kept his ringtone turned off after he'd hung up with his parents—he didn't even want to know how many missed calls and texts he had now.

Carter grumbled something and reached for his phone. "Oh. It's Anna." Then he laughed and turned the phone so Levi could see it. The message read, *Couldn't resist. Don't worry—it won't go public. Deleting after it's sent to you. P.S. You guys are HAWT together.*

Below that was an attachment to a video. Carter hit Play, and the footage made Levi's heart stop. He could see the exact moment he'd broken character, when he could no longer hold on to Max Fuhrman and he wasn't looking at Gabriel anymore. It was Levi, not Max, who spoke, and the words came through on the video clear as day:

"*I love you, Carter.*"

He kissed Carter's shoulder as the video kept playing, and Carter found his hand and grasped it.

"Jesus," Levi whispered.

"She'll delete it," Carter said. "I trust Anna not to post something like that publicly."

Levi chewed his lip. After a moment, he leaned over the edge of the bed and searched through his pants pockets for his phone. Then he lay back beside Carter again. His phone was vibrating and showed a shitload of missed calls and texts, as he'd expected, but he scrolled past them, searching for one in particular. Sure enough, Anna had sent the video to him too. "You have any objections to this getting out on the internet?"

Carter laughed. "What? You think I have a problem with the whole world witnessing Levi Pritchard breaking character to tell me he loves me?"

Levi chuckled. "Well, in that case, here's one tweet to end them all . . ."

Carter slid closer to him, and Levi wrapped his arm around Carter's shoulders. With his other hand, he texted Anna: *Tweet this on your secret account. Title it "The wolf has landed."*

Carter snorted. "Really?"

"You have a better title?"

"No, but good God. That is a terrible pun."

"It is. You sure you don't mind if I post it?"

"As long as you never accuse me of coming up with that horrible title."

"Deal." Levi hit Send. "And with that, I think we may have single-handedly broken Twitter and Tumblr."

Carter laughed, but then his brow furrowed. "You're really sure about this?"

"There's no taking it back now, is there?" Levi gestured with his phone, then set it on the nightstand before wrapping his arms around Carter again.

Carter touched his face. "I didn't mean you had to blow the doors off the closet. I . . ."

"It was long overdue," Levi whispered. "And I'd rather be out to the whole world than be without you. You're the first person I've let in since . . . God, I don't even know." He ran his fingers through Carter's hair again. "I just didn't want to lose you."

Carter smiled, but it faltered. "And your family really knows now?"

Levi nodded. "I told them this morning."

Carter's drew back a little, eyes widening. "You didn't know if we'd get back together, though."

"I know. And I was scared to death you wouldn't take me back. But I've kept way too much of my life hidden because I didn't want to offend them. If they don't like it, that's on them." He caressed Carter's cheek. "I let their bullshit cost me way too much already."

"How did . . ." Carter searched Levi's eyes. "How *did* they take it?"

Levi flinched recalling the disgust in his mother's voice. "It doesn't matter. Honestly, out of everyone I had to show my cards to today, the only reaction I actually cared about was yours." He kissed Carter lightly. "That's how I knew I was doing the right thing."

Carter smiled and pulled him into another gentle kiss. "God, I love you."

"I love you too." Levi smoothed Carter's hair. "We don't have to keep it a secret anymore. All we have to do now is take it a day at a time and enjoy it."

"I like that plan. A lot."

"Me too."

They lay there in silence for a while, just holding each other and letting the boat's gentle rocking lull them to sleep. Carter's breathing slowed down. His body relaxed against Levi's. Levi couldn't even keep his eyes open anymore, and was starting to doze off too.

Then his phone buzzed. "Fucking thing."

"Huh?" Carter lifted his head.

"My phone." Levi almost shut it off, but then saw the message was from Anna.

Just a heads-up—I had to fight HARD for it, but you've still got a job. YOU'RE WELCOME.

A second later, another message followed: *And you're going to hear from Finn. Dude is pissed.*

He laughed. "Well, I'm not fired, but Finn is fired up."

Carter chuckled. "When is he not?"

"Right?" Levi set the phone facedown and wrapped his arms around Carter again. "He'll get over it."

"Eventually." Carter grinned. "So how many condoms do we have left?"

"More than enough." Levi kissed under Carter's jaw. "When we run out, there's plenty more at my place."

"Mine too." Carter ran a fingernail along the center of Levi's spine, making him shiver. "Think we should put another one to use?"

Raising his head so he could look in Carter's eyes, Levi pressed his growing erection against him. "What do you think?"

Carter didn't answer. He pulled Levi down into a dizzying kiss.

Even wrapped up in Carter's arms underneath the sheets, Levi could hardly believe they'd made it back here. He couldn't believe Carter felt the same for him.

On top of it all, he couldn't believe that for the first time in his life, he wasn't pretending to be something he wasn't. He wasn't afraid of people finding out he was gay. He was acting again. He was in love with the most amazing man he'd ever met, and instead of trying to keep it a secret, he wanted the whole world to know about it.

And lying there with Carter, Levi had never been so thankful that Hollywood came to Bluewater Bay.

Explore more of *Bluewater Bay*:
riptidepublishing.com/titles/universe/bluewater-bay

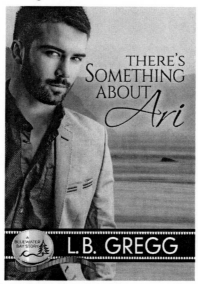

riptidepublishing.com/titles/theres-something-about-ari

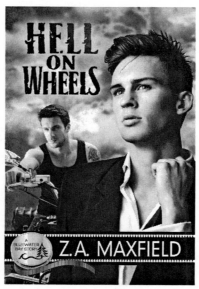

riptidepublishing.com/titles/hell-on-wheels

Dear Reader,

Thank you for reading L.A. Witt's *Starstruck*!

We know your time is precious and you have many, many entertainment options, so it means a lot that you've chosen to spend your time reading. We really hope you enjoyed it.

We'd be honored if you'd consider posting a review—good or bad—on sites like **Amazon, Barnes & Noble, Kobo, Goodreads, Twitter, Facebook, Tumblr,** and your blog or website. We'd also be honored if you told your friends and family about this book. Word of mouth is a book's lifeblood!

For more information on upcoming releases, author interviews, blog tours, contests, giveaways, and more, please sign up for our weekly, spam-free newsletter and visit us around the web:

Newsletter: tinyurl.com/RiptideSignup
Twitter: twitter.com/RiptideBooks
Facebook: facebook.com/RiptidePublishing
Goodreads: tinyurl.com/RiptideOnGoodreads
Tumblr: riptidepublishing.tumblr.com

Thank you so much for Reading the Rainbow!

RiptidePublishing.com

Tucker Springs novels
Where Nerves End
Covet Thy Neighbor
After the Fall
It's Complicated

Hostile Ground, with Aleksandr Voinov
Static
A Chip in His Shoulder
Something New Under the Sun
O Come All Ye Kinky
Finding Master Right
The Left Hand of Calvus
Unhinge the Universe, with Aleksandr Voinov
Noble Metals

The Market Garden Tales, with Aleksandr Voinov

Coming soon
Precious Metals
Dark Soul
Lone Wolf, A Bluewater Bay Story, with Aleksandr Voinov

Writing as Lauren Gallagher
Razor Wire (coming soon)
Damaged Goods
Who's Your Daddy?

For a complete list, please visit www.loriawitt.com

ABOUT THE AUTHOR

L.A. Witt is an abnormal M/M romance writer currently living in the glamorous and ultrafuturistic metropolis of Omaha, Nebraska, with her husband, two cats, and a disembodied penguin brain that communicates with her telepathically. In addition to writing smut and disturbing the locals, L.A. is said to be working with the US government to perfect a genetic modification that will allow humans to survive indefinitely on Corn Pops and beef jerky. This is all a cover, though, as her primary leisure activity is hunting down her arch nemesis, erotica author Lauren Gallagher, who is also said to be lurking somewhere in Omaha.

Website: www.loriawitt.com
Blog: gallagherwitt.blogspot.com

Enjoy this book?
Find more contemporary romance
at RiptidePublishing.com!

Illumination
ISBN: 978-1-62649-051-2

Glitterland
ISBN: 978-1-62649-025-3

Earn Bonus Bucks!

Earn 1 Bonus Buck for each dollar you spend. Find out how at RiptidePublishing.com/news/bonus-bucks.

Win Free Ebooks for a Year!

Pre-order coming soon titles directly through our site and you'll receive one entry into a drawing to win free books for a year! Get the details at RiptidePublishing.com/contests.

RIPTIDE
PUBLISHING

CPSIA information can be obtained at www.ICGtesting.com
Printed in the USA
LVOW10s1627031014

407163LV00005B/492/P